Time Traveler's Playlist

A Classic Rock Time Travel Adventure

David Homick

Copyright © 2024 David Homick

All rights reserved.

Published by Blue Knight Media

ISBN 979-8-9869326-2-0

This book or any portion thereof may not be reproduced or used in any manner whatsoever without the express written permission of the publisher or author except for the use of brief quotations in a book review. Please purchase only authorized electronic editions, and do not participate in or encourage electronic piracy of copyrighted materials. Your support of the author's rights is appreciated.

The characters, incidents and dialogs in this book are fictional and are not to be construed as real. Any resemblance to actual events or persons, living or dead, is completely coincidental.

DISCLAIMER: The song "Waiting for a Girl Like You" was released in 1981 on the *Foreigner 4* album. It was co-written by Lou Gramm and Mick Jones. The information provided in this novel is fictional and meant for entertainment use only.

"We don't belong in any one time or place.
We belong wherever we find love."

Contents

1. Who'll Stop the Rain - Creedence Clearwater Revival (1970) — 1

2. Turn the Page – Bob Seger (1973) — 7

3. Bad Company – Bad Company (1974) — 12

4. Hidden Treasure – Traffic (1971) — 19

5. Money – Pink Floyd (1973) — 26

6. Free Ride – The Edgar Winter Group (1973) — 34

7. Baby Hold On – Eddie Money (1978) — 41

8. Jump – Van Halen (1984) — 47

9. Stranger in a Strange Land – Leon Russell (1971) — 53

10. Renegade – Styx (1978) — 58

11. Green-Eyed Lady – Sugarloaf (1970) — 65

12. Gimme Three Steps – Lynyrd Skynyrd (1973) — 71

13. Radar Love – Golden Earring (1973) — 76

14. Don't Stop Believin' – Journey (1978) — 82

15. Waiting for a Girl Like You – Foreigner (1981)   87

16. Let's Go – The Cars (1979)   91

17. The Boys Are Back in Town – Thin Lizzy (1976)   98

18. It Don't Come Easy – Ringo Starr (1971)   103

19. Paranoid – Black Sabbath (1970)   109

20. Dirty Laundry – Don Henley (1982)   114

21. Wild Horses – The Rolling Stones (1971)   121

22. Do It Again – Steely Dan (1972)   126

23. This Is It – Kenny Loggins (1979)   131

24. Born to Run – Bruce Springsteen (1975)   139

25. Bad Moon Rising – Creedence Clearwater Revival (1970)   143

26. Tell the Truth – Derek and the Dominos (1970)   150

27. Tight Rope – Leon Russell (1972)   156

28. Right Place Wrong Time – Dr. John (1973)   163

29. Baby It's You – Smith (1969)   168

30. Look Into the Future – Journey (1976)   174

31. I Wanna Be Sedated – The Ramones (1978)   181

32. Smoke on the Water – Deep Purple (1972)   186

33. Carry On Wayward Son – Kansas (1976)   191

34. Your Song – Elton John (1970)   195

35. More Than a Feeling – Boston (1976)   203

36. Hold the Line – Toto (1978)   208

37. I'm Coming Back for You – Elf (1972)   215

38. Stairway to Heaven – Led Zeppelin (1971)   222

39. You Really Got Me – Van Halen (1978)   227

40. Dirty Deeds Done Dirt Cheap – AC/DC (1976)   232

41. Rock and Roll Fantasy – Bad Company (1979)   237

42. We Are the Champions – Queen (1977)   243

43. I'm Losing You – Rare Earth (1970)   249

44. Bad Time – Grand Funk Railroad (1974)   254

45. Tangled Up in Blue – Bob Dylan (1975)   260

46. Love Hurts – Nazareth (1975)   267

47. Don't Look Back – Boston (1978)   273

48. Just What I Needed – The Cars (1978)   278

49. Wish You Were Here – Pink Floyd (1975)   284

50. Baby, Come Back – Player (1977)   291

51. TNT – AC/DC (1975)   299

52. All Right Now – Free (1970)   305

53. Utah Sunrise – Grace Monroe (2024)   310

54. Epilogue   315

Chapter One

Who'll Stop the Rain - Creedence Clearwater Revival (1970)

Did you ever notice how it always rains at funerals? Today is no exception, even though the average rainfall in this part of Utah is less than five inches per year.

Raindrops splash against the granite headstones and drum against a black umbrella held above the preacher's head by a young assistant who looks like he'd rather be anywhere else. The preacher's voice drones on, but rain is all I hear.

Despite my opinions about rain and funerals, I didn't bring an umbrella. The rain on my face hides the tears of an only child set adrift at the ripe old age of twenty-two. Every time I blink, the world around me blurs, as though my eyes refuse to adjust to this new reality.

I shove my hands into my pockets, desperately trying not to feel anything. Not the dampness seeping into my bones. Not the lump in my throat. Not the fact that I'm forced to bury both of my parents at the same time.

A single-car accident took them in one cruel blow. No one knows how it happened. Pop had a little lead in his foot now and then, but the sheriff ruled out excessive speed. I need someone else to blame for this tragedy. Maybe a coyote ran out in front of them. Maybe a freak gust of wind knocked them off course. Maybe fate just decided to screw me over.

My name is Angus Walker. I don't know what my parents were thinking when they named their newborn son after a cow. Maybe they thought it was funny. The kids at school sure did. Entering high school thirty pounds overweight with a name like Angus? I might as well have had a sign on my forehead that read "Bully Me." I've shed some weight since then, but the damage was done.

My mind wanders—memories I didn't ask for creep in. Mom's laugh, Pop's calloused hands. The fights. The silences. The way we were never the perfect family but also somehow couldn't let go of each other.

I reckon it was love. That's what families have, whether they like each other or not. Don't get me wrong, I loved my parents, even if I felt like the son they never had. I should have been bigger, stronger, and able to ride a horse or throw a football. The only thing I'm any good at is playing the guitar, which isn't much use on a ranch.

I watch the raindrops glisten and roll off the polished wood of the caskets like so many tears. None of it matters now. They're gone, and I'm an orphan, alone and unloved, in a world where I don't fit in. Perhaps if my girlfriend stood by my side, her hand in mine, I'd feel different. But she doesn't exist. Perhaps she never will.

What will become of me?

I don't know our family's financial situation. Never needed to. Parents take care of those things. Where will I live? I've had my fill of this desolate, two-hundred-acre stretch of rocks and sagebrush that's been in my family for three generations. I need more. Denver. Austin. Nashville. Somewhere with a real music scene.

I'm not aware the service has ended until Uncle John, who made the three-hour trip from Salt Lake City, rests a hand on my shoulder as the crowd thins. We never saw much of him while Pop was alive, so I'm not sure why he's here. Maybe guilt. Maybe duty. Maybe he just wants to see if the ranch is worth anything.

He lights a cigarette and the smoke curls around his head.

It's rude to smoke so close to the dearly departed, but he doesn't seem to care. I hope he doesn't flick the butt into the open grave when he's finished.

"What are you gonna do now, Angus?" he says.

I glance at the caskets. "Guess that depends on the will."

"Did your parents have life insurance?"

I shrug as I watch the ash at the end of his cigarette grow.

"If you need a place to stay, you can come live with me for a while."

Even though he's the only family I have left, I don't know him well enough. "I appreciate that."

He takes another drag and shakes his head. "I've always believed that ranch was cursed."

"Didn't you and Pop grow up there?"

"Yes, but our father—your grandfather—lost his mind there, and it had something to do with that property."

My frown deepens as I try to pull up some old memories. He left when I was eight years old. "Pop didn't talk about it much, just to say Gramps would wander off by himself, sometimes for days."

He flicks the ash from his cigarette. "Then one day, he wandered off and never came back."

"Where do you think he went?"

"Nobody knows. Some say he ran off with one of those trailer park whores. Others say he was senile and got lost up in the mountains, but we never found a body."

I don't know what to say. Gramps had taught me about truth and regret and always taking the high road. I was only seven, but his words meant something—except for the high road part. No way in hell did he run off with another woman.

The wind changes direction and blows his smoke in my face. I wave my hand to chase it away, but Uncle John either doesn't see or doesn't care.

"Your grandmother took a lot of heat from people she thought were her friends."

I'd been close with Gran until she pulled her own disappearing act. Gran was a tough old bird, but she had a soft spot in that no-nonsense heart for me. I kissed her goodnight one evening twelve years ago, and the next morning she was gone.

Uncle John looks at his watch, then hands me a business card. "Here's my number, kid. Keep in touch."

We hug. It's awkward.

"Will do," I say. "Thanks for coming."

He waves over his shoulder as he walks away.

The last of the mourners have gone. I say a silent prayer over the caskets while the gravediggers stand by, waiting to lower them into the ground. As I turn to leave, I notice her. An old woman dressed in black, hunched over the caskets, her frail silhouette clutching a black umbrella. She'd been standing by a tree at the edge of the crowd earlier. The brim of a felt hat, long out of fashion, shadowed her eyes.

She must feel my stare because she looks up and our eyes meet. Tears cling to the edges of my eyes, and I fire off a few rapid blinks to clear them. *No. It can't be her.* The woman I'd spent half my childhood idolizing and the other half mourning—the grandmother I'd given up for dead years ago.

She's thinner than I remember, and her coat hangs on her like it belongs to someone else. Her face is more wrinkled, her hair a muted silver instead of the wild gray I'd known as a kid. But it's her. The sharp cheekbones. The way her mouth presses into a thin line. The same hat she used to wear to Sunday service.

I once loved this woman. Now, I can barely look at her.

My stomach twists into knots until I can't hold it in any longer. "What the hell?" The words come out too loud.

She flinches, her hands tightening on the handle of her umbrella. "Angus…" Her voice is thin.

My heart pounds as I step closer. "I thought you were dead." The words tumble out in a rush. "I cried for a week. Where the hell have you been?"

Her eyes—so much like my father's—meet mine. There's something in them I can't quite read. Regret? Sadness? Fear?

"I—" she starts, but her voice breaks.

"That's it?" I snap, louder now. "I? That's all you've got? You disappear for over a decade, let your grandson think you're dead, and now you show up at the funeral like—like some stranger?"

"What about your other son?" I press. "Uncle John was here. Does he know you're alive?"

"Angus," she says again, this time firmer, like she used to when I was acting up. "This isn't the place."

"You're damn right it isn't the place." My voice rises again. "There *is* no place. You're still dead to me."

Her gaze drops to the ground as her umbrella dips like she's wilting under the weight of my words.

I watch the preacher's car drive away. I want to demand answers, to make her explain herself right here in the rain. But something stops me. She'd made a fool of me, maybe all of us.

"Have you found it?"

I turn my attention back to her. "Found what?"

"We need to talk," she says softly.

I shake my head, backing away.

"Sorry, Gran." My voice is cold, but my chest is burning. "You're twelve years too late."

Chapter Two

Turn the Page – Bob Seger (1973)

I walk to my car. Correction: Mom's car. Mine is up on blocks in the barn.

When I earned my driver's license in my third and final year of high school, I cashed in my savings bonds and paid three hundred dollars for the rusted-out shell of a 1970 Pontiac GTO. Everyone said I should have bought a car I could drive, but my heart belonged to a lost breed of classic muscle cars. I planned to restore it to its former glory someday. Pop called me a shithead. I like to think he didn't mean it the same way as the kids at school.

The rain eases up by the time I make it back to the ranch, but the clouds still hang low and gray over the hills. The silence presses in like a weight. As I slip the key into the door lock, I hear Ozzy's paws scratch along the tired linoleum floor and the thud of his tail against the kitchen table.

I open the door, and there he is, tongue hanging from a big, sloppy grin. He has no clue. I guess ignorance is bliss. I'd trade places with him in a heartbeat.

Ozzy follows me into the living room, and I sit cross-legged on the worn carpet beside him. He lets out a whimper and rests his head on my thigh, as if he feels my pain.

Seeing Gran threw me. At first, I thought she was a ghost. She'd been the only stable thing in my life when Mom and Pop were busy working the ranch. She helped my world make sense when I felt like I didn't exist.

Gran taught me how to play my first chords on Stella, the guitar she'd pawned half her jewelry box to buy me. She'd spin her records—Seger, Fleetwood Mac, Bowie—and dance around the kitchen like no one was watching, daring me to join in. She's the reason I fell in love with music, the reason I can lose myself in a melody when the world gets too loud.

She told me stories about life in the '60s and '70s, how she'd hitchhiked to concerts, fallen in love too many times to count, and marched in protests because "what's the point of living if you're not fighting for something?"

One thing stuck with me more than any other. She said, "Everyone has a time where they fit in, where they're supposed to be. I call it the time of your life. You missed yours, kiddo. We would have been a great team back in the seventies."

She made me believe there's magic in the world. And then she was gone. And so was the magic.

I was ten. It was a Tuesday. I remember because Mom made pancakes for breakfast, and Pop told me while I poured the maple syrup. He said it like it was nothing: "Your grandma died. She went in her sleep." Why would he say that?

I didn't believe it at first. She'd been too full of life to just… stop. When I asked if I could see her, he said there wouldn't be a funeral. She didn't want one. Pop said something about keeping things simple.

That was it. No closure, no goodbye. Just gone.

I cried for a week. Every day, I'd sneak out to the barn, sit with Stella, and play until my fingers bled, pretending she could still hear me. I stopped asking questions after a while because it didn't matter. She wasn't coming back.

Except she did.

And what did I do when I saw her? I tore into her like she was a stranger. Like she hadn't been the only person who'd ever truly seen me.

I lean forward, elbows on my knees, and rub my face with my hands. Why didn't I let her talk? Why didn't I ask her where she'd been or why she'd left? Instead, I yelled at her like some spoiled, angry kid who didn't know what to do with the hole in his chest.

Maybe she'd had a reason. Maybe it wasn't her choice. Or maybe she *did* abandon me, and I was right to be angry. I guess I'll never know, but it wrecked me. Never again will I fall into such an emotional trap. People leave. They always do. So no—I'm not handing over my heart like it's some free sample at a grocery store. Putting yourself first isn't selfish. It's survival.

I let out a long exhale that leaves me feeling hollow. She came back to attend my parents' funeral, and I might have driven her away again.

"Damn it, Gran," I mutter, my voice cracking. "Why did you have to show up now?"

Ozzy barks and I stroke his back. "It's okay, boy."

But it's not. The truth is, I'm not sure if I'm mad at her for leaving, at my parents for lying to me, or at myself for not being the man who could handle seeing her again.

"What would I do without you, huh?"

Ozzy looks up at me with big sad eyes, and I remember those eyes looking the same on the day I found him.

Ten months ago—I don't even remember why I was upset—I had to get out of the house. I tossed a couple of bottles of water into a backpack and went for a hike. It's a half mile from the house to the north end of the property, where the flat land gives way to the mountains. It's a good place to get your head straight.

I passed a herd of cattle grazing on clover and wheatgrass. Cows aren't the smartest animals in the world. A few looked up at me, mouths chewing away, and I wondered what they were thinking. Probably nothing.

Half our land is leased to two farmers who raise cattle and grow alfalfa and other forage crops. My parents didn't grow anything themselves but used the rental income to help keep the lights on and food on the table. I grow my own cannabis on a small patch of fertile ground that nobody knows about. It's as close to ranching as I plan to get.

Clusters of sagebrush and wild grasses dotted the loose stones and packed earth underfoot. The Indian paintbrush and balsamroot, which normally added some much-needed splashes of color amid the rocky outcrops, were muted that day. Higher up, the scrubby terrain yielded to sharp rocks, their granite faces scarred and weathered by ancient glaciers.

I found a spot to rest and hydrate. While sitting there wallowing, I noticed a four-legged creature moving slowly toward me. There are plenty of coyotes in these hills, but they're mostly active after sunset. And then it barked. Strange. I'd never seen a dog up this high. I whistled, and he picked up his pace.

The black Lab's coat was dull and matted. A hollow whimper escaped his throat as he sniffed at my backpack. He probably hadn't eaten in days. His tongue hung limp, and his breathing was labored. I uncapped a water bottle, and he attacked it, causing me to lose my grip as he guzzled it. I wished I'd had some food in my bag for him.

"What are you doing out here alone?"

I guess he could have asked me the same question.

His collar had a tag with no name, just a phone number with an unfamiliar area code. The back had only a date: March 11, 1975. Converting that to dog years was beyond my level of math skills, but it seemed like too much.

The date couldn't be his birth date, but I hadn't a clue what else it might be. "We'd better get back to the house and get you something to eat."

I stood, and he stared up at me. I took a few steps, but he didn't follow.

"It's okay. I'll take care of you now, but you need to come with me."

Nothing. It's a half mile walk back to the house. I couldn't carry him, and I couldn't just leave him there. This poor soul was lost or maybe abandoned. I knew the feeling.

"Where did you come from, boy?"

Dogs are smarter than cows, but I didn't expect an answer. Holding his head in my hands, I looked into his dark, soulful eyes and saw myself.

Chapter Three

Bad Company – Bad Company (1974)

The dog eventually followed me home and decided to stay. I named him Ozzy, after the lead singer in the band Black Sabbath. I like to think I saved him, and I'm pretty sure he's doing the same for me.

I'd expected more pushback from my parents, but Pop had a dog many years ago, and he accepted him on the spot. Mom needed a bit more convincing, but she came around when she realized I'd only made one friend at school, and he'd left for college.

Looking back, high school was like a bad B-side track—awkward, out of sync, and something I'd rather not replay. I spent most of it dodging wedgies and avoiding cliques that looked at me like I was some weird alien experiment gone wrong. The pretty girls never gave me a second look.

In my defense, I believe I had a timing issue. I've always felt I was born fifty years too late. Nobody wants to talk about '70s rock bands or muscle cars today.

It's not that I have anything against the present, but I have a passion for the past, especially the music. With help from Gran, I taught myself how to play guitar when I was nine. My parents, God rest their souls, didn't know what they were getting themselves into when they bought me an electric guitar for Christmas.

I practiced with a determination that, if channeled into my studies, might have earned me a nod for valedictorian. But that never happened. I dropped out after my junior year to hit the road with a mediocre rock band. It felt less like giving up and more like an escape.

We played bars and county fairs within a hundred-mile radius. Our sets included classic rock, southern rock, and some heavy metal. But we lived in the middle of nowhere, with no large music venues. Salt Lake City or Denver would have been ideal.

In addition, like many bands, we had other problems—creative differences, power struggles, and financial disputes. The band imploded after eighteen months.

Pop had tried to stop me from leaving, but I wouldn't listen. Nothing was going to stand in the way of my dream. Fortunately, he took me back like the prodigal son when I came home with my tail between my legs.

That was four years ago, and I haven't done a lot with my life since then. Thankfully, my parents left me with a roof over my head. The insurance money from the accident pays the taxes on the ranch, and the rental income helps with the rest. I thought about selling, but nobody is buying. I have little interest in ranching. I spend most of my time with my guitar and my record collection, often served with a side of homegrown cannabis. The little money I earn from my part-time job at Rusty's Auto Parts should keep me in vinyl and guitar strings for the foreseeable future.

I live alone except for Ozzy, who eats a lot and isn't much of a watchdog, but when you live in the middle of nowhere, it's nice to have someone to talk to.

When I finish figuring out the chords for a song I'm working on, I return my Ibanez Flying V to its stand. I bought it when I still dreamed of becoming a rock star, thinking if I had a cool guitar, it might make me play better. Don't get me wrong, I'm no slouch on the strings, but I've all but given up on any prior delusions that I could be the next Jimmy Page or Eddie Van Halen. When you've been called mediocre and a loser enough times, you begin to believe it.

Time to chill. I fire up a doobie, stretch out on the couch, and retreat to my safe place. Pink Floyd's *Dark Side of the Moon* is playing on the stereo. The couch feels like a hammock, and the breeze from the open window an ethereal wind blowing in from, well, the dark side of the moon. Marijuana isn't legal in Utah yet, but that's where living alone in the middle of nowhere comes in handy.

I live my life one vinyl record at a time, just me and my dog, Ozzy. My routine rarely gets disrupted—until today.

A knock on the door shatters my reverie. No one ever knocks on my door. Paranoia sets in. I crush out my joint and wave away the smoke as panic thrums in my chest. It's my day off, and I want to spend the afternoon comfortably numb on my couch. Ozzy looks at the door and then at me. I shrug.

"Who is it?"

Another knock.

"All right, I'm coming." I steady myself before opening the door.

"Hey, Retro. Long time no see."

Standing on my porch is the last person I expected—or wanted—to see: Jackson Carr. His name tops my if-I-never-see-you-again-it'll-be-too-soon list.

I play dumb with a blank stare. "Do I know you?"

Jackson frowns. "Of course you do. Jackson Carr? From high school?"

"Still nothing." I recognize him, all right. He always had a pretty girl on his arm. I try to close the door, but he wedges his foot inside and flashes a grin that's as obnoxious as I remember.

"Look, man, I'm sorry for all the shit I gave you in school. It wasn't personal. I did the same to everybody."

Like *that* makes it better. I open the door wider, without a word.

"I want to make it up to you."

I narrow my eyes and fold my arms across my chest. "You've got a lot to make up for."

His grin widens. "See? You *do* remember me."

Wow, still a jackass. "I'll probably regret this, but how exactly do you propose to make it up to me?"

"Can we come inside?"

Jackson stands on my porch with his usual smirk, but it's the girl at his side that catches my attention now. She's stunning—like she stepped out of a magazine. My heart stumbles, then speeds up as I realize my face feels like sandpaper. I haven't shaved in days.

I hesitate, tilting my head and pinching my bottom lip, trying to gauge Jackson's sincerity. My eyes are drawn to the girl again. I don't recognize her. If we went to school together, I'm sure I'd remember her. Her smile is warm, but her stare makes me feel even more like a slob.

Jackson gestures to her. "This gorgeous creature is Zoe, a friend from college. Zoe, meet Angus Walker—a.k.a. Retro."

"Hi," she says, giving me a little wave.

I offer a tight nod, but my tongue feels glued to the roof of my mouth. I've never had a female friend, not even one of the skanky girls from shop class.

My mind scrambles for something cool to say, but all I can think about is how I must look to her—unkempt and awkward. Her gaze is friendly and patient, like she doesn't notice my internal meltdown. Jackson, of course, is oblivious.

"We were in the area and figured we'd stop by," he says, already stepping through the door like he owns the place. The smell of Zoe's shampoo lingers in the air as she follows.

I see myself in the hallway mirror as they pass, and my face flushes. *Great.* I look like a hermit who just emerged from his cave.

"Cool place," Zoe says, looking around. "It's got a lot of character."

That's one way to put it. I clear my throat. "Uh, thanks. It's... a work in progress."

Her eyes land on me, and I'm certain she's about to comment on my rough appearance. Instead, she smiles. "I like the scruffy look. It suits you."

I blink, unsure if I heard her right. "What?"

She tilts her head, studying me. "You know, rugged. Like a rock star."

Rock star? The words momentarily short-circuit my self-doubt.

"Uh… thanks," I manage, my voice cracking.

Jackson snorts from the kitchen. "Don't let it go to your head, Retro. She's just being polite."

Zoe throws him a sharp look. "No, I'm serious."

Glancing at the mirror again, I see myself through her eyes. Maybe I don't look so bad. Or maybe she's being nice because her hotshot boyfriend wants something from me.

"How did you get the name Retro?" she asks.

"I… well… I guess it's because I've always been into classic rock, and pretty much everything from the seventies. If I'm not mistaken, Jackson was the first to call me that, as well as other names I'm too embarrassed to mention."

Jackson waves a dismissive hand. "Whatever."

"I like it," Zoe says, her smile warm and genuine.

Her approval sends a flicker of pride through me, but I don't let it show. Truth is, I've always felt I belonged in that era, so the name doesn't bother me. But I wouldn't admit it to Jackson.

I realize I'm staring, so I turn to Jackson, who leans in with an irritating confidence.

"I can make you a rich man," he says. "But not without your help."

Rich? I'm intrigued. He's always been a bullshitter, but people sometimes change. I haven't seen him in three years.

Ozzy approaches to give our visitors the sniff test. Zoe kneels to scratch behind his ears. I'm envious as I watch her, but I can't tell Jackson that either.

Jackson pauses and looks around the room with condescending eyes. The house was built in the '60s, and it shows.

Faded wood-paneled walls and low ceilings make the place feel small. Except for a flat-screen TV, this room resembles a low-budget 1975 movie set.

"What's his name?" Zoe asks.

"Ozzy."

"Like that old rock star?"

At least someone in the room has a little culture besides me.

"Yes. He was the frontman for Black Sabbath." I flash a crooked smile. "You get it? Black Sabbath, Black Labbath?"

Silence.

Seriously? Am I the only one who sees the humor in that?

A polite smile lifts the corners of Zoe's mouth. "How long have you had him?"

"About ten months. I found him wandering around on the ranch. He looked like he hadn't eaten in a few days, so I took him home and fed him. He's been here ever since."

"Aww."

Jackson clears his throat. "Uh… Girls? Are we done with the small talk?"

I sigh and lead them along a flat, well-trodden path in the carpet to the living room. Jackson makes himself comfortable in my recliner while Zoe perches on one end of the couch. I sit on the opposite end and try not to stare as Ozzy plants himself in her lap.

I turn to Jackson and wait. He could give an aspirin a headache.

He slides to the edge of his seat. "How would you like to go on a treasure hunt?"

Chapter Four

Hidden Treasure – Traffic (1971)

It sounds like a scam, but I'll hear him out before I throw him out. "I don't have to put up any cash, do I?"

"No, no, nothing like that."

"Why me?" I glance at Zoe, then back to Jackson. "You never liked me in school. Now, five years later, you show up at my door asking for my help?"

Jackson clears his throat and shoots a nervous glance at Zoe like he doesn't want her to think any less of him. "That's not true. We traveled in different circles."

Different circles. The haves and the have-nots. The cool kids and the nerds. "What kind of treasure?"

Jackson leans forward and rests his elbows on his knees. "Three billion dollars in gold."

My eyebrows shoot up. "Did you say *billion*?"

"Billion—with a B."

I lean back, trying not to look as intrigued as I feel. "I'm going to circle back to my earlier question. Why me? There are plenty of people who know more about treasure hunting than I do."

Jackson leans in even closer, his eyes darting toward the windows like he's checking for spies. "Because I think the gold is buried under your ranch."

And there it is. Perhaps this ranch is not so bad after all. "Technically, that would make it *my* treasure." I slide to the edge of my seat. "What makes you think it's here?"

"Legend has it, during the sixteenth century, eight thousand Aztec warriors carried King Montezuma's gold from Mexico City to the U.S. to protect it from the Spanish conquistadors. I've done some research—old maps, aerial surveys, accounts from early settlers—and everything points to the Uinta Mountains."

"And?"

"I did some aerial reconnaissance and found drawings on the rocks at the northern edge of your ranch that appear to be Aztec petroglyphs."

"You saw them from a plane?"

"A drone."

"That's illegal, isn't it?"

"It was just a drone. No harm done." He waves the concern away. "Does it matter if it makes us both rich?"

He has a point. "So, what do you need from me?"

"Your permission to do some treasure hunting."

"And what's in it for me?"

"Twenty-five percent of anything we find."

I laugh. "That's a little light, don't you think? It's my land, after all."

Jackson's jaw tightens, but he forces a smile. "Twenty-five percent of three billion is still… well, a boatload of money."

"True, but I'm not convinced I need you. I could follow the petroglyphs myself."

Jackson's face flushes. He's not used to people telling him no, and the muscles in his jaw flex like he's biting back a retaliation. I let him stew before I throw out my counteroffer.

"Fifty-fifty sounds fair."

My counter lands like a Mike Tyson right hook.

Jackson stands, chest out and nostrils flared. "You can't be serious."

I rise to meet him. Zoe steps between us, her hand on Jackson's chest.

"I'm sure we can work something out that's fair for everyone," she says.

I look at her and wonder what percentage he's promised her, if any. Whatever it is, it needs to come from his cut. I realize at that moment, an even split isn't possible. He'd make less on this deal than me. But he needs me, or at least my land, so I wait for him to counter.

Jackson exhales. "Fine. Sixty-forty. That's my final offer."

Sixty-forty still sounds too good to be true. But can I trust him? If there's even a nugget of truth in Jackson's story, I can't ignore it. This ranch barely pays for itself.

"I'll think about it."

His eyes narrow. "What's there to think about?"

"I need to sleep on it. I'll let you know tomorrow."

With an annoyed grunt, he grabs my hand, flips it over, and scribbles his phone number on my palm like a middle school slut. His glare tells me he's furious.

"Come on, Zoe. We're done here."

I follow them to the door and lock it behind them. My brain still spins. What just happened? If someone asked me to name the most bizarre moment of my life, I'd have to say this one.

I flip my record to the B side, flop back onto the couch, and settle into my vegetative state. Halfway through the second track, another knock pulls me out of my daze. You've got to be kidding me.

"Coming!"

I swing the door open, ready to send Jackson packing again, but instead, I find a tall, lanky figure with round glasses and wavy brown hair.

The adrenaline fizzles and my shoulders relax. "Waldo!"

"Hey."

I grin. "Home for the summer?"

"Just got back."

His real name is Walter Hastings—the smartest kid in our high school and my only real friend. Someone called him Waldo after he showed up to a Christmas party in a red-and-white striped sweater and matching hat. His wavy brown hair and round glasses made him the spitting image of that cartoon character you have to look for in a crowd in those children's books. The name stuck, much to the annoyance of his sister, who fielded "Where's Waldo?" jokes daily.

Ozzy wags his tail as he sniffs Waldo's hand.

"I see Ozzy's still here."

"Yeah, he's my *second-best* friend."

"As long as I remain the first, you can have as many as you like."

I step aside to let him in. "How was school?"

"At Stanford, pretty much everyone is smart, so I fit in better." He glances around the living room. "I'm sorry about your parents. That sucks."

"Yeah. Thanks." I head to the kitchen. "Want a beer?"

He hesitates.

"Come on, man. You probably pulled a 4.0 last semester, and now we've got the entire summer to hang out. Let's celebrate."

"Fine, but let's make it a toast to your parents."

I return with two bottles, hand one to Waldo, and settle into my chair. We clink the bottles together in a quiet toast, and I take a long sip.

Waldo tilts his bottle to his lips but pauses halfway, studying me with unexpected seriousness. "It must be strange without them here."

I stare at the bottle in my hand, the label already peeling under my thumb. "Yeah. Quiet, too. Feels like the house is holding its breath." I glance at my guitar in its stand. "I guess that's why I play so much. You know, to fill the void."

He nods, his gaze shifting to the family photos on the wall. The silence stretches for a moment.

"It feels like this is it for me." The words tumble out unplanned. "Like I might spend the rest of my life here alone."

Waldo looks up with a frown. "Don't be ridiculous. There's someone out there for everyone." He cracks a small grin. "Even you."

I can't help but snort. "That's rich, coming from you. I don't recall you ever making any inroads with the ladies."

He leans forward and rests his elbows on his knees. "Do you believe in soulmates?"

I hesitate, surprised by the question. "I don't know. It sounds like something Hollywood cooked up to sell movie tickets."

He shakes his head, leaning forward. "No, it's more than that. The idea's been around forever. A soulmate. Someone you're meant to find, no matter what. Someone who gets you like no one else can."

The conviction in his tone makes me pause, and I roll the idea around in my head for a moment. "I don't know. I guess it's… possible… for some people."

I pick up my phone and Google *soulmate*. "A connection that goes beyond mere physical attraction. A person with whom you click on every level. It's effortless and natural, and all you have to do is be yourself."

The words offer hope. But the chances of finding her are slim to none, living alone on a ranch in rural Utah.

Waldo nods toward the dog curled up on the carpet. "Hey, maybe Ozzy's your soulmate."

I roll my eyes. "Just my luck, right?"

The tension breaks, and we share a laugh.

Waldo lets out a sigh as his shoulders relax. "Sorry I didn't make it to the funeral."

"It's okay." I shrug, not wanting to linger on the subject. "You'll never guess who I saw there."

Waldo tilts his head, curious but cautious.

"Gran."

His eyes widen, and he sits up straighter. "Wait—your grandmother? I thought she was… dead?"

I let out a dry laugh. "She fooled us all."

"Did you ask her where she's been all this time?"

"Not exactly." I shrink a bit in my seat. "I was too pissed."

He nods. "I guess I'd be mad, too. What did she have to say?"

"This is where it gets weirder." I lean forward. "She asked me if I found it."

"Found what?"

"No clue. She said we need to talk, but not there."

Waldo slides to the edge of his seat. "Did she say where?"

I drain my beer. "Didn't stick around long enough to find out."

"You ran away?"

"It was more like a fast walk." I gesture vaguely, hoping to change the subject again. "Anyway, you'll never guess who else showed up today."

He tilts his head again. "More riddles?"

I smirk. "J.C."

"Jesus Christ makes house calls now?"

Mr. Serious made a decent joke. "Not *that* J. C., Jackson Carr."

"The douchebag from high school?"

"That's the one."

Waldo sits back. "Jackass Carr? Out of the blue? That makes no sense."

"And yet, it happened."

Waldo leans in and studies my face. "You're high."

"Maybe a little. But I'm telling the truth."

Chapter Five

Money – Pink Floyd (1973)

Waldo pushes his wavy hair out of his eyes before he speaks. "As bad as Carr acted toward anyone who showed a hint of weakness, I have to give him credit for bringing us together."

He isn't wrong. Jackass Carr, as we called him, was the catalyst for one of the most defining moments of my high school life—and the reason I ended up taking two years of judo lessons.

Being different doesn't play well in a small-town high school. Waldo and I were opposites, but outsiders in our own ways. He was the brainy kid at the top of the class, while I treaded water around C-level. He was thin as a fence post, while I was overweight. He was grounded in the present, while I lived in the past.

It didn't matter that we both existed on the outskirts of teenage society; I didn't feel like I belonged even with the other misfits. Lunchtime was a study in solitude—Waldo at one table, me at another, each of us eating alone.

The incident Waldo's referring to was the first time we ever spoke.

On this particular day, I noticed Jackass Carr and one of his jock buddies sit down at Waldo's table. Big red flag. I froze, my sandwich halfway to my mouth, and watched. Normally, I'd mind my own business—high school was tough enough without making enemies—but this felt different. I could see their intentions before they even said a word.

Carr grabbed Waldo's lunch bag and rummaged through it. He tossed his friend an apple and kept the sandwich for himself. I watched Carr and his sidekick laugh like hyenas, hoping one of the lunch monitors would intervene. No such luck. When Carr slapped the back of Waldo's head, I couldn't just sit there.

I'm not a violent person—make love, not war, and all that. I had no experience with either, but a person needs to start somewhere. My tray clattered on the table as I got up and marched over. Carr had two inches on me, but I had thirty pounds on him.

"Back off, Carr," I said, my voice steadier than I felt.

He looked up and smirked. "Who's gonna make me?"

Ignoring him, I turned to Waldo. "You okay?"

Waldo nodded, his face red with humiliation.

I turned back to Carr. "Nobody wants trouble, so why don't you take your pet monkey and scram?"

In hindsight, I could have chosen my words more carefully.

He threw the first punch. I'm not going to lie, it hurt like hell. Adrenaline rushed from wherever it rushes from and flooded my veins. It's called the fight-or-flight response, and for the first time in my life, my brain chose fight. I'm sure he expected that to be the end of it, so when I landed a right hook below his left eye, he went down like a bag of rocks, more stunned than hurt.

The monkey left in a hurry. Carr scrambled to his feet and brushed himself off, embarrassed in front of the entire fifth-period lunch crowd. He puffed his chest out and glared at me before the lazy lunch monitors arrived and dragged us off to the principal's office.

I spent the next three days suspended, replaying the scene in my head. I wasn't proud of what I'd done, but I knew one thing for sure: it wouldn't be the last time I'd need to defend myself. The next day, I signed up for judo lessons.

Judo taught me more than how to defend myself; it taught me how to use someone else's strength against them. Winning my first competition sent a clear message, and no one messed with me after that. At least, not physically. The name-calling continued in earnest, but I could live with that.

Jackass Carr kept his distance when I returned to school. And Waldo? He waited by my locker after second period.

"Why don't you join me for lunch today?" he said, his voice careful, like he wasn't sure how I'd respond. "I've noticed that we both eat alone. Perhaps we could eat alone together."

A grin spread across my face despite myself. "Sure. Why not?"

And just like that, a friendship was born.

When my mind returns to the present, I smile. "It was worth every day of that suspension."

Waldo's smile fades into something more serious. "So, what did Jackson want?"

"Get this—he wants my permission to go treasure hunting on my land."

"You didn't give it to him."

"I told him I'd think about it."

Waldo raises an eyebrow. "Which means no, right?"

"Not necessarily."

A silence stretches between us, and he stares at me like I've grown a second head. Finally, he asks, "What kind of treasure?"

"He thinks three billion dollars of Aztec gold is buried in caves up north."

"Does he have any proof?"

"He claims there's some legend and maps and stuff."

Waldo turns his beer bottle in his hands, his expression thoughtful. "I know the legend."

"You do?"

"There might be some truth to it."

If Jackson says something, you assume it's bullshit. But if Waldo—Stanford egghead extraordinaire—corroborates it, you pay attention. "Can you elaborate?"

"How much do you want to know?"

"Just the important stuff."

Waldo leans forward, slipping into lecture mode. "Okay. Montezuma II, the last emperor of the Aztecs, is said to have amassed an enormous treasure of gold, jewels, and sacred artifacts. When Hernán Cortés and his conquistadors overthrew Tenochtitlán in 1521, some Aztec priests and warriors supposedly fled north with a substantial portion of this treasure to keep it out of Spanish hands."

I nod, encouraging him to continue.

"Over the years, maps and rumors have surfaced, pointing to the treasure's supposed location. Many of the maps are vague, with symbols and descriptions of natural landmarks. Some scholars believe certain petroglyphs in Utah and neighboring states might hold clues. There's linguistic overlap between the Aztec language and the languages of the Ute and Hopi tribes, suggesting the Aztecs traveled through this area."

"You're a walking encyclopedia."

He smirks. "I've been called worse."

I lean back and let it all sink in. Perhaps I should have stayed in school.

Waldo grins, clearly enjoying the chance to show off. "Fun fact: the Aztec word for gold translates to 'excrement of the gods.'"

I can't help but laugh. "In other words, 'holy shit.'"

Waldo rolls his eyes, but his smile lingers.

"Jackson offered me a sixty-forty split."

"That sounds too generous for him."

"It wasn't his first offer."

"What's it going to cost you?"

"Nothing. He wants permission to hunt on my land." I pause. "It'd be a no-brainer if it were anyone but Jackson."

"Indeed." Waldo leans back, tapping his fingers on the bottle. "What would you even do with over a billion dollars?"

"Does that mean you don't think I should do it?"

Waldo smiles. "No, it means you should split your take with me. I can do nothing as well as you can."

He's got a point. And he's practically family. "Okay. We can do nothing together."

"I'm really glad I stopped over here today." His smile lasts only a moment before he pauses, lost in thought. "So, what would you do with your half?"

"Let's see… Fix up the ranch, build a music studio with high-end recording equipment, and maybe add a pool out back for hot days. Wait, I almost forgot. I'd restore the old GTO that's collecting rust in the barn." I grin. "What about you?"

"Easy. I'd build a high-tech smart home with a state-of-the-art lab where I'd work on AI, robotics, or maybe solve the world's problems."

"That's nice," I say. "But what would you do for fun?"

Waldo flashes a devilish grin. "Come over here and enjoy your pool, obviously. We could throw pool parties with lots of hot babes in bikinis."

"We don't know any hot babes."

"We wouldn't need to." His devilish grin returns. "With that kind of money, the girls would find us."

He holds his fist out for a celebratory fist bump.

"Babes in bikinis." I hesitate—like that's ever gonna happen—then muster up a fist bump, not wanting to spoil the moment. But the moment is spoiled.

I grab my fourth beer. Waldo shakes his head when I offer him another. He'd stopped after one, refusing to go down the rabbit hole with me. I try to pull him in, anyway. "So, what's wrong with me, Waldo? I'm lost and alone, and the way things are going, that's the way I'll die."

"It's the alcohol talking. Nothing's wrong with you."

"You're lying."

"Okay. Nothing that can't be fixed."

"The band that I thought would make me famous went nowhere. So, now what have I got? I'll tell you what I don't have—a high school diploma. Or a girlfriend. Or any prospects. Everyone was right, I'm a shithead."

"You need to stop listening to everyone."

"Easy for you to say. You proved them wrong."

"I don't like to see you like this. You need to let go of the past, stop self-medicating, and do something with your life."

"The only time I feel good about anything is when I'm high. But you wouldn't understand."

He stares at the coffee table, strewn with remnants of my daily rituals—an ashtray overflowing with crumpled, half-burned joints and the faint outline of rings left by beer bottles. "You're right. I don't understand."

The corners of his mouth turn up in a compassionate smile. "Jackson Carr is a bigger shithead than you'll ever be."

I study his eyes to see if he's patronizing me again. "You really think so?"

"Of course."

"That might be the nicest thing anybody's ever said to me." I shrug. "Okay. Maybe you're right. After all, you're the smart one."

He nods, and his smile widens. "I know."

Waldo's on his way home an hour later, and I'm left alone with the mess in my head. I grab a leftover taco from the fridge and wash it down with another beer.

My guitar calls, and I plug it into my vintage Fender amp. Turning the volume knob to eight—Mom and Pop never let me go past three in the house—I rip through Black Sabbath's "Paranoid." Halfway through, my fingers falter, and I stop.

Waldo was right. I need to put on my big boy pants and move on with my life, and six hundred million in gold might be just the thing I need to get started.

A smirk tugs at the corner of my mouth as I play the opening riff to Pink Floyd's "Money."

It's time to call Jackson and let him know I'm in. However, when I check my palm for his number, I realize the condensation from the beer bottles has washed away two of the digits.

I collapse backward onto the couch. I know I say this too often, but…

What a shithead.

Chapter Six

Free Ride – The Edgar Winter Group (1973)

I 'm sure Waldo could tell me how many different number combinations I would need to dial to cover the two missing digits, but I fear it's too many to consider. A quick Google search for Jackson Carr turns up nothing. Perhaps it's a sign. My only other choice, short of driving around town looking for him, is to wait until he gets impatient enough to knock on my door again.

Ozzy's ears perk up, and he's out of his bed. He doesn't bark, but he looks uneasy.

"What is it, boy?"

I pull the curtain back and look out the back door. Something moves in the shadows. I grab a flashlight and a shotgun on my way outside.

"Who's there?"

Two eyes glow as they watch me from outside the flashlight's beam. I move the light to illuminate a coyote. Probably the same one that ran Mom and Pop off the road, looking to finish off the rest of the family.

As I raise the shotgun, Ozzy lets out loud bark, and the coyote scampers off.

I turn to Ozzy, relieved I didn't have to shoot. "Attaboy, Ozzy. Good dog."

Back inside, I return Pop's gun to the cabinet. I've only ever shot it once. The kick nearly knocked me off my feet. I pull a dog treat from the kitchen cupboard and toss it to Ozzy.

★★★

I'm in the kitchen the next day making myself a sandwich for lunch when Jackson returns. He's standing alone on my porch.

He follows me into the kitchen, where I continue to make myself a peanut butter and jelly sandwich.

"I've given it a lot of thought," I say as I realize I've put too much peanut butter on the bread and scrape some off with the knife. I look at the knife, then the jar, not wanting to return the excess. I hold up the knife. "Want a sandwich?"

His eyes roll back in his head. "No. I don't want a sand-wich." He shifts his weight to his other foot. "So, what do you think?"

"I think I'm in." I lick the peanut butter from the knife—something I wouldn't recommend in the middle of an important conversation.

His muscles relax. "Great."

I hold up a finger as I try to scrape the sticky mess from the roof of my mouth with my tongue.

Jackson crosses his arms in front of his chest. "What?"

I take a beat to swallow and clear my throat. "I have one condition."

"You're in no position to be dictating conditions."

I could tell he knew I was. "You're paying for any equipment and supplies."

"How's that fair?"

Look who's talking about what's fair. "You said I wouldn't have to put up any cash." I grab a glass of water from the sink and drink it while he watches. I set the glass down and turn to face him.

"How about this?" I offer. "I'll provide the transportation. It's a long hike out to the mountains. I've got two ATVs in the barn that we can use. That's more than fair."

"I can live with that."

Of course he can. I'm saving him a boatload of time and money. We strike a deal, and I shake his clammy hand.

"Okay, partner. Get those buggies gassed up and ready to go. I'll be back at eight tomorrow morning."

Eight? I don't normally roll out of bed until nine. "I'll be ready at eight-thirty."

"It gets hot out there. We need to get an early start."

"Okay. Eight-thirty."

A blank look washes over his face, and he waits a beat. "Fine. But you'd better be ready."

"By the way," I say as he heads for the door. "I'm bringing a plus one."

He stops with his hand on the doorknob. "This isn't a wedding reception. Who's your date?"

"Walter Hastings."

"Waldo?"

"He's smarter than the three of us put together. And he knows about the legend. He might come in handy."

Another blank look. "I don't like it. He'll need to keep his mouth shut about what we're doing. And if he's looking for a payday, it's coming from your end."

"Roger that."

As soon as he leaves, I call Waldo. Unfortunately, he has a prior commitment tomorrow. I'm disappointed, but I convince him to accompany us the following day.

I need to gas up the ATVs, and I know better than to wait until morning.

The heavy barn door squawks as it slides open along the metal rails. Pop says they're noisy no matter how much you oil them. A wave of cool, musty air spills out, thick with the smell of aged wood, old hay, and gasoline. Inside, shafts of sunlight pierce through gaps in the weathered boards, illuminating swirls of dust motes that hang in the air like in a horror movie.

I haven't been in here since last year. I rode one of the ATVs during the summer, but the condition of the other one is suspect. I should have looked it over before offering its services to Jackson.

I put some fresh gas in the tank of the first one and cross my fingers. She starts right up. The second one, not so much. I push it outside, clean the layers of dust off, and inspect the engine. I know something about fixing cars and other vehicles from two years of auto shop at school and working at the parts store.

It appears the fuel filter is clogged after sitting for too long. Fingers crossed there's a spare in the barn. I rifle through a box of spare parts and find one I think will work. I install it, change the spark plug, add some fresh gas, and fire it up. Big sigh of relief. We're ready to roll.

✱✱✱

An alarm that sounds like a meltdown in a nuclear reactor rips me from a hazy dream. I squint at my phone, struggling to make sense of the numbers. *Eight.* Eight in the morning? Instinctively, I tap the snooze button before I remember I can't sleep in today. Jackson will be here at 8:30. I lay in bed for another minute, grateful that I cleaned and gassed up the ATVs the night before.

My bare feet hit the floor, and I find my way to the bathroom mirror. The guy staring back at me looks half-dead, hair sticking out in every direction. I splash water on my face and run a comb through my renegade hair. My face shows another day's growth, but the whiskers feel good under my hand.

"Rock star, huh?" Zoe's words echo in my mind, and I feel more alive.

I find a clean shirt and a pair of shorts, then grab my phone, keys, and wallet. After a quick cup of coffee and a bowl of Cheerios, I'm ready to go.

My fellow treasure hunters arrive on time in a pickup truck piled high with gear. I slip on my work boots and grab a well-worn Colorado Rockies baseball cap.

Jackson's truck is overloaded, looking like something straight out of *The Beverly Hillbillies*—the only thing missing is Granny perched on top in her rocking chair.

"Looks like you're moving in." I send a sideways glance and a quick wink Zoe's way.

"What do you mean?"

"Who packed your truck, Jed Clampett?"

Jackson folds his arms across his chest. "Are we going to stand around telling jokes, or can we get this show on the road?"

I put my hands together. "Okay. Let's load up the ATVs."

It won't all fit, so we'll need to leave some stuff behind. Clearly, he'll need my help with that.

Jackson looks around then smirks. "Where's Waldo?"

Zoe giggles.

"Unfortunately, he can't make it today, but he'll be here tomorrow. ATVs are gassed and ready to go."

"Great. Looks like I'm going to need all the space I can get for supplies. Zoe, you can ride with Retro."

I'm okay with that, but someone needs to tell my sweaty palms. I wipe them on my shorts and help Jackson unload the truck.

I rifle through the pile of supplies in the back of the truck. "A tent? Sleeping bags?"

Jackson grabs the tent. "We may want to work late and stay overnight."

"Correction. *You* may want to stay overnight. Too many coyotes and other creatures out there. Ever heard of a skin-walker?"

"Bullshit. That's a Native American myth."

"Yeah, until you meet up with one."

Zoe frowns. "What's a skinwalker?"

"Skinwalkers are malevolent witches in Navajo folklore that often take the form of coyotes or wolves but can transform into any animal." I shake my head slowly. "Not something I'd want to have wake *me* up in the middle of the night."

"Maybe he's right," Zoe says, looking as uneasy as a vegan at a barbecue.

Jackson looks from her to me, then deposits the tent back in the truck and says, "What a bunch of babies," which earns him a punch on the arm from Zoe.

We move about half the provisions onto the two ATVs, including picks, shovels, flashlights, walkie-talkies, GPS, metal detector, ropes, carabiners, water, and snacks.

"Is that dynamite rolling around in your truck bed?"

"We might need it to open up a cave or something."

I shake my head. "It's staying here."

"That's a mistake." His arms are folded across his chest again.

"I'll tell you what's a mistake. Blowing up one of my ATVs while you're driving it to the dig site. Dynamite is sensitive to shock, friction, and temperature. The older it is the more sensitive it gets. You're lucky you didn't blow yourself and your girlfriend up on the way over here."

The color drains from Zoe's face.

"It needs to be carefully packed for transportation, not allowed to roll around loose like that."

Jackson's raised eyebrow tells me this is news to him.

"Okay, okay. Let's go get rich," he says, unable to admit he was wrong.

"One more thing." I run back into the house.

I return and tuck Pop's shotgun and a box of shells into the back of my ATV.

Jackson flinches. "What's that for?"

I climb into the driver's seat and glance at him over my shoulder. "Skinwalkers."

Chapter Seven

Baby Hold On – Eddie Money (1978)

We roar out into the brush, headed north toward the mountains. Zoe waves to Jackson as we pass him in a cloud of dust. This is my first treasure hunt, and having a pretty girl in my shotgun seat only adds to the excitement. She's laughing, wide-eyed, her hair catching in the wind.

The engine growls as I push it faster, weaving around clusters of brush and small rocks scattered across the ground. The land rolls and dips, the mountains growing closer, their jagged peaks sharp against the brilliant blue sky. Ahead, a rabbit darts across our path, and I swerve. Zoe laughs again as she clings tighter, her fingers white on the roll bar.

When we reach the foothills, we stop and wait for Jackson, who'd collected some GPS coordinates from his earlier aerial reconnaissance.

"Where to?" I ask.

He checks the GPS unit. "Follow me."

We ride along a narrow ledge, my eyes glued to the path ahead of me. The path widens, and we stop next to a vertical wall with drawings etched into the rock.

"Too bad your friend isn't here to tell us what they mean."

"Like I said, he'll be here tomorrow."

I watch him hop off his vehicle and examine a two-foot hole at the base of the wall. "If you're considering going in there, you're crazier than I thought."

Even if I could fit through that opening, you couldn't pay me enough to crawl in there face-first and have it bitten off by whatever creature might call this hole home.

"That's why I brought the dynamite."

"So that's your plan? Blow up every little hole you find up here. That's not gonna happen."

He steps back and studies the rock art.

"There are hundreds of these drawings all over the state," I say.

"Maybe you can call your friend or send him a picture. See what he thinks."

"There's no cell service up here."

"Really?" He pulls out his phone and checks. "Shit!"

"Most of the drawings around here are Navajo or Ute, not Aztec."

He pulls a folded paper from his pocket and hands it to me. "These are Aztec. This is what we're looking for."

I study the images on the paper. "Then we should move on."

Zoe approaches, and I hand her the paper. Jackson checks his GPS and gestures for us to follow him.

After a handful of similar encounters, and a stop for lunch, we pause near a larger opening that could be a cave, or as Jackson suggests, a tunnel to a cavern full of gold. If there's any chance he's right, I suppose we should investigate.

This cave is by far the largest we've found. We spend two hours inside, kicking over rocks, looking for anything that might indicate humans had been there. The back of the cave narrows, and we follow it for fifty feet to a dead end.

Jackson stops and shakes his head. "There's got to be more."

"Maybe in the next one."

I watch Zoe sit on a rock and slump forward with her elbows on her knees, looking exhausted. An eerie silence hangs in the dusty air.

Finally, she looks up at me for help, not expecting any sympathy from her boyfriend. A lock of hair has escaped from her ponytail and hangs across her face. She blows it out of the way, her face streaked with fine layers of dust.

My gaze shifts from Zoe to Jackson. "Maybe we should call it a day."

Zoe's eyes widen. "Yeah, I'm beat."

Jackson glares.

"You're welcome to stay out here," I offer. "But Zoe and I are going back to the house. We can pick up where we left off tomorrow." I surprise myself with the suggestion.

Relief washes over her face, and she stands.

Jackson shakes his head. "I figured you girls wouldn't last."

I let his insult go without comment.

"Hey," he calls out after us. "I don't suppose you could leave the shotgun."

"Yeah, that's not happening."

We're halfway to the mouth of the cave when Jackson calls out.

"Wait up."

Outside, he helps me load the ATVs. I climb in and glance at Zoe before reaching for the ignition. She mouths the words "thank you."

I smile and nod, proud of myself.

Back at the house, we agree to meet at the same time tomorrow.

"Hey, Retro. Mind if I send up the drone again? I want to gather some additional intel for tomorrow."

I'm too tired to think about it. "Knock yourself out."

They leave in a cloud of dust, but not before I remove the two sticks of dynamite from his truck bed and store it safely in the barn.

After dinner, I call Waldo and recount the day's events. He promises to join us tomorrow, which I realize means no more eye candy in my shotgun seat. Treasure or no treasure, I'm encouraged that I held my own in the presence of a pretty girl. Instead of my usual stumbling over words and acting like a moron, one might say I was borderline witty and charming. I fire up a doobie to celebrate the day and play guitar until my exhaustion catches up with me. I call it a night early, set my alarm, and climb into bed.

Day two starts with a call from Jackson to say he won't be able to make it until after lunch. He's on his way to town to pick up a package, then crunch the data from last night's recon flight.

Still tired from yesterday's adventure, I welcome the time off. After I update Waldo about the change in plans, I play guitar for a couple of hours, then straighten up the house. I tell myself it needs a good cleaning, which it does, but honestly, I don't want Zoe to think I'm a slacker.

Waldo shows up at noon like I'd asked, and I throw some ham and cheese sandwiches together for lunch. He sips on a water bottle while I crack open a beer for myself.

Jackson pulls into the driveway at one. He looks more eager than prepared. "Let's hit it." He grins like he's already found the treasure.

We load up and head for the mountains, our game plan sketched out based on drone footage and Jackson's questionable instincts. The video shows some intriguing rock art and what looks like an old opening that someone went to a lot of trouble to cover up. The carvings stretch across a vertical rock face.

Waldo hops out first when we get there and heads straight for the rock wall, clutching a book like it's the Rosetta Stone. He's muttering to himself as he flips pages and nods in that scholarly way of his.

"This is the one," Jackson says as he parks near the opening and unloads his tools like we're about to break into Fort Knox. "I can feel it."

I need more than a feeling from the likes of Jackson Carr. "What do you think, Waldo?"

Waldo glances back at me, one finger marking his place in the book. "These over here are mostly Ute or Navajo. See the horses and the warriors with bows? Standard stuff."

I point to another carving near what used to be the cave opening. It's a spiral, carved deep into the stone, its edges worn smooth by time. "What about that one?"

Waldo adjusts his glasses and flips through his book. "Spirals are common in Native art, and their meanings vary. Some say it represents a coiled snake or the path of the sun."

"And?" I prod.

"It could also represent the afterlife," he continues, "or a geographic marker, like the location of water. Some tribes believed it identified a portal to the spirit world."

He pauses, and I catch the hesitation in his voice.

"What is it?"

Waldo looks up, his expression a mix of intrigue and caution. "The Aztecs sometimes used it as a symbol for gold."

Chapter Eight

Jump – Van Halen (1984)

I call Jackson over so Waldo can tell him what he told me about the spiral marking.

His eyes widen above a triumphant smile. "I knew it!"

"I'm confused." I scratch my chin. "If you're going to hide something valuable, why mark it with a sign that basically says, 'Here's where I hid the gold'?"

Jackson's expression falls.

Waldo has a theory. "Perhaps the Aztecs were the only people who knew what the symbol meant."

This satisfies Jackson, and he returns to his work.

Rocks, which could have fallen or could have been deliberately placed, cover the mouth of the cave. A small opening is visible above the rock pile, so I investigate. The opening appears too small to allow human access, but large enough for an animal such as a wolf or coyote. My flashlight beam does not reveal any activity inside.

Two hours and a half dozen bottles of water later, we've removed enough of the rocks to enter the cave. The air is cooler inside, but heavy with dust from our excavation work. We don masks and search for evidence of human occupation as the dust settles around us. Nothing to note in our search of the outer cavern, except three large openings in the rock walls that appear to be tunnels or mine shafts that require investigation.

Each tunnel heads in a different direction, holding the promise of a secret vault somewhere deep in the bowels of the mountain. I suggest we split up to save time. The others agree.

Jackson walks outside and returns with three strange-looking handguns.

"What are those?"

"Tasers." He smiles as he hands one each to Waldo and me.

Waldo hesitates, then inspects it like it's a science project.

Jackson raises his chin. "I picked them up this morning."

Zoe protests. "Where's mine?"

"You don't need one. You're coming with me."

I hold mine up. "And we need these, why?"

"We need to protect ourselves. Or did you bring shotguns for everyone today?" He pauses to let his logic sink in. "Even if you did, I don't imagine discharging a firearm inside a cave is a good idea."

He has a point. "Okay. Thanks."

"We don't know what animals we might run into."

I look at Waldo and wink. "Don't skinwalkers live in caves?"

My remark earns me a stern glare and a "shut up" from Jackson. He gives us a quick lesson on the use and care of Tasers, then clips it to his belt. "Keep your walkies close and let me know if you find anything."

I watch the others disappear into their respective holes, take a deep breath, and venture into mine. Gravel crunches beneath my boots as shadows flicker over jagged walls that seem to close in on me the farther I go. The air grows mustier, infused with centuries-old dust, and a faint smell that might be guano. I keep an eye out for bats. I hate bats.

As I move farther into the cave, I remember a TV show where cave explorers carried electronic air quality monitors that sounded an alarm when poisonous gas was detected. Years ago, miners took canaries in little cages down into the mines with them because they were more sensitive to toxic gases like carbon monoxide and methane than humans. If the bird keeled over, it was time to bounce.

I guess no one in our party had thought of that. Our inexperience and our enthusiasm have left us vulnerable to such things. I wonder what other dangers we might be ill-prepared to deal with.

The cave walls eventually close in on me, and I squeeze through a crevice that opens up to a hidden chamber. My light illuminates three ordinary rock walls and a fourth that is anything but ordinary. I'm mesmerized. It seems fluid, moving in nearly imperceptible waves, like heat rising from the pavement in the middle of July. But I don't see a heat source. In fact, the space is colder than the rest of the cave.

The air bristles with energy, and the hairs on my arms dance with the vibration as curiosity moves me closer. I've discovered something incredible here, but I'm not sure what it is. I reach out a hand toward it, and the surface parts around my fingers like warm water. I freak out and quickly pull it back.

As I flex my fingers, relieved there's no damage, I remember the spiral image carved into the rock outside the cave. Waldo said it could indicate the location of a portal to the spirit world. What does that even mean? If I step through this portal, where will I be—another dimension or planet or somewhere I can't even imagine? Will I be able to return? I wish Waldo and his gigantic brain were here.

I step backward, and my flashlight reflects off something shiny on the floor. It appears to be a dog tag, the same shape as the one on Ozzy's collar. I pick it up and turn it over to see the word "Shadow" engraved on the front. That's a great name for a black Lab. Has Ozzy been in here?

The cave entrance had been filled in, but an opening large enough for a dog to come and go had remained. Was he living here? For how long? I slip the tag into my pocket. Could he have come through this… this… portal? If so, from where?

I guess there's only one way to find out. But do I really want to?

I stare into the distortion and wonder if this might be it—my shot at something bigger than this lonely, dead-end life. What if, on the other side, I'm not the weird kid with a rusted-out car and no clue what he's doing? What if I could be someone cool, someone with a band, someone with a girlfriend who doesn't exist only in my daydreams? It could be dangerous, but it can't be worse than slowly fading into nothing out here. At least wherever this takes me, I might matter to someone.

My heart pounds so hard it drowns out every rational thought. I take a deep breath, then another, but it does nothing to steady me. My feet feel rooted to the cave floor, my body torn between fight and flight.

I take a step forward. Then hesitate. What if I get stuck? What if this thing vaporizes me on contact? Or worse—what if it tears me apart molecule by molecule and forgets how to put me back together? No body. No bones. Just a cloud of regrets and guitar riffs drifting through the void.

For a split second, I consider turning around, heading home, and pretending I never found this damn thing. *What will it be Angus?* I'm like a radio dial stuck between two stations. *Pick one!*

I step into the unknown, and there's nothing beneath me. I'm falling through a tunnel in slow motion like it's full of water, and I curse my recklessness. But instead of coming up gasping for air, I suddenly find myself on solid ground again, stumbling as my eyes adjust. The air feels thick, dusty, and stale. I blink, disoriented, as the dim light resolves into the concrete walls of a space littered with debris. Rusted metal shelves line one wall, covered in scraps of yellowed paper. This is no cave; it's the basement of a building, some relic of the past.

I find the stairs and ascend to the main floor, but the door won't open, so I give it a kick. It surrenders its hold, and I find myself surrounded by an abandoned office building that has long fallen into disrepair. The boarded-up windows allow slivers of sunlight to filter in, casting eerie shadows on the graffiti-covered walls. Old metal desks are randomly strewn around the room, like the aftermath of a demolition derby.

The remnants of squatters and transient partygoers offer hope there's a way in and out that's not boarded up. The front door is locked and the windows painted over. I grab a guitar pick from my pocket and scrape at the paint in one corner, but it breaks in my hand before I can get a look outside. Not knowing who or what is on the other side keeps me from breaking the glass.

A quick search turns up a side door with no windows. A sign above the crash bar reads, *Emergency Exit. Alarm will sound if opened.* Assuming the alarm has long been disabled, I push the door open.

My eyes take a moment to adjust to the sunlight.

"Toto, I have a feeling we're not in Kansas anymore."

Chapter Nine

Stranger in a Strange Land – Leon Russell (1971)

I'm standing in an unfamiliar alley, flanked by graffiti-stained brick walls. The hum of traffic beckons me to the alley's mouth, and I stumble toward it as my pulse quickens.

I step onto the street, and the world opens like a living time capsule. The cars—long, wide beasts of chrome and muscle—roll by, their engines growling in a way that modern hybrids can't replicate. Each one looks like it just rolled off a vintage car calendar. Drivers sport aviators, mustaches, and hair straight out of a Burt Reynolds movie. The pedestrians wear denim jackets and bell bottoms. Cigarette smoke curls lazily from their lips. I blink hard.

Billboards loom overhead, some advertising cigarettes. Others advertise products that don't exist anymore—relics of a bygone era. I catch snippets of conversation as people pass, their voices laced with slang that sounds foreign.

The sign on the corner reads North Willow and Copperfield. I have no clue where that is. My head swims as I try to make sense of this. I spot a newspaper stand with a rack of magazines and tabloids, their covers plastered with celebrities whose names I know, but faces I don't recognize.

My heart pounds as I reach out and grab the nearest newspaper—The Denver Post. I find the date.

May 25, 1978.

My throat goes dry, and my knees threaten to give out. The newspaper flutters from my trembling hands to the sidewalk as the realization crashes down on me. *Forty-six years. I'm forty-six years in the past.* I squeeze the back of my neck and close my eyes. Everything looks the same when I open them again.

The improbable truth slaps me in the face. I'm in Denver… forty-six years ago.

A pudgy fifty-something man behind the counter points two fingers at me, the stub of a cigar wedged between them. His voice sounds like truck tires on a gravel road. "You gonna buy that?"

"I'm sorry." My voice barely escapes. I fumble to refold the paper and place it back on the rack.

"Then scram," he growls. "This ain't no library."

I stagger away, each step feeling heavier than the last. My mind spins with questions, doubts, and fear. *How? Why?* The rational part of me screams to turn around, head back to the basement, and leap through the portal before this madness consumes me. But another part of me, fueled by reckless curiosity, whispers, *stay.* This is your chance to live the life you've always imagined.

The world plays out around me like a scene from an old movie. I've always wondered what it would have been like to live in the '70s. Now I'm here. But I feel like an intruder, a ghost in a place where I have no business being. I take a deep breath and try to look at this from a different perspective. If I stick around long enough, I might catch Black Sabbath or

Deep Purple or Zeppelin in concert. I think I just blew my mind.

A flicker of movement catches my eye as I walk. A man in a blue hoodie steps into a doorway. My gut tightens, but I brush it off. Coincidence.

A dozen steps later, I glance over my shoulder. He's still there. My unease grows as his gaze drills into me from beneath the hood. Is someone following me? In 1978? I haven't even been born yet.

I park myself on a bench in front of a Woolworth's store and wait. Hopefully, he'll walk by without a second look and put my growing paranoia to rest. I try not to make eye contact as he approaches. I get an uneasy feeling that he's not all there in the head. His hood is pulled up on a day when the temperature is close to eighty.

He sits next to me, and I throw up a little in my mouth. His eyes burn holes into me, so I turn to face him. He's unshaven, with intense gray eyes that make you want to look away, but I can't.

"You don't belong here," he says, his voice low and menacing, like thunder rolling in the distance.

A thousand centipedes with cold, wet feet crawl up my arms and gather on the back of my neck. "Excuse me?" Surely, I heard him wrong.

"Go back where you came from."

Panic bubbles to the surface. "You've got the wrong guy." My voice is shaky, betraying my fear.

What does he think he knows? Before I can process what's happening, he reaches for my belt and snatches my Taser. In a blur, he disappears into the crowd.

A beat cop across the street locks eyes with me as I jump to my feet. I slump back onto the bench and force myself to stay put. I can't risk drawing attention. How would I even explain who I am—or where I'm from? My driver's license won't be issued until 2017.

I shuffle inside the store, but the smell of food from the busy lunch counter chases me back outside. My nerves are so jangled I can't even think about food without getting the dry heaves. Whoever was underneath that hood sure knows how to suck the joy out of this once-in-a-lifetime adventure.

Back on the bench, I try to process what just happened. Hoodie Man singled me out to deliver his cryptic message. My heart pounds as I replay his words. *You don't belong here.* How does he know?

Were hoodies even a thing back in the '70s? I don't think so, but I can't be sure. Could Hoodie Man be another time traveler? I guess it's foolish to assume I'm the only one. Well, Ozzy and me.

The thought clings to me like a shadow. A couple of deep breaths slow my heart rate, and I redirect my thoughts to my fellow treasure hunters back home and wonder what they're up to. Did they find anything in the other two tunnels? Gold? Silver? Another portal? Do they even know I'm missing? At this point, I'm not sure I can go back. Does the portal work both ways? Will I be able to find it again in that God-forsaken building?

I pull the dog tag from my pocket. There's a good chance Ozzy, or Shadow, or whatever his name is, came through that portal in the opposite direction. I'm not sure if there's more than one portal that connects with the one on the ranch, but the area code on his tag matches a number on the billboard across the street. Denver must have been his point of origin.

Encouraging, but I still need to make sure I can find the portal. It had been difficult to see much when I arrived; the basement was dark, with junk strewn around. I need to remember exactly where I landed, so I'll go back there and scope it out before I do anything else.

A poster in a window for a bar named *Thunder Road* catches my eye as I stand to leave. They're just down the street, and they feature live music. *Now, we're talkin'.* No schedule is posted, so I make a mental note to check it out later tonight. A more positive experience while I'm here would be nice.

I wave to Gravel Mouth as I pass the newsstand on my way back to the portal, but he's not one for pleasantries. There's only one door on the side of the building. I scan the alley to make sure Hoodie, or anyone else, won't see me enter, then pull on the handle. *It's locked.*

This day keeps getting better and better. How could I be so stupid? Emergency doors lock automatically. I know that, but I was a little preoccupied, having just stepped through a FREAKING TIME TRAVEL PORTAL. Now what? Am I stuck here?

Heat rises from under my collar until I feel my ears turn red. Fear and frustration finally erupt like a volcano. I slam the bottom of my boot into the door, but the only thing that gives way is my ankle.

Chapter Ten

Renegade – Styx (1978)

I clutch my throbbing ankle as I lie on the ground in the alley. I want to scream, cry, and punch something. *Breathe, Angus. Breathe.* Brilliant move—trying to kick in a door like I'm some action hero. My ankle might be broken, and all I've accomplished is making myself look like an idiot.

Unless Ozzy had a key, there has to be another way in. Hobbling along the alley, I spot a loading dock in the back of the building. The overhead door is stuck at an awkward angle, raised just enough for someone desperate—or stupid—to crawl under. That's me. Wincing, I drop to my hands and knees and shimmy through.

On the other side, the smell hits me like a wall—stale piss and something that could be wet dog or a dead raccoon. I gag and press my nose into the crook of my arm. My injured ankle protests with every step, but I limp toward a metal door at the far end of the room.

The hinges groan in protest, but it opens and I slip through. I close it behind me quickly, leaving the stench on the other side. The air here is cooler, still musty but bearable. I pause until my eyes adjust to the dim light, and glance around. The silence presses in on me as I approach the basement stairs. Each step sends a dull throb through my ankle.

I reach the bottom of the stairs and rest on the last step, cradling my foot. The pain isn't as bad now—maybe it's just gone numb—but I need to figure out where the portal is. My earlier landing had been chaotic, so I scan the room to piece together the orientation of the space. I move cautiously through the darkness, looking for any sign of those energy waves.

Then I feel it—a faint buzz in the air, like static electricity crawling over my skin. I turn, and there it is. The distortion. It's subtle, like looking through rippling water, but it's unmistakable. My heart skips a beat. If Ozzy had been down here, which seems likely, he might have walked right through it without even knowing.

I reach out cautiously and let my hand pass through the distortion. The energy parts like liquid, warm and alive. I wonder if it might help my injured foot. The moment my foot enters, I feel a soothing and oddly pleasant sensation. I pull it out and tentatively place weight on it. The pain is gone. I bounce on my toes, testing it further. Nothing. No pain.

I pace in front of the portal, rubbing the back of my neck. It's still here—a literal doorway home. I should go. Step through right now before I do something stupid, like get too comfortable. If I stay too long, will the portal disappear, stranding me here forever? The thought sends a cold shiver down my spine. But the idea of leaving now feels just as impossible. I glance at the waves of energy rippling in front of me. Stay or go? Risk or regret? For now, I tell myself I'll stay just a little longer.

Back outside, I pull my phone from my pocket, but of course, there's no cell service in 1978. The clock still works. It's dinnertime, but my nerves are too shot to eat.

I'm standing in history. I can't waste it. A walk around the city sounds like a nice way to spend some time before I check out Thunder Road. With any luck, they'll have a band tonight.

Hoodie is back, but he's busy reading something on the newsstand rack. My pulse quickens, and I turn onto Copperfield and head in the opposite direction. I keep my head down and walk briskly until I'm two blocks away. I don't slow my pace until I'm sure he's not following me.

The large, colorful *Music Emporium* sign across the street catches my eye. Hoodie and my other troubles slide to the back of my mind as I cross at the crosswalk, giddy with anticipation.

A bell over the door jingles as I step inside, and I stand frozen just inside the doorway. I feel a rush of envy, disbelief, and awe. A record spins on a turntable sitting atop a vintage Marantz receiver flanked by two free-standing Bose speakers that fill the space with the energy of Led Zeppelin's "Whole Lotta Love". It's the opening track from *Led Zeppelin II*, the album boldly featured on the front of my t-shirt. Coincidence? I think not. I've always felt a deep connection to the past, a sense of belonging in a time when music was more than just sound—it was an experience, a way of life.

I could live in this place. Maybe I'll ask if they have any rooms to rent. I'm not picky. I could live in a storage closet if they had one big enough.

A voice calls out from behind the counter. "Need help with anything?"

I turn and spot a dude in his late 20s, his long hair tied back in a ponytail, and a pair of round glasses resting on his nose.

"I'm new in town. Just checking out the place."

"Welcome, friend. Make yourself at home."

"Thanks." No problem there.

He takes a long drag on a short cigarette, then crushes it out in a glass ashtray on the counter. "We've got some new arrivals in the first bin on your left."

I smile and nod, amused by how *new* and *vintage* can apply to the same items.

A series of long, waist-high wooden record bins stretch in neat rows from the front to the back. Each bin is divided into labeled sections: *Rock, Jazz, Funk & Soul, Country,* and even a small one for *Soundtracks.* Customers hover around the bins, their heads bent in quiet concentration. Some tap the beat of the music playing overhead as they flip through the records with rhythmic clicks.

To my right, a collection of guitars hangs on the wall, each one suspended like a work of art. They're all classics—Gibsons, Fenders, a Rickenbacker 360 in cherry red that makes my mouth water. These aren't reissues or relics in some collector's glass case; they're brand new, gleaming under the glow of the overhead lights.

I wander over to the record bins. Browsing here is a ritual. Each bin has a slanted top shelf to display the covers of featured albums, while the rest are tucked into alphabetized rows underneath. The records are packed tightly but loose enough to flip through with ease.

Each cover feels like an unearthed treasure as I flip through albums with reverence. They're all shrink-wrapped—brand new, no scratches or fingerprints. My fingers pause on Van Halen's debut with pictures of Eddie, Alex, David, and Michael tearing it up on stage. It isn't retro here; it's now.

After more than an hour of browsing, I'm lost in a rock and roll coma, flipping through a bin of nostalgia when someone bumps into me.

"Sorry, man—" I start, then freeze.

It's him. Hoodie.

Every hair on my body stands at attention, but I try to play it cool, swallowing the lump of fear rising in my throat. "You really know how to ruin a good time."

"You're the one ruining things," he says, his voice low, like he doesn't want to be overheard.

I square my shoulders, refusing to show how much he unnerves me. "Why'd you take my Taser?"

He glances around the store like we're being watched. "We can't talk here."

"Then we don't talk." I turn back to the bin and flip through the records with shaking hands.

Before I can walk away, he grabs my arm. His grip is firm, but not threatening—at least, not yet.

"In the back." His hood shadows his face.

I wrench my arm free, aware of the store owner's stare from behind the counter, his eyebrows raised above the rims of his glasses.

I give him a nervous wave and plaster on the most con- vincing, nothing-to-see-here smile I can muster. My pulse pounds, but I need answers, so I follow Hoodie to the back of the store.

He leads me to a nook where a couple of stools sit beside an amplifier where customers can try out instruments. I grab a stool and drag it farther from him before I sit.

I don't wait for him to speak. "I want my Taser back."

"I destroyed it," he says flatly.

I'm on my feet before I realize it. "You what?"

"Sit down." His tone is sharp.

"Why would you do that?" I sit and match his glare.

"It's for your own good. For everyone's good."

I cross my arms, still seething. "Who the hell are you?"

"That doesn't matter. What matters is that you march back through the portal you came from and stay in your own time."

I freeze. "You know about the portal?"

"Of course I do. Your being here is unnatural. It's dangerous. You're playing with fire every second you're here."

"How do you know so much? Did you come through it too?"

"No," he says, and his face hardens. "I came through a different one."

The air feels heavier. "There's more than one?"

He nods.

I wait for him to elaborate, but all I get is his piercing stare. The silence stretches, and my frustration boils over. "Why destroy the Taser?"

He leans forward, his voice a harsh whisper. "Everything you do here has consequences in the future. Some are minor, while others can be catastrophic. Let's say you lose the Taser. If it's found and reverse-engineered, they could become popular years sooner than they're supposed to. That could amount to a lot of criminals walking around in the future who would have otherwise died from a police gunshot. What if one of them kills your parents before you're born?"

I clench my fists, the weight of his words sinking in. "Okay. I get it. Point made."

"Then go home," he says. "And don't come back."

My jaw tightens. I won't let him control me. "If I do, it won't be because you told me to."

I must've said it louder than I intended because the store owner appears, his arms crossed. "That's enough," he says. "You're disturbing my customers. I'm going to have to ask you to leave."

I exhale and turn to the owner with an apologetic smile. "Sorry for the trouble."

I'm relieved when I step outside, and Hoodie doesn't follow.

For the next two hours, I wander aimlessly to kill time before I head to Thunder Road. I stop by Radio Shack, mess around in a pool hall, and linger at a Chevy dealership, where I drool over a shiny new 1978 Camaro Z28. It's a steal at only $5600. I hear Hoodie's voice in my head, warning me about consequences.

I shove my hands in my pockets and walk on.

A movie theater catches my eye, and I stop to stare at the posters: *Animal House, Grease, Jaws 2*. I've seen them all, just not like this. Not first runs.

Chapter Eleven

Green-Eyed Lady – Sugarloaf (1970)

Thunder Road is a gritty-looking building of brick and weathered paint in the middle of a block of gritty-looking buildings. A neon sign displays the bar's name in jagged letters. I'm in luck. A smaller neon light announces "LIVE MUSIC TONIGHT."

Small groups of people lean against walls or huddle on the sidewalk in front of the building. The faint hum of a muffled bass riff vibrates through the cool evening air.

I pull open the heavy wooden door and step into the dimly lit room. The place is everything I ever imagined a '70s bar to be. Cigarette smoke hangs in the air, mingling with the stale scent of spilled beer. My nose detects the familiar aroma of someone smoking a joint in the back corner. It's a heady mix, almost overwhelming, but strangely comforting.

A familiar tune from Boston's self-titled debut album drifts through the air from the jukebox in the corner. The low hum of conversation and the occasional clink of glass bottles fill in the spaces. The jukebox is a colorful relic with lights that blink in sync with the music.

A small, elevated stage has a few instruments and amps scattered around—evidence of the band that's currently on break. The guitars, leaning against their stands, gleam under the stage lights, and I feel a rush of anticipation.

I stop and survey the standing-room-only crowd. It's tight, but not uncomfortably so. Denim and leather, band t-shirts, and platform shoes are everywhere. The women wear their hair in feathered layers or natural afros, while the men sport shaggy hair and mustaches.

I get some odd stares from the few who notice me walk in. I've never felt the need to grow a mustache, but I'm not the only dude in here with a clean upper lip. Fortunately, the Led Zeppelin album on my t-shirt was released in 1969. However, cargo shorts won't become popular for another ten years.

Posters of iconic bands—The Rolling Stones, Deep Purple, The Eagles—adorn the walls of the bar, interspersed with neon beer signs that would fetch a pretty penny where I come from. I'm parched and my appetite is back, so I thread my way through the crowd, hoping to find a seat at the bar and get a burger and a beer.

The bar is shoulder to shoulder. As I look for a place to squeeze in and order my food, I notice a woman in a denim jacket adorned with patches of my favorite bands. I'm intrigued by the large, unfamiliar logo emblazoned across her back. I consider myself a '70s rock band aficionado, but I can't for the life of me remember a band named "Hallowed Ground." A wolf howls at the full moon in a cemetery above the name, written in a distressed Gothic font.

She turns around, leans back against the bar, and my breath catches. Her black hair cascades over her shoulders in soft waves, and her striking green eyes grab my attention and don't let go, making it impossible to look anywhere else. The room suddenly feels smaller, the noise of the crowd muffled.

She's magnetic. I should stay in the shadows and keep my distance like I always do. But my feet betray me and pull me forward through the crowd as if they have a mind of their own.

I pause as the old familiar voice whispers in my ear. "Leave it alone, Angus. She's out of your league… if you even have a league."

I've grown tired of that voice always putting me down. Why do I continue to listen? This time will be different. I need to give it a try, big boy pants and all. It's not like I'm going to ask her to marry me. I just want to have a little harmless conversation. It's a different place, a different time, perhaps a different Angus.

The voice is back. "She's gonna break your heart."

"Shut up!" I say out loud.

A Sasquatch in a leather jacket turns and snarls beneath his Fu Manchu mustache. I hold up my hands, palms out, before he gets any closer. *Think fast!* I point into the crowd, hoping to indicate my words were meant for someone else. He buys the charade and lets it go.

I need to meet her. This is so far outside my wheelhouse that I take a deep breath to center myself. The jukebox switches tracks, and the opening chords of The Eagles' "Hotel California" fill the room, drawing appreciative murmurs from the crowd.

She turns and our eyes meet. For a moment, my entire existence is frozen in time. She raises an eyebrow, like she thinks she might know me. How could she? Not only have I not been born yet, I can't imagine how or why a girl like her would know someone like me. She continues to stare, daring me to believe it might be possible. The rest of the bar seems to fade, like when you adjust the depth of field in a photo so everything blurs except the subject.

My pulse quickens as I take a step closer. My burger can wait. There's something about her—like the universe has shifted to bring us together.

"Hey." The word slips out easier than I expect. "I like your jacket."

A faint smile parts her lips. "Thanks."

"Those are some of my favorite classic rock bands."

Her smile falters, and a flicker of confusion crosses her face. "Classic?"

Crap. I forgot. In 1978, it was just rock. "Yeah, you know, bands that'll still be great decades from now."

She studies me, her head tilted, as though deciding whether I'm serious. Then, to my relief, she nods. "I like the way you think." After a pause, she adds, "Do you have a name?"

What planet is this? The prettiest girl I've ever met is asking my name.

"Angus." I spit it out like it's been stuck in my teeth, and brace for the inevitable comment.

Her eyes brighten. "Like Angus Young."

She's right. The lead guitarist for AC/DC and I share the same hideous name.

"Exactly."

"I'm Grace."

I fire back with another iconic classical rock reference. "Like Grace Slick."

She laughs, and for a moment, the air feels a little lighter.

"I don't recognize the band logo on the back of your jacket. Hallowed Ground?"

"You've never heard of them?" Her smile widens, and she hooks a thumb toward the stage. "They're playing tonight."

"Can't wait to hear them."

An awkward silence stretches between us. I shuffle my feet, as I scramble for something to say.

Out of nowhere, I blurt, "Can I ask you a personal question?"

Her eyebrows lift, and she studies me like I'm some peculiar creature she's just discovered. The silence stretches, and I'm certain I've crossed some unspoken line.

I backpedal. "I'm sorry. I should buy you a drink before I ask personal questions."

Her lips twitch into a small smile. "Yes."

"Yes, I should buy you a drink, or yes to the personal question?"

Her smile grows. "Both."

The bartender is a shaggy-haired dude with an eye patch who looks like he wandered off a pirate ship. I order two beers and drop a five-dollar bill on the bar.

I turn to her when the drinks arrive, and my mouth moves before my brain can stop it. "Do you believe in soulmates?"

What the hell, Angus? Did you say that out loud? Maybe back in 1978, Redford, or Reynolds, or perhaps even Travolta could ask a stranger such a question, but not some overweight high school dropout who looks like a Muppet.

She blinks, then tilts her head, amused but curious. "Where did that come from?"

Panic grips me. I take a long gulp of beer, wishing I could disappear into the foam. "Forget I said anything. That was… weird."

But instead of brushing it off, she narrows her eyes thoughtfully, like she's turning the question over in her mind.

Before she can answer, the pirate calls out from the end of the bar, "Hey, Grace."

She downs the rest of her beer in one smooth motion and stands. "Thanks for the drink. Gotta go."

"Wait. Where?"

"It was nice meeting you, Angus." She flashes a quick smile over her shoulder.

I'm still trying to piece together what just happened when she strides toward the stage. I watch in stunned silence as she picks up a bass guitar. The band members greet her with nods and smiles as she takes her place and adjusts the strap and tunes her instrument.

The drummer counts them in, and they launch into a cover of the Rolling Stones' "Jumpin' Jack Flash." The music vibrates through the floor and into my bones.

Grace glances my way as she plays, a smile on her lips. I raise my beer in a silent toast, grinning like an idiot until I notice the guitar player next to her doesn't share her enthusiasm.

Chapter Twelve

Gimme Three Steps – Lynyrd Skynyrd (1973)

The band finishes the song to wild applause, and I stand and punch my fist in the air. I adjust my phone in my back pocket when I sit. A lot of good that'll do me here. It's not like I can get her phone number and add her to my contacts list. Googling her is also out of the question. *Sheesh!* How did people communicate? I guess you don't know what you don't know, and you don't miss what you never had.

I feel a tap on my shoulder and turn to find the bartender glaring at me with his good eye.

He holds up a five-dollar bill, but I'm staring at the patch. "What's with this?"

I refocus. "It's for the two beers. Why? How much were they?" A fiver should have covered them and then some. I'm not sure what his problem is.

"A buck and a quarter each."

"Okay. You can keep the change."

"Gee, thanks." He shoves the bill in my face, and his eyes narrow into suspicious slits. "This a joke?"

I blink, thrown off. "No, it's a fiver."

"Look at it again."

There it is, mocking me: SERIES 2016. My stomach plummets like I've just missed the last step on a staircase.

"What are you trying to pull with this funny money?"

"Nothing, no pulling, I—" The realization dawns that my money is worthless here. How could I have been so stupid? My pulse spikes as I glance around the bar. When in doubt, get the hell out.

I don't even think—I bolt for the door. Behind me, the bartender shouts something I don't catch. Sasquatch rises from his stool like an angry bear.

An unsuspecting patron on the way in opens the door in time for me to barrel through.

"Thanks," I mutter without breaking stride.

My feet pound the sidewalk as adrenaline pushes me forward. I don't want to miss the show, but clearly, that ship has sailed. And I sure as hell don't want Sasquatch to follow me back to the portal.

I veer toward a busy intersection, hoping the crowd will shield me. After sprinting for two blocks, my lungs burn, and my side feels like I've been stabbed. I double over and try to catch my breath, but Sasquatch is still coming. He's fast for a guy who looks like he's never skipped a meal. How is this my life?

Relief floods me when he stops, shakes his head, and heads back toward the bar. Apparently, I'm not worth chasing this far for five bucks. Good call, big guy.

I stagger into a nearby park, my nerves shot. Twenty feet down a stone path, I collapse onto a bench, pull a joint from my pocket, and light it with shaky hands. The first drag calms my nerves. The second clears my head enough for me to laugh at how close I came to being flattened.

"Thought I smelled weed." The voice snaps me out of my reverie.

A wiry dude in a leather jacket approaches. When I offer him the joint, he slaps it out of my hand.

"I don't want your grass," he sneers, pulling a knife from his pocket with a flick. "I want your money. Now."

I'm caught off guard and stand to protest. The blade glints under the streetlight.

"Sit down!"

I oblige. My only other run-in with a bully took place back in high school. It didn't turn out so bad, but Jackson didn't have a knife.

"Now about that money…"

My hands tremble as I pull the wad of useless bills from my pocket, and my phone tumbles out with them.

"Stop," he says as I reach for it. He takes my money with his free hand and shoves it in his pocket, then picks up my phone.

He inspects the sleek glass rectangle like it's an alien artifact. "What's this?"

"It's an Apple iPhone," I say, trying to keep my voice steady.

"It don't look like no apple." He laughs and pretends to take a bite out of it. "It don't taste like one either."

What a moron. But when he accidentally presses the side button and the screen lights up, his expression shifts to wide-eyed terror. He drops the phone like it burned his hand.

"What the hell?"

An idea hits me. "Hey Siri, play 'Back in Black.'"

The phone lights up again, and Angus Young's iconic guitar riff blares from the speaker. Knife Guy jumps back, his face pale.

"How did you—?"

"Hey Siri, call the police."

That's all it takes. He disappears into the shadows as fast as his feet can carry him, seconds before Siri informs me that cell service is required to complete my request. I grab my phone, relieved to find it intact, though I wish I could say the same for my nerves.

Okay, that's enough excitement for one night. My buzz is long gone, and I'm ready to call it quits.

I backtrack, intending to give the bar a wide berth, but I need to talk to Grace. Believe me, I know it sounds crazy—not only do I not know her last name, but we're about the same age and I haven't actually been born yet—but I think I'm in love.

Bigfoot is perched on a stool near the door, his back toward me. I see Grace on stage, her passion for her music contagious. We made a connection, and I think she felt it, too. There's no way I can go in there. But I can't just walk away either.

The backstage door is near an unsavory-smelling dumpster behind the building. I crouch in its shadow and wait for the show to end. The things we do for love.

An hour passes, then another. My eyelids grow heavy, and before I know it, I'm startled awake by the sound of voices. I spot Grace helping load equipment into a van. My heart leaps, but before I can make my move, a familiar voice growls from the shadows.

"Hey!"

Bigfoot. Of course.

My feet pound the pavement as I beat a hasty retreat. He yells after me. "You better run, you little shit!"

Did he recognize me, or does he say that to anyone who hangs out at night by his dumpster? I don't stop until I reach North Willow and Copperfield. Something moves up ahead in the dark alley. I'm skittish after being held at knifepoint and chased by a Sasquatch. Hopefully, it's a cat or the wind kicking up some trash.

"Suck it up, buttercup. You need to get home," I tell myself, chest heaving. I take a moment to let my heart rate stabilize.

Hoodie's words echo in my mind. "Go home and never come back."

Sorry, Hoodie. I've made my decision. I need to talk to Grace again.

But for now, it's back to the future.

Chapter Thirteen

Radar Love – Golden Earring (1973)

The air hits me first—cool and damp with that unmistakable earthy smell of the cave. Ahead is darkness, complete and absolute, like the world has folded in on itself.

I fumble in the dark, heart racing, until my fingers brush against the smooth metal casing of the flashlight I'd left behind. The beam slices through the suffocating black and the familiar surroundings of the cave come into focus. I let out a shaky breath. "Okay... I'm back." My voice echoes, hollow and strange, like it doesn't belong to me.

The flashlight carves a narrow path ahead of me until I'm outside. There's no moon, but the stars spill across the blackness, so bright and sharp they almost don't seem real. The chilly night air rushes at me, carrying the faint scent of sagebrush and dry earth. I'm back. But after everything I've seen, everything I've felt... will it ever feel like home again?

My phone has no service, but the clock shows it's after eleven, and I have a twenty-minute trek back to the house in the dark. As I walk, I wonder how everything played out while I was gone. What happened when they couldn't find me? What am I going to tell them? Certainly not the truth.

I need to come up with a plausible story. Jackson is a dumbass. He'll believe almost anything. Waldo, not so much. I consider telling Waldo the truth. I can use his help to figure out what's going on. But I'll need to sleep on that one.

I'd be lying if I said I didn't miss Grace. I don't even know her last name. We talked for all of ten minutes. She was a looker, for sure, but it felt like more than that. I can't explain it, but it's like we've known each other forever.

Five minutes into my walk, cell service is back, and my phone blows up with a dozen missed calls and voicemail notifications. A couple are from Jackson, but most are Waldo's. I'm sure he's been worried about me. I don't need to listen to voicemails now. I'll come up with a story and straighten everything out in the morning.

The porch is dark. The outside light burned out a week ago, and I keep forgetting to replace the bulb. Something moves in the dark. I drop my key and grab the flashlight. The beam illuminates Waldo sitting on the porch swing.

He rubs his eyes. "I must have fallen asleep. Where the hell have you been?"

I didn't expect to have to answer any questions tonight. "Uh… I got lost." It sounds lame, but it's the best I can come up with. In my defense, the ranch covers around two hundred acres.

"Lost? Where?"

I'd bailed on him, and he's been sitting here worried for hours. I try to lighten the mood. "If I knew where, I wouldn't have been lost."

His glare cuts through the awkward silence as I pick up the key and unlock the door.

"We searched inside and out, calling your name for over an hour."

I shrug. "Sorry, man."

More silence.

"Can I crash here tonight?"

"Sure." It's the least I can do for what I put him through.

He follows me in, and I set all my stuff on the kitchen table. "I'm beat. I'm going to bed."

After my parents died, I moved into the master bedroom, so I offer Waldo my old room.

"Okay. But we're going to talk about this in the morning."

"Sure. Help yourself to anything in the fridge."

I hate giving my friend the bum's rush, but I need time to decide how much to tell him and to fabricate a story for the rest.

Despite how tired I am, sleep eludes me. Tension builds in the back of my neck, so I get up and take some painkillers. I'm having a hard time wrapping my head around the day's events. The range of emotions, compressed into such a short period of time, is too much to process. Between Hoodie, Grace, the '70s vibe, and that switchblade, I can't think straight.

Eventually I fall asleep, disappointed when I awake in the morning and realize nothing has been resolved. What do I tell Waldo? Do I heed Hoodie's warning to stay away, or go back to find Grace? I think I know the answer to that one, but it frightens me on multiple levels.

I wander downstairs, hungry, but not sure I can keep anything down. I'm feeling under the weather. Did I catch a bug, or is it a residual effect from spending yesterday in 1978?

Waldo is dressed and playing X-box in the living room. He pauses the game and stands when he sees me.

"What time is it?" I ask, rubbing my eyes with both fists.

"It's nine-thirty, but it feels like noon."

"Sorry. I couldn't fall asleep last night."

"I'd say you made up for it this morning." He hesitates. "You'd better get cleaned up. Jackson will be here soon."

"I'm not going. I need a mental health day." That's an understatement.

Waldo follows me into the kitchen. "What will you tell Jackson?"

"I won't tell him anything yet."

"Well, I'm not leaving until you tell *me* what's going on."

I still don't have a plan. Waldo waits. The worried look in his eyes makes me want to spill my guts. I will eventually. I need an objective opinion from someone who can think with his head instead of his heart. "Let's go wait in the living room, out of sight."

Jackson rolls up just before ten and bangs on the door. "Let's go, girls. We're burning daylight."

I hold an index finger up to my lips. Waldo nods.

Ozzy barks. *NOW he's a watchdog?*

Another bang on the door. "Stop wasting time. I know you're in there."

I look at Waldo and shrug.

"Waldo's car is in the driveway, and I can see your flash-lights and radios on the kitchen table."

Busted!

I pull a blanket off the back of the couch and dive underneath it. "Get the door and tell him I'm sick."

Jackson marches into the living room with Zoe close behind. "What happened to you?"

"You probably don't want to get too close," Waldo says. "He might be contagious."

Zoe takes a step back. "You poor thing."

"He got lost out there and had to walk back in the dark."

Jackson looks at me. "How the hell did you get lost?"

Waldo steps in. "He can't talk. Laryngitis."

"How did he just disappear yesterday? I'm glad he's all right, but we searched for an hour and there was no sign of him."

"I waited here for him last night. He got back around midnight. Before he lost his voice, he said his tunnel was a bust, so he went looking for another. A coyote chased him into a nearby cave. He was terrified. He stayed there for hours until it was safe to come out and walk back home."

"Jeez. I guess he's lucky to be alive." He glances at Zoe, who's about to burst into tears, then back at me. "You rest up and take it easy today. The treasure's not going anywhere." He looks at Waldo. "What about you?"

Waldo shifts his weight. "You two go on without me. I think it's best if I stay here with Angus."

They agree and head for the door.

Before he leaves, Jackson turns around. "Tomorrow is Sunday. I've got church in the morning, and something to do in the afternoon. So, I'll see you guys on Monday. Retro should be better by then, right?"

Waldo nods and closes the door behind them as I pull the blanket up over my head. I still don't know how much to tell him.

Squeaky springs and vinyl creaking let me know Waldo is back in the chair and waiting for my explanation.

I lower the blanket and sit up. "The coyote was a nice touch."

Waldo props an elbow on the arm of the chair and rests his chin in his hand. His expression says, *This better be good.*

"Okay." My stomach twists. "What do you know about time travel?"

Chapter Fourteen

Don't Stop Believin' – Journey (1978)

Waldo stares at me with a mix of confusion and skepticism. "The general consensus is, it's not possible," he says slowly. "But a few theories are floating around that suggest it could be."

"Has anyone proven any of those theories?"

He shakes his head.

"What if I told you I've proven one?"

That gets his attention. "Which one?"

Which one? Does it even matter? "I don't know," I admit. "I just know I traveled back in time."

He leans back and crosses his arms. "Alright, I'll play along. Where'd you go?"

"It's not a game, Waldo," I snap. "I spent most of yesterday in 1978."

His expression shifts from curious to flat. "How long have we been friends?"

"Since freshman year."

"And you still don't trust me enough to tell me the truth?"

"Damn it, this is the truth!" I clench my fists. "I can prove it to you."

He doesn't look convinced. "I'm waiting."

"Not here, dumbass."

"How am I supposed to know?" He shrugs. "Some people claim they can train their minds to project their consciousness into another time or dimension."

"Do I look like I'm trained in anything?"

"Good point."

"Remember the spiral drawing we saw near the cave?" I ask. "You said it could indicate a portal to the spirit world. Well, I found a portal inside the tunnel and walked through it—straight into 1978."

Waldo steeples his fingers and taps his lips. "What did this portal look like?"

"It looked like heat waves rising off pavement, but the air in the cave was cold. I felt its vibration before I saw it."

"Where exactly?"

"In the left tunnel," I explain. "There's a small chamber at the end. I had to squeeze through a narrow opening to get inside."

"It sounds like a traversable wormhole."

"Call it whatever you want. To me, it's a time machine."

Waldo rubs his chin. "We searched that tunnel looking for you and didn't see or feel anything."

"I can show you, but we can't go when Jackson or Zoe are around."

"We can go tomorrow morning while he's at church."

For the next hour, I recount everything: the portal, Hoodie, Grace, and getting held up at knifepoint. Waldo's eyes light up when I mention the dog tag.

"So you think that's where Ozzy came from?"

I nod. "His real name is Shadow."

"What are you going to do with him?"

"I guess I should take him back," I say reluctantly, glancing at Ozzy asleep in the corner.

Waldo nods his approval. "This is incredible. A wormhole is like the ultimate cheat code through space and time."

"That guy in the hoodie said there are more. He came through a different one than I did."

"You need to find him," Waldo says, his tone serious. "He might know more."

"That'll be your job. I need to find Grace."

"Wait. My job?"

"You're coming with me."

Waldo holds up his hands. "I'm interested in seeing this portal, but that's as far as I'm going."

"You have to come with me. I need a wingman."

He stares for a moment with a vacant expression. "I don't even know what that is."

I smirk and clap him on the shoulder. "A wingman is like... a co-pilot. Your job is to have my back, keep me out of trouble, and make sure I don't do anything too stupid."

Waldo adjusts his glasses. "Sounds like a full-time job."

"Exactly. Which is why I need the smartest guy I know."

He hesitates then sighs. "I guess I don't have a choice, do I?"

"Nope."

I look over at Ozzy, asleep in the corner. "What about Ozzy?"

Waldo glances in his direction. "He looks content for now. Perhaps we should wait for another time. We need to get the lay of the land first."

Probably a good idea. Besides, I'm in no hurry to give him up.

★★★

The next morning, I pick out something to wear that doesn't include cargo shorts. I call Waldo to make sure he does the same, then pour a cup of coffee and return to my bedroom to search for old money. I'd cleaned out Pop's dresser and filled it with my clothes, but Mom's is still the way she left it.

I pull out her drawers one by one and inspect them. I find an envelope taped to the back of her pajama drawer. Inside are twelve bills, but only two—a ten and a twenty—were printed prior to 1978. I shove the two bills into my pocket, toss the envelope back in the drawer, and head outside to prep the ATV.

"You won't be able to use these," I tell Waldo as I check his cash when he arrives.

"Why not?"

"They were printed after 1978. Trust me, I learned the hard way."

He mulls it over for a moment. "I think I'll take them with me to prove I'm from the future. I hear chicks dig that kind of stuff."

"Chicks?" I raise an eyebrow. "Since when are you interested in girls?"

"I'll have you know I dated a lovely woman at school."

"Your physics professor?" I ask with a smirk.

He smiles. "Biology."

Inside the cave, I lead Waldo to the crevice, squeezing through while he strolls in with ease.

"You really should think about a diet."

I ignore him and scan the chamber, flashlight in hand. But there's nothing. No waves. No energy. Nothing.

"Where is it?" Waldo asks, looking around.

"It was here," I insist, circling the space. My stomach bottoms out.

"There's nothing here, Angus."

"I promise you, there was a portal right here!" My voice cracks as I wave my arms at empty air.

His face is unreadable, but I see the doubt creep in.

I stagger back, my legs giving out beneath me. "Where is it, Waldo?" My voice trembles. "What am I going to do now?"

Waldo kneels beside me, and his expression softens. "We'll figure it out. You're not crazy. We'll find a way."

But his words don't reach me. All I can see is the empty chamber and the fading hope that I'll ever see Grace again.

Chapter Fifteen

Waiting for a Girl Like You – Foreigner (1981)

The mood is somber on the ride back to the house. A woman I didn't know two days ago has hijacked my heart. How did I let this happen?

Waldo turns to me, his eyes shadowed with concern, or perhaps pity. "What are you going to do now?"

"I don't know. What I do know is that I'm not giving up. Hoodie Man said there are more portals. All I have to do is find another one."

"Is that all? Seems like a stretch that they would all go back to 1978."

"Whose side are you on?"

"I'm just being realistic."

"Thanks for the support."

"Sorry." He pauses for a moment. "Perhaps it's only gone temporarily. There might be some atmospheric or astrophysical condition that allows the portal to come and go."

That's better. "You think?"

"It's possible."

We ride in silence the rest of the way, except for the sounds of our two brains hard at work. Mine's the one that sounds like a hamster wheel.

It's lunchtime, and Waldo's stomach does not suffer from the same nuclear meltdown as mine, so I make him a sandwich. I chase him away when he finishes, so I can wallow without an audience. He understands.

"How about if I come over later tonight and check on you?"

I want him to leave, so I nod.

When he's gone, I curl up on the couch and nod off. An hour later I'm up, pacing around the living room. I fire up a doobie to calm my nerves.

Whatever this is that's eating away at me has to come out somehow. They say the best songs are written from pain. I've never suffered the kind of pain I hear about in those songs, but I know what it's like to wait your entire life for the right person to come along.

My guitar and a pad of paper get me through the next four hours. Hunched over my guitar on the couch, I alternate between playing, taking notes, and writing lyrics.

"Did you eat dinner?" Waldo asks from the living room doorway.

"Dinner? What time is it?"

"Almost seven."

"I had some Doritos earlier."

"What have you been doing all this time?"

"I was in a funk, so I wrote a song."

"Finally." He drops into the recliner. "You always play everyone else's music. I knew you could do it."

"I guess I needed some inspiration."

"Grace?"

"It's called 'Waiting for a Girl Like You.'"

"Appropriate. Let me hear it."

I hesitate for a moment before I nod and play.

After the first chorus, he holds up his hands. "Dude. This is really good."

"You think so?"

"Hell yeah. Are you going to play it for her?"

"That's the plan." My shoulders slump. "If I ever see her again."

"I've been thinking about that," Waldo says. "The portal was there two days ago when you went through. Now it's gone. There has to be a pattern."

A portal pattern? I guess I'm in over my head.

"If it's cyclical," he continues, "something in the environment must be turning it off and on. A wormhole is based on gravity and negative energy."

"The moon's gravity affects ocean tides." I can't help flashing a smile, having finally used something I'd learned in high school.

"That's correct. In fact, the moon's phases have different effects on the tides. When the Sun, Moon, and Earth align during full and new moons, their combined gravitational forces cause spring tides, which are higher than usual high tides and lower low tides. When the Sun and Moon form a right angle relative to Earth during the first and third quarters of the Moon, their forces partially cancel each other out, causing neap tides, which are weaker."

"That's great, but what does it mean for the portal?"

"It means we might be able to determine when the portal is here and when it's not."

"So, it might only be open during a full moon? Like a werewolf?"

"I think at a minimum it would be roughly twice a month, at both the full and new phases. Two days ago, when you went through, was a new moon."

"Okay…"

"The next full moon will be in roughly two weeks."

"If what you suggest is true, then we need to wait two weeks before we can go back?"

"I'm afraid so, unless the portal operates on some other cycle. Because phases last for roughly three days, you would have a three-day window twice a month."

"I don't want to wait two weeks. I want to leave tomorrow."

"Not possible."

He's probably right, but my heart won't let me believe it. "We don't know if any of this is actually true. I'm going to check the portal every day."

"What are you going to tell Jackson? He's moved on to the next site. If you keep going back to check on the portal, he'll get suspicious. He might think you found the treasure and are trying to cut him out."

"I don't care about any treasure. He can keep it all."

Waldo holds up his hands. "Slow down, Dude. Let's not get hysterical."

Chapter Sixteen

Let's Go – The Cars (1979)

I tell Jackson I won't be able to join him anymore because I have to work. Rusty's pretty understanding when I ask for time off, but I don't want to push my luck. I figure it's better to work extra hours now, so I can take time off when the portal opens. Waldo needs to look for a summer job, so he backs out, too.

Jackson doesn't take the news well. "So, what? I'm out there alone?"

"You can still use the ATVs." I try to sound diplomatic. "Waldo and I will just… stay in the background from now on. Silent partners, like we originally agreed."

He crosses his arms. "Fine. But I'll need the Taser back."

I wince. "Yeah… about that."

"What about it?"

"I don't have it."

"Where is it?" His voice rises, and the vein in his temple twitches.

"It must've fallen off my belt when I was, uh, running for my life."

Jackson throws up his hands. "What a shithead! That thing cost me three hundred bucks!"

"Take it out of my cut."

He glares at me like he wants to deck me. Finally, he mutters under his breath and storms off.

After work, I stop by the gas station and fill up three five-gallon cans for the ATVs. Jackson assumed that when I said he could use them, it included gasoline. I hadn't thought that far ahead, so I guess that one's on me.

My next stop is Timeless Treasures, an antique shop in town. I hope to find some vintage bills to avoid any future "funny money" incidents like the one at the bar. The shop owner rifles through a drawer and produces forty-five dollars in bills from the late sixties. I pay a twenty percent premium, but I'm okay with it. By the time I leave, I've got seventy-five dollars in old money, which translates to about three hundred fifty bucks in 1978 buying power. That should cover me for a while.

On the way home, I stop at Burger King to grab a Whopper and a Diet Coke—I'm trying to cut some calories. The barn is quiet when I pull in. The ATVs are back where they belong, and Jackson is gone for the day. It's the perfect time to check on the portal.

I head out to the cave, heart pounding with a mix of anticipation and dread. I search for that telltale shimmer in the air when I reach the spot. Nothing. The portal still isn't there.

According to Waldo's theory, the portal only cycles back every two weeks. He's the smartest person I know, but no one's right one hundred percent of the time, so I'll keep checking. It's not like I have much else to do.

I drive to the gym with my coupon for a three-month trial membership. Rock stars need to be in shape, and I could stand to lose twenty pounds.

The gym smells like sweat and something medicinal. The woman behind the counter hands me a towel and a key to a locker.

"Do you need a trainer?"

"I'm fine." I stuff the key into my pocket. I'm really not fine, but I'll pretend I have a clue what I'm doing.

The main workout area buzzes with activity. The thump-thump of treadmills, the clang of weights, and the occasional grunt from a guy who looks like he's lifting a compact car.

I wander toward the treadmills, figuring I'll start with something simple. Running. Walking. I know how to do that—been doing it since I was a toddler. The machine jerks to life, and the belt moves faster than I expect. I grab the side rails for dear life and settle into a brisk walk.

"Piece of cake," I whisper under my breath, though my lungs are already questioning my life choices.

After ten minutes, I hop off and pretend I've got a plan. I pick a machine that looks safe—something with a padded seat and handlebars—and set it to the lowest weight. It feels… okay, like I'm doing something productive. I increase the weight until my arms shake, and I wonder if I'll be able to lift a fork later. Perhaps that's the point of all this.

I finish with a few half-hearted stretches in a corner, avoiding eye contact with anyone who looks like they know what they're doing. As I leave, the same woman at the counter waves and says, "See you tomorrow?"

Tomorrow. Sure. I give her a thumbs-up. As I step outside and feel the cool air on my face, I realize something. I did it. Not gracefully, but I showed up.

My workouts become a daily ritual, and I'm feeling better about myself. It also helps pass the time as I wait for the portal to reopen.

On the seventh day, I feel it the moment I step into the chamber. The air crackles, and my skin tingles. It's back. The portal is back. But wait—it's too early. Waldo's calculations were off.

I extend my hand, and the waves part around it. The energy pulls at me like an invisible current. The temptation to walk through is overwhelming, but I can't. I'm wearing cargo shorts, no money in my pockets, and I'm completely unprepared. Besides, I want Waldo with me this time.

Outside the cave, I check my phone—still no signal. I jump on the ATV and drive faster than I should, glancing at the screen every few seconds. I slam on the brakes when the first bar appears and frantically dial Waldo's number.

"The portal is back!" I shout into the phone.

There's a pause, then, "Who *is* this?"

"Stop fooling around. Why is it back so soon?"

"Hmmm..." I can almost hear him adjust his glasses. "Today is day... seven. It must be reacting to four lunar phases—new, first quarter, last quarter, and full—instead of two. That would shorten the interval to roughly one week."

"That's way better."

"Did you check yesterday?"

"Yes. Nothing."

"Good." He sounds pleased. "This must be the start of the first quarter phase. Each phase lasts about three days, so the portal should stay open for another couple of days. Tomorrow will be the safest day to travel."

"Did you find a job yet?"

"I did. At the hospital."

"That's great."

"Is it? I start tomorrow."

"Ouch. So, what are you going to do?"

"What would you do?"

I grin. "See you in the morning."

The excitement bubbles under my skin like a caffeine high. Sleep doesn't come easy that night. I feel like a five-year-old on Christmas Eve, straining to hear reindeer hooves on the roof and imagining all the shiny new toys under the tree.

Four hours later, it's 8 AM. Any other day, I'd be draggin' my wagon, but not today. I hop out of bed with purpose.

Waldo shows up after breakfast wearing a backpack like it's the first day of school. He's dressed appropriately for the '70s, so he gets points for that. But I still make him turn around.

"What's in the bag?" I unzip it before he can respond.

"Just stuff I might need." His tone is edged with resistance.

Inside, I find notebooks, a textbook titled *Wormhole Theory*, pens, pencils, and—of course—a calculator.

"You look like you're going to math camp." I remove the calculator.

"Don't worry. It's vintage. My dad bought it in 1975. Texas Instruments."

"Okay. Let's go. Don't want to be late for class."

I smirk. Waldo groans.

The ride out is quiet as the weight of what we're about to do settles over us. When we reach the crevice, I slip through first, and Waldo follows, his breath already uneven.

"There it is." I gesture toward the waves. The energy distorts the air, bending light like a heat mirage. Waldo's jaw drops, and he stares at it, clutching a hand-drawn schematic of something he calls "potential wormhole theory."

"This is insane," he whispers, his voice almost reverent. He adjusts his glasses as he leans closer. "I've read about phenomena like this, but seeing it..."

"Go ahead, touch it."

He hesitates, then slowly reaches out. The waves part around his hand, and it disappears. He jerks it back as if burned, his eyes wide.

"Freaky, isn't it?"

"I've never seen anything like it," he murmurs. "It's... beautiful."

"All right. I'm ready. Let's go."

Waldo holds up a hand, his nervous energy bubbling over. "So, wait. We just... walk through the waves? Like a waterfall?"

"Yep. But instead of getting wet, we end up in 1978."

His Adam's apple bobs as he swallows hard. "If we disintegrate, I want you to know this is the worst idea you've ever had."

"Noted." I grin wider, but Waldo doesn't look amused.

He stares at the portal like it might lunge at him. "I'm sorry, I just—"

"Some wingman you turned out to be," I tease. "Come on. Together, on three. One."

"Wait, shouldn't we—"

"Two."

"Angus, are you even sure—"

"Three!" I grab Waldo's arm and step into the portal, dragging him behind me.

Chapter Seventeen

The Boys Are Back in Town – Thin Lizzy (1976)

We fall through the tunnel and stumble onto the basement floor.

"We're here." I brush the dust off my shorts.

"It doesn't look like much." Waldo does a quick inventory of his body parts.

"You gotta see this to believe it. Follow me."

We walk to the corner, and I point at the muscle cars parked along the curb, their paint jobs gleaming in the sunlight. A sandwich board in front of a diner advertises hamburgers for fifty-nine cents. Waldo spins in a slow circle, taking in the sights: the newsstand stacked with vintage magazines, a phone booth on the corner, and a kid racing by on a bike with a banana seat and sissy bar.

He fires off a few quick blinks. "This… this is impossible." He flips open his notebook and scribbles furiously. "It's—"

"1978, baby." I pat him on the back. "Now, put that thing away."

Although we try to blend in, I'm afraid we look like tourists. My head is on a swivel, looking out for Hoodie. No sign of him yet. Waldo fiddles with his notebook and mumbles about "anomalous gravitational effects."

I grab his arm. "Put the book away. I need your help with something. You can do your calculations later. Look around, man. Soak it in."

He nods and stows his notebook. "What do you want me to do?"

I point up ahead. "See that bar, Thunder Road? I can't show my face there, but you can go inside and ask about Grace's band, Hallowed Ground. Someone in there might know where they play next."

Waldo approaches the building while I hang back.

"Hey. See if anyone in there knows Grace's last name."

He flashes me the thumbs-up sign before he pulls on the door handle. It doesn't budge.

Shit! I pull out my phone. Ten-thirty. They probably won't open for another six hours.

Waldo's back. "They're closed. What do we do now?"

I don't have a Plan B. As my brain sifts through the options, the smell of fried… everything derails my thoughts. I nudge Waldo. "Follow me."

A bell above the door jingles and the smell of grease, coffee, and something sweet mix together in a way that feels like home. The diner is small, with booths along one wall and a counter along the other. Red vinyl seats, cracked and patched with duct tape, tell me this place does a brisk business. I pause to take it all in.

The breakfast crowd has thinned out, and I can hear the activity in the kitchen as they prepare for lunch. I figure the owner will be more inclined to give out information to paying customers. Besides, my throat is parched.

We take our seats at the counter.

Waldo's eyes dart around the room like a kid on Christmas morning. "This is incredible." His voice is hushed. "Like we've cracked open a history book and somehow stepped inside."

The owner approaches with a tired smile. His salt-and-pepper hair is combed back, and his glasses rest low on his nose. He wipes his hands on a checkered dish towel slung over his shoulder.

"What'll it be, boys?"

I rest my forearms on the counter. "We'll have a Diet Coke and—"

"A what?" He stares at me like I'm speaking Chinese.

"Diet Coke?"

"Never heard of it. We got Coke, Pepsi, or root beer. Take your pick."

"Uh… two Cokes, please."

He returns with our drinks and sets them on the counter. "Will that be all?"

I nod.

"That'll be fifty cents."

I hand him a dollar bill, and he sets the change on the counter.

"Do you know anything about the band that played across the street last Friday night? Hallowed Ground?"

"They've got a different band in there every weekend. I live upstairs, so I hear them all, whether I want to or not." He removes his glasses and polishes the lenses with the towel while he thinks about it. "Can't say I know any of their names."

"Sometimes they drop off fliers," he continues. "Too much work to put them in the window every week." He gestures toward a small table against the front wall. "You're welcome to look through that pile over there."

"Thanks." I push the two quarters toward him. "Keep the change."

The stack is about three inches high and most of them are outdated. I give half to Waldo. It doesn't take long to find the wolf logo. "Here it is. It's got a list of their concert dates for this month. They play tonight in Englewood, wherever that is."

Waldo pulls out his phone. "I'll Google it."

"Put that away. Besides, you can't Google anything here. The Internet doesn't exist yet."

"Oh, yeah. I forgot." He slips the phone back in his pocket. "How did anyone find anything?"

"The old-fashioned way. Come on. I have an idea."

We walk to Woolworth's and buy a map of Denver and its suburbs. While we're inside, Hoodie walks past the front window. Does he know we're in town? I point him out to Waldo.

"He's the guy who told you to leave town?"

"Yep. Let me know if you see him on the street. We'll need to steer clear."

It's lunch time, so we grab a seat at the counter. We order cheeseburgers, fries, and Cokes, and study the map while we wait for our orders.

The Viper Room in Englewood is about five miles away. Too far to walk, so we'll need transportation. Unfortunately, we can't call an Uber. We'll need to find a bus schedule or call a cab from a payphone. We have plenty of time for that, so the next stop is the record store.

I pay for lunch with a fiver and a one-dollar tip—I could get used to these prices—and ask the cashier if she knows where I can get a bus schedule. She walks to the end of the counter and returns with a trifold Regional Transportation District pamphlet.

Buses run until midnight, which solves the how-do-I-catch-the-show-and-get-back-to-the-portal dilemma. We'll take the four-thirty bus to Englewood, have dinner, and get to the Viper Room early enough to talk to Grace before the show. In the meantime, we can spend an hour at the record store, then do some sightseeing.

Waldo talks about negative energy and temporal displacement and asks me all kinds of questions I can't answer. Otherwise, we're having a great time.

After we get off the bus in Englewood, we have dinner at a Howard Johnson's, and top it off with one of their famous twenty-eight flavors of ice cream.

Chapter Eighteen

It Don't Come Easy – Ringo Starr (1971)

It's still early, and the Viper Room's front door is locked. We walk around back to find the band's van parked next to what might be the stage door. Eventually, the door opens and a big dude, who could be Sasquatch's twin brother, props it open with a cement block. He shakes his head when he sees us. "Sorry, boys. Band members only."

"I need to talk to Grace."

"You and everyone else."

"Can you tell her Angus needs to speak to her? It's important." That's a stretch—I don't know yet what I plan to say.

"She's busy setting up."

"Please. Just tell her I'm here. I'll make it quick."

He sizes me up for a moment, then rolls his eyes, shakes his head, and disappears inside.

Two minutes later, Grace appears in the doorway. "Angus?"

"Hey."

Confusion clouds her eyes. "What are you doing here?"

I thought I'd drop in from the future again to say hi. "Uh…"

"Why did you run out on me during my set last week at Thunder Road?"

I hold up my hands. "I can explain." No, I can't. Telling her I paid for a drink with a five-dollar bill that won't be printed for another forty years won't help my case. I need to think of something quick. "That's why I'm here. I wanted to stay and talk last time, but I got a call that my mom was in the hospital, so I had to leave."

"I don't understand. They called you at the bar? They don't take personal calls for customers."

Yikes! I forgot. No cellphones. "Uh… the police called. She had a car accident." Please forgive me, God.

"Oh, no. I'm sorry."

"Can I buy you another drink on your break?"

Before she can answer, a man who I recognize as the band's guitarist steps outside. "Come on, Babe, we need you for sound check." The muscles in his chiseled jaw tighten when he spots us. "Who are these guys?"

"This is Angus and…"

"Walter. Pleased to meet you."

Pleased to meet you? Come on, Waldo. Whose side are you on?

This beast of a man flings his long blond hair back out of his face. His fists are like sledgehammers that he rests on his hips. "What are they doing here?"

What's it to you, big guy? Why don't you flex those tattooed guns somewhere else where you can mind your own damn business? Of course, I can't say that to his face. He's wearing a black leather vest and nothing underneath except a silver chain around his neck. Another silver chain runs from a belt loop around to his back pocket. Like someone's gonna try to steal *this* guy's wallet.

"I met Angus last week at Thunder Road," Grace says.

He puts his arm around her and leans over to kiss the top of her head, clearly marking his territory. "Let's go, they're waiting."

As they walk away, he turns and, with his free hand, points two fingers at his eyes, then turns them toward me.

Message received.

He kicks the cement block aside, and the door slams behind them. My heart drops to somewhere below my stomach.

"Well, *that* just happened," Waldo says.

I'm pacing now. I can't believe it. I should have seen it coming, like it always does. I thought this time would be different, like we were meant to be together and nothing could keep us apart. *What a shithead.*

Hallowed Ground's sound check bleeds through the closed door. Grace's voice, clear and electric, cuts through the muffled thrum of the instruments, adding insult to injury. It should've been a moment of hope, a chance to make a connection, but all I can think about is that smirking, leather-clad behemoth who draped his arm over her like a "Keep Out" sign.

"Angus!" Waldo's voice pulls me out of my thoughts. "Stand still. You're making me dizzy."

I stop and run a hand through my hair. "I—why the hell is she with *him*?"

Waldo gives me a look, the kind he reserves for when I'm being particularly dense. "Did you see that guy? I love you, man, but he looks like Thor, and you look like, well, Angus Walker."

I glare at him and lean against the wall. "Thanks for the pep talk."

He sighs, folds his arms, and leans against the wall beside me. "He looks like the kind of guy who punches first and asks questions never."

"I don't care." I stand straighter. "All my life, I've been the guy who gives up. The guy who decides it's not worth the fight because I think I don't deserve it. But this isn't high school. This isn't some girl I'll forget about in a week." I pause and clench my fists. "If there's even a chance she could feel the same way about me, I won't let fear, or some Norse god, stand in the way."

Waldo adjusts his glasses, clearly uncomfortable. "Okay, I get it. But maybe we don't go all Braveheart on him. Remember, this is 1978. We don't belong here. How would this even work?"

"It's meant to be, that's how." My fists tighten, fingernails biting into my palms. "Didn't you see what he did? It was a challenge."

"A challenge to what? A duel?" Waldo cocks his head then shakes it. "You're not going to win her by storming the stage with a guitar solo and a declaration of love."

"Why not?" I shoot back and a grin breaks through despite myself. "Worked for Marty McFly."

"You're not really basing your romantic strategy on *Back to the Future*, are you?" Waldo groans as he rubs his temples. "This is exhausting."

"Then go home. But I'm staying. And I'm going to prove to her we should be together."

I surprise myself with such a bold declaration. But am I really going to put myself out there again? This could be the universe's way of reminding me what a broken heart feels like. Do I really want to go there again?

Waldo pushes himself away from the wall. "Okay, let me add a little reality check to your grand, romantic gesture. What if messing with this—messing with her—is a bad idea?"

"What are you talking about? I'm not trying to destroy history or anything. I want her to know how I feel."

"Yeah? Then what?" he shoots back, his voice sharp. "What if she leaves the band because of you? Or the band falls apart because Thor is too busy brooding about losing her to focus on their music?"

I open my mouth to argue, but he isn't done.

"What if her band never makes it big because of something *you* did? What if Grace never gets the career she's supposed to have? What if..." He gestures wildly. "What if you change everything about her life because you think you're 'meant to be'? You're talking about rewriting *her* future, Angus. Not just yours."

The words hit me like an invisible fist to the gut. I hadn't thought about it like that. I hadn't considered that Grace's life—her path—might be something I wasn't supposed to mess with.

"That's not fair." My voice is softer. "I'm not trying to ruin her life. I just... I want her to see me, Waldo. To know I'm here. We *are* meant to be together. I know it."

Waldo sighs and his shoulders drop. "I get it. I do. But, man, this isn't just about you. If you're serious about her, you've got to think bigger. Her career, her band, maybe even her happiness—it's all tied to this moment in time. You start pulling threads, and the whole thing could unravel."

I clench my fists. "But what if—"

"No." He holds up a hand. "Listen to me. What if she's meant to be with him, at least right now? What if he's part of what makes her the person she is?" He softens a little, tilting his head. "You ever think about that?"

"You're saying I should leave her alone? Walk away and hope she ends up happy with someone else? You think she'll be happy with *that* guy?"

Waldo hesitates. "Maybe there's a way to be in her life without blowing it up. Figure out what she wants, what she needs, before you decide what *you* want. And if you're going to fight for her, do it the right way—without trampling on the things she's already built. If you're meant to be together, as you say, then it will be."

I let his words sink in. I can tell he wants to let me down easy. If he had his way, we'd leave now and never come back. But as my friend, he's laying out the facts to let me decide.

Part of me hates how much sense he makes. But the other part—the stubborn part—knows I can't walk away. Not this time.

"Fine." I meet his gaze. "I'll try not to ruin the timeline. But I won't give up, Waldo. I can't."

He nods. "Fair enough. But if we go back to 2024 and it's an apocalypse because you couldn't resist the girl in the band... I'm blaming you."

"Deal."

Chapter Nineteen

Paranoid – Black Sabbath (1970)

We go around front and wait for the place to open. A line forms behind us, a testament to the band's popularity, and I'm happy for Grace. When the doors open, we grab a couple of seats at the end of the bar. The band's instruments and equipment are set up on the small, dark stage. I remember the simultaneous feelings of excitement and fear as our band had waited to take the stage.

I order a couple of beers, and we wait for the show to begin. Mine goes down too easily. Waldo nurses his, so I order another.

"Hey. Slow down. I know you feel bad, but the show won't start for another half hour."

I reluctantly take his advice.

Finally, the lights dim, and the low hum of the crowd's anticipation is electric. Hallowed Ground's drummer strikes the first beat, and the stage comes alive. Grace steps forward, and everything else falls away.

She stands in the glow of a spotlight. Her black hair shimmers as it catches the red and blue hues from the stage lights. She sings, and it pulls everyone in the room into her orbit. I can't look away. Her voice is smoky but powerful, and it cuts through me, sharp and unrelenting.

But then *he* moves closer to her and shatters the spell. His long blond hair whips and sways with every sharp motion. It falls in front of his face one moment, then flies back as he rips into a solo that is pure fire. His name is Lars—I'd overheard someone in the crowd say it earlier—and he plays like he owns the stage. His sharp eyes pierce the crowd and find mine. This is his kingdom, and I'm a trespasser.

He leans in toward Grace as he plays. She turns to him and her eyes meet his with a familiarity that twists my stomach into knots. Grace smiles at him—a quick grin that lights up her face—and I have to look away.

I hate him. Not only for being with her, but for being the kind of person who fits—the kind of person I've always wanted to be but felt I could never be.

He sits next to her at the bar after the first set. She's clearly on a short leash tonight. She gives me a sideways glance from time to time, and I order another beer to dull the pain of watching them together.

"Don't you think you've had enough? You're going to get us kicked out of here, or worse."

"Okay, Mom."

Waldo grabs my arm. "I'm not the bad guy here. I'm just looking out for you… and me by association. Isn't that why I'm here?" He stands. "I think we should leave."

Once again, he's right. I need to go back and regroup. I pull the folded flier from my pocket to see when the band plays again—next Friday at Thunder Road. In the meantime, I'll go home and Google the band. I might be able to find out what's going on with her and Lars.

The clock behind the bar reads ten-fifteen. "Fine. We can catch the ten-thirty bus."

We're standing in my kitchen by eleven-thirty.

"You're welcome to stay," I offer. "I'm going to pet my dog, smoke a joint, and sleep for three days."

"Thanks, but I need to go home and get some sleep so I can smooth things over with my new boss in the morning."

I exhale and the tension bleeds out of me as I drop my keys on the kitchen table. Something's not right, but I can't put my finger on it. Then it hits me. It's too quiet. Ozzy usually greets me at the door. There's no scrabbling paws, no joyful bark, no familiar thud of his tail against the furniture. My chest tightens as I scan the room.

"Ozzy."

Nothing. Probably asleep, like I should be. I walk into the living room and stop dead in my tracks. Not only is Ozzy not in his bed, his bed is missing. So is his food bowl, his leash, and the basket of toys I trip over on a regular basis.

"Ozzy?" I call again, louder this time, but don't expect an answer. I turn to Waldo, who is standing in the doorway, his brow furrowed.

"He's gone." My voice is hollow. "His bed, his toys... It's like he was never here."

Waldo pauses, his lips pressed into a thin line. "Angus," he says slowly, his tone careful, "is anything else missing?"

"You think I've been robbed?"

He raises his hands, palms out. "I'm just asking, because... what if this isn't the same timeline we left?"

The words hit me like a slap, and for a moment, I can't breathe. "What are you talking about?"

Waldo slips off his backpack and sets it on the couch. "Look, you've seen *Back to the Future*, right? Or read science fiction? What if... I don't know, something we did in 1978 shifted us into an alternate timeline? A version of 2024 where Ozzy was never part of your life?"

"That's ridiculous." The words feel weak in my mouth. "We didn't do anything to change the past... did we?"

"You met Grace. You talked to her. We spent an entire day in 1978. Who knows what kind of ripple effects that could've created? For all we know, Ozzy's disappearance is just the beginning."

My mind races through every interaction I'd had in 1978—every word, every glance. Could something as simple as talking to Grace again have done this?

Waldo shakes his head. "I told you this was a bad idea."

"No." The dog tag—the one I found near the portal, and I've carried around in my pocket. I reach in to grab it, to feel the metal between my fingers, but it's not there. "That doesn't make sense. Ozzy was here. He was here, Waldo. He's gotta be—"

My voice falters, and I sink onto the couch, burying my face in my hands.

Waldo sits beside me.

"What if I'm only allowed two friends in this lifetime? I know it sounds crazy... and cruel, but it might be why Ozzy is gone. I know it's too early to call Grace a friend, but maybe Ozzy has left me to make room for her. It's either a good sign, or a very, very bad one."

"I don't think that's how it works." Waldo folds his hands in his lap. "I know this is hard to wrap your head around. But we need to figure out what's different. Ozzy might not be the only thing that's changed."

The implication of his words settles like a weight on my chest. If Waldo is right—if we've come back to a world that isn't entirely ours—what else might have been erased? "We have to fix this."

"I'm not sure that's possible. But first, we need to figure out exactly what's broken."

I look around the room, now unbearably empty, and clench my fists. The timeline isn't the only thing at stake here. My whole life—everything I care about—is at stake.

Chapter Twenty

Dirty Laundry – Don Henley (1982)

I'm up early the next morning, even though I don't need to be to work until after lunch. My head feels like a drum solo, so I take some pain meds. I'm sad about Ozzy and wonder what else might have changed. What I really want to do is sleep until Friday when I can see Grace again.

I grab my laptop, sit cross-legged in bed, and Google *Hallowed Ground*. A picture of the band comes up. I linger on Grace's image then read the text below. *A local Denver band made the wrong kind of headlines when guitarist Lars Steele was arrested on a domestic violence charge that put girlfriend Grace Monroe, the band's bassist, in the hospital. The band subsequently split up, losing their shot at national recognition.*

NO! I break out in a cold sweat as I open up a few more articles. Nothing.

Grace *Monroe*. Not the way I wanted to find out her last name. I type it into the search box. Apparently a common name, but none of them are my Grace.

Unable to sit still any longer, I pace around the room in my skivvies. I have no way to contact her, to warn her. I can't call 1978. Even if I could, what would I say? "Hi, this is Angus calling from the future. You need to dump that asshole who plays guitar in your band before he puts you in the hospital. How do I know? I Googled it."

Now, I need to wait another week to see her. What if I'm too late? I'll leave on Thursday morning instead of Friday. The portal's three-day window should be open by then. I need to see her as soon as possible. I take a deep breath and feel a little better, but not much.

Disappointment takes over when I see my reflection in the bathroom mirror. I'm still carrying too much weight, and I'm overdue for a haircut. I can't compete with Lars on a physical level, but I can at least do something to up my game.

I suddenly know what I need to do. Still in my underwear, I march downstairs, open a kitchen cupboard, and transfer anything that tastes good into a trash bag. Doritos, potato chips, and Oreo cookies are the first to go. I tear open a bag of Pop-Tarts and stick one in my mouth—gotta have breakfast—and throw the rest of the box away.

With the Pop-Tart hanging from my mouth, I open the freezer and pick up two tubs of ice cream. I toss the first into the bag and stare at the second. Cookies and Cream, my favorite. An image of Lars kissing my Grace on the head flashes in my mind, and I slam-dunk the ice cream into the bag. Anything processed or full of fat is unceremoniously discarded.

I'm not sure what I'll eat from now on, but it'll damn sure be healthy.

A knock turns my attention to the door. Probably Waldo here to check on me on his way to work. I set the bag down and open the door.

"Gran?" I'm frozen like a deer in headlights.

"You gonna stand there like buzzard bait, or you gonna let me in? This used to be my house, you know."

I step aside and let her pass. She waltzes through the door like she still owns the place. Gramps used to say she was so ornery she could start a fight in an empty room. Somehow, she'd always been nice to me as a child. Perhaps I've outgrown her good graces.

"You always answer the door in your drawers?"

"Uh… no… I—"

"Go put on some clothes."

"Yes, ma'am."

She walks through the kitchen and into the living room while I run upstairs.

"I love what you've done with the place," she calls up after me.

"Thanks, but I haven't done much."

"Don't you know sarcasm when you hear it?"

I slip on a shirt and a pair of shorts. When I reach the bottom of the stairs, I fold my arms across my chest. "Why are you here?"

"Like I said, we need to talk."

"About what?"

"Your grandfather." She sits in the recliner. "You need to know the truth about why I left."

"Why are you telling me this now?" I lower myself onto the couch, ready to finally hear her side of the story.

"Not much left of this family, and it's about time you knew where you came from."

"I don't follow. I thought I was born here on this ranch."

"You were, but your grandfather was born in Denver… in 1896."

Denver? I might know where this is going. "That would make him 114 years old when he disappeared. How is that even possible?"

"Normally, it wouldn't be. But he had a secret, and I think you know what that secret is."

Do I admit anything to her? "He never said anything to me about a secret."

"Don't play dumb with me, Angus. I know about your treasure hunt up in the mountains. I think you found something else up there."

How the hell could she know that? "You know about the portal?"

She nods slowly. "Best and worst thing that ever happened to me."

I wait for an explanation.

"Your grandfather found the portal in Denver in 1920. He was twenty-four, the same age as when he came out this end in 1966. When he found this ranch unoccupied, he went back to Denver and made some money in the stock market, trading on information he'd gained while in the future. He returned here and put a down payment on it."

So, I'm not the first in my family to time travel? You could have blown me over with a hair dryer. "Did he know anything about ranching?"

She tips her head back and laughs. "Not a lick. He was more interested in owning that portal."

"Was he rich?"

"He had enough to throw around every weekend at the local saloon. That's where we met. Mr. John Walker swept me off my feet. Mind you, I don't usually fall for time travelers, but he was different."

"What? You knew he was a time traveler?"

She smiles a crooked smile. "I'm kidding. I didn't learn that until years later." She raises her hand to her mouth and coughs to clear her throat. "I'm parched. You got anything to drink around here?"

"Water, iced tea…"

"I'll take a beer."

I stare through squinted eyes. "You know it's nine o'clock in the morning, right?"

"Are you gonna get me a beer, or do I have to get it myself?"

I walk to the kitchen and return with two bottles.

After a long draw, she continues. "We married in 1968, same year your father was born. John Jr. came two years later. For the next thirty years, we learned a lot about ranchin'. We raised horses and cattle until the ranch fell on hard times. That's when he told me about that damn portal. I didn't believe him at first. He said he wanted to go back in time and buy stock in companies that he knew had done well—like he'd done the first time. We'll be rich, he said."

"That's not a bad plan. Did he do it?"

"He certainly did. We paid off our debts, including the mortgage. Then he decided we didn't need to work so hard, so he sold all the animals except a couple of horses. Your father got a job at the feed store. I think he was happy to have regular hours."

"Didn't my parents wonder where the money came from?"

"John liked to tell tales. When he returned from his trips, he'd cash in the stocks and tell everyone he'd hit it big in

Vegas. After a while, they all suspected he had a gambling problem. He didn't care."

"Did you ever go with him?"

"Lord, no."

"Weren't you curious?"

"Sure. He almost talked me into going with him once. I made it all the way to the cave, but I chickened out when he disappeared into that thing."

"So, what happened to Gramps?"

The corners of her mouth twitch upward in a tight, restless expression. "You've probably heard stories. That's because no one knows what really happened, including me."

"He traveled again and never came back?" I'd considered doing the same thing until I met Lars. Truth is, I'm still considering it.

"That's exactly what he did. I ask myself why, but I don't like any of the answers I come up with."

Perhaps he met his soulmate, not that I would suggest the possibility. "What if something happened to him that kept him from coming back?"

"Everyone had their version of what happened, and none of them were very nice. I certainly couldn't tell them what I knew, so I suffered through it until I couldn't take it anymore. I moved away, quickly and quietly."

"Did Mom and Pop know?"

"They knew your grandfather disappeared, but I kept the portal a secret. I told them I needed to leave, that I couldn't deal with all the gossip and condescending looks anymore. I was embarrassed and swore them to secrecy."

"They told me you died."

"I know. Don't hate them. They had to come up with something you might believe."

They're both dead now, so hating them serves no purpose.

Gran leans in. "On a related subject... how would you like to go on another treasure hunt?"

Chapter Twenty-One

Wild Horses – The Rolling Stones (1971)

I didn't see that coming and manage a smile. "I'm not sure I can handle two treasure hunts in less than a month. What have you got in mind?"

"I'm pretty sure John never spent all the money he made trading stocks. He told me the portal sent him forty-six years into the past, to 1964, so he couldn't bring any money with him since all of it was printed in this century. If he did take it, he'd be dead before he could spend it."

"So, you think it's somewhere on the ranch?"

"He thought the manager down at the bank was so crooked he had to unscrew his britches at night. So, yeah, I think it's here somewhere."

"You don't think Mom and Pop found it?"

"I reckon I would've known."

"How?" My eyes narrow. "You left soon after Gramps disappeared."

"Your parents kept in touch. They visited now and again. Even came out for Thanksgiving one year."

"They had Thanksgiving with you? I don't remember that. Where was I?"

"You were on the road with your band." She shakes her head. "I always thought you were too good for that bunch."

"Let's get back to this so-called treasure. Where do you suggest we look?"

"You'll have to do the looking. I'm getting too old for such things. You can keep half of anything you find. Deal?"

She drives a hard bargain. I can't contain an enthusiastic smile. "Sure. Where should I start?"

"John was clever. If I were you, I'd search every inch of this place, from top to bottom. He was also handy as a rope at a hanging, so he may have built something to hide it in or stashed it in a wall or under a floorboard."

"I can't just open up the walls and rip up the floors."

"You'll figure something out."

"What if I go back to 1978 and look him up and ask him where he hid it? I could find it myself and keep it all."

She gives me a wary glance. "First, that's not how we raised you. You're better than that. And second, if you ever see that son-of-a-bitch, tell him he's got some explaining to do."

I take a deep breath and stand to suggest our time together is up. "How do I contact you if I find something?"

She writes her phone number, but no address. I guess you can't trust anyone, not even your own grandson.

I'm not ready to begin Treasure Hunt 2.0 yet, so after she leaves, I pick up my guitar and play for an hour before work. I miss my best friend—apologies to Waldo—and audience of one. Ozzy never made much noise, but it sure seems quieter around here without him.

I plan my trip at the breakfast table the next morning. I'll have a day, maybe a day and a half, to find Grace and get her alone to talk. I'm not sure what I'll say. I can't travel for another five days, so I have time to think of something.

I need to be careful that I don't appear as some lovesick groupie, or worse yet, a stalker. Music seems to be our common ground. We can start there.

Waiting is hard, but at least the portal is predictable. Having it open randomly would be a logistical nightmare. Waldo figured out the schedule, but there's one issue that concerns me. It takes about 29.5 days to complete a lunar cycle, which doesn't line up neatly with a weekly schedule. While I enjoy having the portal open on Fridays when Grace's band plays, that won't always be the case.

I may have to stay in 1978 for a week at a time. What about my job? Then there's the question of where I will stay. What if Grace and I hit it off right away, and she invites me to stay at her place? That would be awesome, but it scares the bejesus out of me. I've never been with a woman before. Wait. What if she lives with Lars?

Take a breath, Angus. Don't get ahead of yourself.

I work extra hours through Wednesday so I can have Thursday and Friday off, but not without a warning from my boss.

On Thursday, I'm up early and stumble out on the Denver side of the portal by nine. The room blurs for a moment before snapping into focus. I'm still amazed I can be in 2024 one minute and 1978 the next. This should be a ride at Disneyland.

Moving quickly upstairs to escape the musty air, I pause to breathe in air that's only slightly better. A shadow shifts in the corner of my eye.

"Back again, are you?" The voice is calm but laden with menace. "I thought I made myself clear."

My heart pounds as I spin around to find Hoodie standing several yards away. His hood casts a shadow across his face, but it's not enough to obscure those piercing eyes. I really don't need this today.

"You don't belong here."

"And yet here I am." I force a cocky grin to mask my growing unease. "What's it to you, anyway?"

He ignores the question and steps closer. "What are you doing here?"

I give a casual shrug, unwilling to divulge the real reason I'm here. "Just sightseeing."

"Don't lie to me." The man's voice sharpens. "Every time you come back, you risk unraveling the timeline. Do you understand the stakes? The damage you could cause?"

I've seen it firsthand with Ozzy's disappearance, but I'm willing to sacrifice to be with Grace. Who knows? I may save her life. Unfortunately, it doesn't look like this guy is going to give up. I cross my arms and stand my ground. "If you're so worried about the timeline, why don't you tell me who you are and what this is all about?"

Hoodie doesn't answer. Instead, he lunges.

My high school judo training kicks in. I pivot on my back foot and sidestep the attack. The man's arm shoots out, but I twist beneath it, breaking the grip before it can do any damage.

He spins to face me again, and my muscles coil with adrenaline. When he swings out a hand toward my shoulder, I duck low and grab his arm. I use his momentum to redirect the strike.

"Nice try." I step back to create distance.

Hoodie advances again, faster this time, his movements sharp and deliberate. He's stronger than he looks, and I can feel the air shift with each swing.

He reaches for me again, and I pivot to the side and hook a foot behind his ankle. I sweep his leg, and he stumbles. He catches himself before he hits the ground.

"Go back. Before it's too late."

"I can't do that."

He lunges again, but I step into him this time. I grab his sleeve and twist it in a classic judo grip. I pull him forward, using his own weight against him, and send him crashing into a desk.

I don't wait for a counterattack. My heart pounds as I bolt through the side door and into the alley.

The man's voice echoes behind me, sharp and cold. "You don't know what you're doing!"

I run toward the sound of traffic and don't look back. My lungs burn, and my legs ache by the time I reach the newsstand. I stop momentarily to catch my breath as Hoodie's warning lingers in my mind. Something about the way he said it makes my throat tighten.

Chapter Twenty-Two

Do It Again – Steely Dan (1972)

I need a place to shake off my encounter with Hoodie and figure out how to find Grace. It's difficult to think straight in the aftermath of the attack. Another headache is coming on.

The bell above the record shop door jingles as I step inside another world, one that doesn't care about time travelers or mysterious hooded strangers. The low hum of classic rock plays over the shop's speakers—steady, familiar, grounding.

The door swings shut behind me, and I stand there for a second, taking it all in. My pulse is still racing from the encounter with Hoodie. Every shadow on the street had felt like it watched me, but here, surrounded by music, the world feels... manageable.

It's not busy—just a couple of guys flipping through the bins near the back as the owner leans on the counter. I walk over to the rock section and let my fingers brush along the edges of the albums. They're all crisp and new, unblemished by decades of handling. My breath slows as I flip through them. I stop when I find Blue Öyster Cult's *Spectres*. The vivid artwork jumps out at me. Next to it is Cheap Trick's *In Color*, a gem I've always wanted but never thought I'd hold in mint condition. I pull them both out and tuck them under my arm. Two albums, and I'm still in the letter C. I brought extra money, but I'll need to pace myself.

The tension in my head and shoulders eases as I keep flipping. I add Pink Floyd's *Animals* to my finds and head up to the counter. The shop owner sorts through the mail, his movements slow and deliberate, like he's in no hurry. I glance at the stack he's working through.

I set my finds on the counter. "I'll take these."

He glances up, nods, and sets the stack of mail aside. A flash of handwriting catches my attention. A name on one of the envelopes—Grace. My heart skips. The letter is addressed to someone named Grace at this address.

I look away before he notices, and turn my attention to the records on the shelf behind him. "No way!"

He stops what he's doing and looks at me over the top of his glasses. "What?"

"Is that a copy of Badfinger's *Wish You Were Here*?"

He smiles. "Sure is. It's rare."

"I know. It was released in November 1974 and pulled from the shelves seven weeks later."

"You know your music."

"Can I see it?"

He grabs it from the shelf and hands it to me.

My hand shakes as I slide it out of the inner sleeve, careful not to touch the grooves. It's in excellent condition. "Is it for sale?"

"Maybe." He pauses. "I'd have to get twenty dollars for it."

It's more than I'm paying for the other three combined, but it's worth it. "Sold."

He smiles and adds it to the stack. I need to create a distraction to get a better look at that letter. I point to a container full of brightly colored guitar picks behind him.

"That's quite a selection of picks you have. Mind if I look through them."

He sets the container on the counter. "Here you go." He pauses. "I've got another bin in the back, if you're interested."

Perfect. I thought I'd have to spill these to distract him. "Thanks. That would be great."

As soon as he turns and disappears behind the curtain, I lean over the counter and look at the letter again. It's addressed to Grace Monroe. That's my Grace! My pulse quickens. She must be connected to this place somehow—maybe she works here, or...

I nudge the letter to see the next one in the pile. Everything is the same, but "Apt. 2" has been added to the end of the second line. An apartment upstairs?

"Find one you like?"

The owner's voice snaps me back. I straighten up so fast my elbow almost knocks over a display of 8-tracks.

"Uh, not yet." I flash an awkward smile.

He sets the second bin of picks on the counter. "Maybe you'll find one in here."

"Thanks."

He watches my hand shake as I sift through the picks. "Are you okay?"

"I'm fine." I gesture to a poster on the wall. "I'm a big fan of Hallowed Ground. They ever shop here?"

"Sure." He hooks a thumb toward the posters. "A lot of those local bands stop in from time to time. I sell them quite a few instruments."

I press harder, keeping my tone light. "You ever see her? The bassist, I mean."

"Grace? Yeah, she's around."

"I'd love to meet her sometime."

He chuckles. "You and every other guy that comes in here." He pauses, then flashes a wry smile. "Can't miss her if you hang around here long enough."

I set a couple of picks on the counter. "I'll take these, too."

I hand him the cash and wait for him to bag the records. He doesn't mention she lives here, but now I'm almost sure of it.

"Enjoy the music," he says as I leave.

Outside, I glance at the second-story window above the shop. A narrow staircase leads to a door marked with the number 2.

My pulse quickens. "This has to be it."

Two cars sit in the driveway: a shiny blue Camaro that screams Lars, and an older Chevy Nova. My gut twists as I try to figure out my next move.

I tuck the records under my arm, cross the street, and find an inconspicuous spot with a clear view of the door.

Why is *he* here? I don't want to go up there and start trouble for her. But what if he's in there hurting her? I'd never forgive myself for just standing around out here. Before I can decide what to do, the front door bursts open. Lars storms out, his long blond hair all over the place, clutching his hand like it's busted. His face twists in anger, and he mutters under his breath.

Every muscle goes rigid as I watch him stomp over to the Camaro and yank the door open with his good hand. Tires screech as he tears out of the driveway.

That son-of-a-bitch.

I grab my records and run toward the stairs. My heart hammers harder with every step. By the time I reach the door, I'm out of breath and my palms are sweating so much I almost drop the albums.

I knock lightly at first, then louder.

The door opens. Grace freezes when she sees me, her eyes red and puffy, like she's been crying. She wipes at her cheeks, so I don't notice, but it's too late.

"Angus?" Her voice is soft, and her eyebrows pull together with a mix of surprise and unease. "What... what are you doing here? How did you even...?"

I suck in air, trying to hide the fact that I ran up her stairs. "Long story."

"Are you all right?"

"You've got a lot of stairs." Thankfully, my breath has returned to normal.

She shakes her head slowly. "What are you doing here?"

Chapter Twenty-Three

This Is It – Kenny Loggins (1979)

Nothing I say is going to make sense. "I, uh, was shopping downstairs. When I left the store, I saw Lars. I recognized him from your gig at the Viper Room."

"Yeah, I'm sorry about that."

I shift my feet. "I saw him leave. He looked pissed. And he held his hand like he was hurt. I had to see if you were okay."

I hold my breath and hope her next move isn't to slam the door in my face.

"That's sweet." She sighs, glancing over her shoulder into the house. "Lars has got a temper. And no respect for drywall, apparently."

She steps aside and motions for me to come in. "I can't believe I'm letting you in. This is weird, Angus..." She pauses. "I don't even know your last name."

"Walker. My last name's Walker, and I know it's weird." I step into the cozy little apartment. "I don't mean to show up like this. I just... I want to make sure you're okay."

The place is small but full of personality—mismatched furniture, band posters covering the walls, and a collection of vinyl stacked in the corner. Everything appears to be normal, except the jagged hole in the wall near the kitchen.

"Let me guess," I nod toward the hole. "Lars?"

She follows my gaze and grimaces. "Yeah. He's an asshole, but you probably already knew that."

Asshole is putting it mildly. I say nothing at first, just set the records down on her small dining table. "Are you okay?"

Grace sighs again, deeper this time. Her posture goes limp like her bones have all dissolved, and she sinks into the couch. "I will be. I guess I'm just... tired of all the drama."

I hesitate, then sit beside her, keeping a respectful distance between us. "You deserve better than that."

She lets out a small, nervous laugh. "You don't even know me, Angus."

"Maybe not." I slide to the edge of my seat. "But I know what I saw. And that's not how I would treat someone I care about."

She doesn't answer right away. I lean back into the cushion, and for a moment we sit in silence.

Before it gets awkward, she rubs at her temples and mutters, "It's not just about me. Lars is our lead guitarist, and now we'll have to cancel tomorrow night's gig at Thunder Road because of his stupid hand."

She's clearly better off without him. I hatch a brilliant idea. "I could play in his place." *Yikes!* Did I say that out loud? Maybe she didn't hear me.

She snaps her head toward me, her brow furrowed. "You?"

Okay. I guess she heard. "I mean... I play guitar. I played in a band for a while."

"What band?"

"I'm sure you've never heard of us. We played small gigs in Utah. That's where I'm from... originally."

Her eyes narrow, like she's trying to figure out if I'm joking. "The guy who unexpectedly shows up at my door just happens to play guitar well enough to stand in for Lars?"

"Crazy, right?" I shrug, wondering if I really am good enough. Perhaps I should have kept my mouth shut.

Her eyes hold a mixture of disbelief and frustration. "You don't even know our songs."

All I do anymore is play guitar and listen to my records. This is *my* music. I bet there isn't a song on her set list that I haven't heard or played.

The silence stretches out between us as she rubs her temples like her head might explode. I feel better about my chances. "Come on, Grace. What do you say?"

She turns her head enough to catch my gaze. "Don't mess with me, Angus. Do you think you can do this?"

"Give me a couple of hours with the set list. Then *you* tell me." I surprise myself with an unfamiliar confidence. It feels good. "What have you got to lose?"

I can almost see the gears turning in her head as she stares. "I know a couple of people who could replace Lars, but not on such short notice."

My foot taps the floor, and I place my hand on my knee to stop it.

Finally, she sighs and leans back against the couch. "I can't believe I'm even considering this." She studies me for what feels like forever before finally nodding. "All right, Angus. Let's see if you're as good as you say you are."

I'm blown away by how this day has played out. I'm sitting in Grace's apartment, which I located within an hour. Lars injures his hand—fortunately, not on her face—and

can't play for the foreseeable future. And… wait for it…
Angus Walker from 2024 is his replacement in the band.

"What kind of guitar do you have?" she asks.

Yikes! In all my excitement, I somehow forgot a guitarist
needs a guitar. "An Ibanez Flying V." Unfortunately, it's
forty-six years away in another state.

She raises her eyebrows, apparently impressed. "I didn't
see that coming. Don't take this the wrong way, but… even
if you're as good as you think you are, you're no Eddie Van
Halen."

I anticipate her next question. "I won't be able to bring
it tomorrow, so… I was hoping you might have one I can
borrow."

Disappointment flashes in her eyes, but she makes a quick
recovery. "I've got the perfect fix for that." She disappears
and returns a few moments later with a black Stratocaster.

"Fun fact," she says, brushing her hair out of her face. "I
used to play guitar before I switched to bass. She hands me
the Strat. "This was my favorite because it matches my hair."
She smiles and playfully fluffs her hair with one hand.

It's an original. Finding one in this condition in 2024
would be difficult. "She's a beauty."

"Don't ding it. I'm still attached."

"I'll treat it like gold."

We sit in her living room, surrounded by amps, cables,
and half-filled coffee mugs. Grace spreads out the set list
on the table between us, tapping it with a pen. "It's mostly
covers, but we sometimes do a couple of originals."

"The originals. Did you write them?"

"I've written a couple of songs. They're not very good."

"But you perform them live."

"What about you?" she says, ending that part of the conversation.

I'm sorry I asked. "I've only written one."

"Play it for me."

I shake my head.

"Come on." She flashes a playful smile. "I'll show you mine if you show me yours."

I want to ask her if we're still talking about songs, but I think it might be too soon. "Maybe another time."

"Fine." She pouts, then turns her attention to the list. "You know 'Don't Fear the Reaper,' right?"

"Of course." I play the intro. The Strat hums beneath my fingers. "Who doesn't?"

She watches as I play, her arms crossed and lips pressed together in what looks like skeptical concentration.

"Not bad," she finally says. "Let's try the solo from 'Hotel California.' That one's a bit trickier."

The next two hours fly by. We go through song after song, and every time I hit the right note or nail a solo, she relaxes a little more. Her instructions are sharp but never harsh, and by the third run-through, I've got most of it down.

"You're not half bad, Walker." She leans back against the couch with her arms behind her head.

I nod and flash an I-told-you-so smile.

She tilts her head and her curls spill over one shoulder. "You said you were from Utah. Where do you live now?"

I freeze for a second but force myself to keep strumming. "A little outside the city."

"Like where?"

I fake a cough and switch topics. "The second chorus in 'Black Magic Woman'—do you want me to double the rhythm there or stick to the lead?"

Her eyes narrow for a moment, like she knows I'm dodging the question, but she lets it go. "Lead. Definitely lead. Lars usually goes overboard there, but if you keep it tight, it'll sound cleaner."

"Got it."

By the time we finish running through the set list, it's almost two, and my stomach growls loud enough for her to hear.

"Sounds like you're hungry," she says with a smirk.

"Starving."

She heads to the kitchen. "I make a mean grilled cheese."

"Grilled cheese sounds perfect."

As she works, I stay in the living room and practice one of the solos. Her voice drifts in from the kitchen. "Did you drive here?"

Shit! "No. I don't have a car." I cringe, anticipating her response.

"Really? Why not?"

My mind scrambles, and I pause mid-note. "It's complicated."

"How complicated can it be?"

I hesitate, my fingers hovering over the strings. "Let's just say I've been... between vehicles for a while."

She leans around the corner, a spatula in her hand. "Between vehicles?"

"Yeah, like, you know... one broke down, and I haven't had the cash to replace it yet." It's a lame excuse, but I hope she buys it.

She studies me for a beat before ducking back into the kitchen. "Fair enough. Do you need a ride tomorrow night?"

"Thanks, but I can make it there myself," I say as she sets a plate of perfectly golden grilled cheese in front of me.

"In case you were wondering, the band makes four hundred a night, so if this works out, your share will be one hundred, okay?"

I hadn't thought about payment. "Sounds good."

She sits across from me, picks up her sandwich, then pauses it in front of her mouth. "Lars might show up and cause problems. What do we do if that happens?"

I chew my first bite slowly, thinking. "If he shows up, we'll deal with it then. He can't play with a busted hand. If he causes trouble, you've got every right to have him arrested and kick him out of the band."

She snorts. "Easier said than done. He's a hothead. I don't want you to get hurt."

"I can take care of myself."

"No offense, but I've seen him fight. He's an animal. A big one."

"None taken." I pause before I ask something that might be none of my business. "If he's such an asshole, why are you still with him?"

She lowers her head and takes a bite of her sandwich, a signal that the conversation is over.

"I'm sure everything will be all right tomorrow, but if it isn't, do I get combat pay?"

She smiles unconvincingly.

"Don't worry. I've got your back." I surprise myself with the conviction in my voice.

"Thank you, Angus." Her eyes are soft, and her gaze lingers.

I think we just had a moment, but I can't be sure. Perhaps if I'd had more experience with this kind of thing.

We finish eating, and the conversation drifts back to music—safer territory. But my nerves continue to buzz under the surface.

It's after four when I pack up her Strat.

"Can I give you a ride somewhere?" Her expression is genuine, but her eyes search mine for a clue.

Where will I go? I'll probably have to stay at a hotel tonight. "I'm good. Thanks."

"You said you live outside the city. How will you get home?"

"I'm staying with some friends." Howard and Johnson.

She clears her throat. "You're not going to skip out, are you?"

"Not a chance."

"Good." She hands me a piece of paper. "Here's my phone number in case you need to get ahold of me."

Her eyes linger, and it feels like another moment.

"Thanks." I grab my records. "See you tomorrow."

As I walk out, I glance back at the house. Did that really happen? My mind races as I head down the street, staring at the digits on the paper in my hand.

Chapter Twenty-Four

Born to Run – Bruce Springsteen (1975)

I decide to return home for the night rather than stay in Denver. I have twenty dollars in old bills and would need to spend that much for a hotel room. Besides, I don't want to show up tomorrow wearing the same dirty clothes.

I'm nervous about leaving Grace alone, but I'd be of little use to her unless I camp out on her street… with Pop's shotgun. I'll have to live with the fact that I can't watch her 24/7.

Thunder rumbles in the distance, and I pick up my pace. I'm not concerned about another run-in with Hoodie, because I'm doing exactly what he told me to do. I'm leaving.

I return to Utah, records under my arm, without incident.

The house is quiet. I call Ozzy's name. Wishful thinking, I guess. I skip dinner and practice Grace's set list for a few hours before bed. I'm nervous about the gig tomorrow and don't sleep well. I can normally handle the pressure of a live performance, but having to impress Grace takes it to a whole new level. If she thinks I'm a hack, I won't stand a chance with her.

In the morning, I go over the set list a couple more times. After a shower and a protein shake for lunch, I fall back into bed, my head pounding. Two hours later, I splash cold water on my face and run my wet hands back through my hair. I pick out the studliest outfit from my touring days and check myself out in the mirror. I can do this.

I arrive early at Thunder Road to smooth things over with the bartender. I apologize for the misunderstanding and lay a fiver on the counter to cover my debt. I lay another beside it for his trouble. After that, we're cool. He nods to Bigfoot, who's been watching from his stool by the door.

Grace arrives happy to see me, and we hug. She hands me her guitar, which feels good in my hands, and I can't wait to get up on stage again. In the meantime, I help the band haul the rest of their equipment inside and set up.

We open up with Deep Purple's "Smoke on the Water" to get the crowd fired up. Everything is cool until Lars walks in a half hour later. The place is packed, but he's hard to miss. I'm sure people wonder why he's not up here instead of me. I look around and realize the crowd is into us, hanging on every note. And I've been hitting all of them on time. I'm no Norse god, but I've lost a few pounds, and I'm feeling confident. People are here for the music, not a beauty contest. All things considered, I'm crushing it.

I look over at Grace, but she's not smiling. The blood has drained from her face. She shoots a sideways glance in Lars's direction, then back to me. I nod.

By the time the song ends, her color has returned. She calls for a quick huddle and changes the next song. We take our places and play Carly Simon's "You're So Vain." Grace holds the mike with her middle finger in the air as she sings.

Lars doesn't stick around long, and I throw a big smile and a thumbs-up in Grace's direction when the song ends.

I guess he's seen enough to know we don't need him anymore.

After the last set, we bow to wild applause. It feels good.

Backstage, Grace hugs me and gives me a peck on the cheek. "Thank you, Angus. You did great."

My heart jumps around in my chest like it's loose. I should say something, but my brain is mush. "Thanks for trusting me," I finally say.

Lars approaches as we load our equipment into the van outside. He looks at me like he's a bull and I'm wearing a red cape. My heart attempts to hammer its way through my chest.

A small crowd gathers as Grace steps between us.

"No, Grace. Stay out of his way."

She tries to reason with Lars, and he swats her away like a bug. I run toward her, but he scoops me up in a choke hold. It's hard to breathe. I turn my head into the crook of his elbow to reduce the pressure on my airway. Escaping a choke hold is all about bodyweight and leverage.

I unbalance the beast backward by dropping my weight and executing a leg sweep, then use my hips to throw him over my back. He hits the ground like a felled redwood. The crowd lets out a collective gasp.

He's up quickly and takes a run at me, swinging his oversized fist.

No time to celebrate. I duck under it, and his momentum corkscrews him into the ground. I take a few steps backward to put some distance between us. The crowd is enjoying this. I'm too terrified to share their enthusiasm.

Lars is on his feet again. "Stand still, you little shit."

Grace is crying. I have to work hard to breathe. I can't overpower him. All I can do is outmaneuver him, so I hope he tires soon. He bears down on me like a Scandinavian freight train.

One wrong move and he'll rip off my arms and eat them like chicken wings. *You can do this, Angus. Focus.* I stand my ground until the last second, then sidestep his attack and sweep his leg again. He's airborne and crashes to the pavement with a thud. A siren wails and stops abruptly on the other side of the gathering crowd.

It doesn't matter who's at fault here, I can't stick around to answer questions. I'm a ghost—no ID, no birth record, no record of anything.

I grab Grace by the shoulders and look into her puffy, red eyes. "I'm sorry. I can't stay."

Car doors slam, and I run.

"Wait. Angus!"

I don't look back.

Chapter Twenty-Five

Bad Moon Rising – Creedence Clearwater Revival (1970)

I second-guess leaving Denver as I drive the ATV back to the house. Maybe I should have gone to Grace's apartment and waited for her—made sure she was all right. I should have offered to stay with her in case Lars follows her home. But I ran. Scared as a sinner in a cyclone, Gran would say.

On one hand, I'm glad the cops showed up when they did. I don't know how much longer I could have continued the David vs. Goliath show. On the other, they forced my hand. I couldn't stay, right? I hope Grace sees it that way. But how could she? She doesn't know my situation. That needs to change, but it presents another problem. She might think I'm batshit crazy and never want to see me again.

Things were going so well until Lars came along and blew it up. Does Grace feel the same way? Or is she pissed at me for bailing on her? I can't live a lie. She deserves to know the truth. "We're soulmates. She'll understand."

Famous last words of every poor bastard who said something stupid that ended a relationship.

I slam on the brakes and skid to a stop. Should I go back? I pull out my phone. It's after midnight. I'm exhausted. I'll try to get some sleep and figure it out in the morning.

Sometime during a fitful night's sleep, I decide to return the next day to straighten things out with Grace. My eyes open to the sound of an alarm I forgot to cancel. I shut it off and drift back to sleep until I'm awakened around noon by a noise outside.

I splash water on my face and stumble out the back door to find Jackson loading his truck with the equipment he'd stored in the barn.

"Hey, Jackson. What's up?"

"Just getting my stuff out of your way." He loads a metal detector into the truck bed. "No more treasure hunting."

"Is there a problem?"

"You can say that." He wipes his hands on his jeans. "My girlfriend's pregnant."

"Zoe?"

"No. Callie. I don't know anyone named Zoe."

"Of course you do." I rake a hand back through my hair as I try to make sense of this. "You brought her here the first day. We all drove out together. Zoe…? Cute. Brown hair, blue eyes, built like—"

"I don't know what you're talking about." He gives me a wary glance. "My girlfriend's name is Callie. She went home to Provo for the summer."

"So, you don't know anyone named Zoe?"

"Sorry."

An image of Ozzy flickers through my mind, and realization hits me like a sucker punch.

Jackson picks up a crowbar and tosses it into the truck. "I'm on my way to Provo next week to look for a job."

"What about the gold?"

"I've turned over every rock out there. If you find anything, it's all yours."

"Good luck with the job search."

He gives me a quick salute. "Thanks."

"Wait. Did you get the dynamite?"

"No way." He shakes his head and offers a sigh of resignation. "I can't take any chances. My kid needs a father."

"Yeah. Good luck with that, too."

As soon as he drives off, I run into the house and get dressed in my 1978 clothes. The gym will have to wait until Monday. I chug a protein shake and drive out to the portal. I need to talk to Grace *now*. I can't go radio silent for a week.

I'm rehearsing my explanation as I step into the chamber. "NO!"

The portal is gone. No waves, no vibrations, nothing but a dark, empty chamber.

I wave my arms wildly around the space, but it's no use. I'm just flailing at air. My chest tightens, and I grit my teeth. I need to talk to Waldo.

My phone shows no signal. I curse it for that, then again for not being able to call Grace in 1978 Denver. I drive back until I show a cell signal and skid to a stop.

"Waldo, I need help. The portal's gone, and I'm trying to get back to 1978 to fix things with Grace."

"Who *is* this?"

My blood pressure spikes. *Please be joking.* "Not funny. We need to talk."

"I can meet you at your place in twenty minutes."

"Thank you."

I sink into the porch swing. Its creak matches the rhythm of my restless thoughts. The wind chimes, suspended from the corner of the roof, translate the afternoon breeze into a soft, disjointed tune. It's the soundtrack of my life—random notes, no order. No sheet music, no theory, just me hammering away, hoping the noise turns into something that makes sense.

Waldo arrives and drops into the swing beside me. "Okay, I'm here. Talk."

I exhale hard before I unload everything, starting from the moment I stepped into 1978 on Thursday until I stumbled back out last night.

Waldo stares at me when I finish, like I just confessed to robbing a bank. "You took down Thor? Dude, you're a superhero."

"I don't feel like one." My sigh is sharp and heavy. "If I don't talk to Grace *yesterday,* I'm going to blow everything."

He shakes his head. "You know where I stand on this. I loved our trip to 1978, but I don't think you should go back."

The words hit me like a slap. "Not an option, Waldo. I need to do this. I need to tell her how I feel and find out if she feels the same."

"And if she doesn't?"

My chest tightens like a vise. "I don't know. My life will be over, okay?"

"Stop it." He gives me a firm pat on the back. "You're twenty-two. You've got your entire future ahead of you."

"You only get one soulmate, right? Grace is mine. I know it."

He throws up his hands. "Fine. Then go. But the next time you see her, tell her the truth."

"And how do you think *that* will go?"

"It doesn't matter. You can't keep lying to her. You've spent what?" He pauses to calculate. "Ten hours with her? Look where it's gotten you. You need to shit or get off the pot. Whatever happens, accept it and move on."

I glare at him as my frustration boils over. "What would *you* think if we just met, and I told you my story?"

He raises an eyebrow above a mischievous grin. "Maybe she's a time traveler, too."

"I'm serious!" I snap. "It was a mistake calling you. You should leave."

His grin vanishes, and he raises his hands in surrender. "Okay, okay. I'm sorry. But chill, man."

I push off the swing and storm into the house. I return with a joint and a lighter, sparking it up without a word. The first drag hits my lungs like fire. My hand trembles as I hold it out toward him.

"No thanks."

"Suit yourself." My voice is flat, the words curling out with the smoke.

"What's wrong with your hand?"

"Nothing."

He watches me carefully. "Look, if the portal's already unstable, this could get worse. You said it worked Friday. There's a three-day window, so it should've been open Thursday and today."

I take another drag, coughing hard before I manage a response. "And?"

He shrugs. "The window will shift a little, but this feels like something else. Gravitational fluctuations can mess with stability—like trying to build a house on shifting sand. It's almost impossible to keep it steady."

I lean back against the porch rail. "So, you're saying it's a crap shoot?"

"We know the moon's phases are the driving force. However, these fluctuations, together with the strength of its energy source, most likely determine the timing and duration of its availability."

My shoulders slump. "In other words, a crap shoot."

"I think it's dangerous," he whispers.

"Everything's dangerous," I mutter. "I Googled the band again. Lars puts Grace in the hospital."

His expression shifts and concern creases his brow. "That's not on you."

"It doesn't matter whose fault it is. I'm going back to stop it."

Waldo leans forward, elbows on his knees. "You might make it worse. Whatever you do to stop it could cause bigger repercussions."

"I know." My voice is brittle. "But I can't just do nothing."

He sighs. "Please be careful. I don't want to lose my best friend."

An awkward silence hangs between us until I finally break it. "Jackson came by this morning. Picked up his stuff and said he's done with the treasure hunt."

"Why?"

"He knocked up his girlfriend and needs a job." I hesitate, then ask, "Do you remember Zoe?"

Waldo gives me a puzzled look. "No. Should I?"

"Jackson's girlfriend. He brought her on the treasure hunt."

He shakes his head. "I don't remember any girl."

I push off the rail and pace. "I was afraid of that. Jackson doesn't remember her either. It's another timeline change. But what could I have done to affect Zoe?"

Waldo leans back and rubs his temples. "Could be anything. Say Grace's band becomes famous. They're scheduled to play a concert in Salt Lake where Zoe's parents meet and fall in love. No offense, but if Lars is out and you're in, maybe the band doesn't do as well, and the concert never happens. No concert, no love story, no Zoe."

Yikes! I stop pacing and stare at him. "I never thought of it that way."

"That's the problem," he says grimly. "If you go back, things here could get worse."

My hand shakes again, and I shove it in my pocket.

"How long has your hand been doing that?"

"Doing what?"

"Dude, you've got a tremor, and I bet you've only had it since you traveled."

I shrug. "It comes and goes. I don't recall when it started."

Waldo shakes his head.

Chapter Twenty-Six

Tell the Truth – Derek and the Dominos
(1970)

I ask Rusty for next Thursday and Friday off. Instead of granting my request, he fires me. I don't care. It was a crummy job, anyway.

I practically live at the gym for the next four days. Punching bags, free weights, and endless laps around the track become my therapy. I can't sit still, can't let my mind linger on Grace for too long without spiraling. The wait is killing me. Five days feels like an eternity when the clock is counting down to something that could change everything—or ruin it.

Every time I close my eyes, I see her face. Her green eyes lock onto mine, and I see the flicker of confusion when I bolted without explanation. What's she thinking now? That I'm a coward? A flake? Either way, I let her down. I committed to help her with her band. She took a chance on me. I imagine the band will rehearse a couple of times this week. She won't be happy when I'm a no-show.

I push harder and faster. Sweat pours off me, but it doesn't erase the thought of her smile, the sound of her voice. The truth sits heavy in my gut: if I don't go back and tell her everything—about why I left, about the portal—then I'll never know if we could have had something real. And not knowing might be worse than losing her.

Driving out to the portal Thursday morning, I'm as nervous as a long-tailed cat in a room full of rocking chairs. I avoided two calls from Waldo this week, for fear he might try to talk me out of going back. My mind's made up, and I don't need to have that conversation again.

Shit! No portal.

What if it's gone for good? Even someone as smart as Waldo doesn't know for sure how these things work. Hoodie said this isn't the only portal, but where are the others, and do any of them connect to 1978 Denver? I'm spiraling.

Breathe, Angus. Try not to get ahead of yourself. It'll be here tomorrow. Like last time. Yes, that's it. One more day. I can do one more day.

That night is pure torture. I lie in bed, staring at the ceiling, my mind running circles around every worst-case scenario. What if Waldo was wrong? What if the portal is gone forever, and I blew my only shot? What if I'm stuck here while Grace lives out the rest of her life in the past, never knowing why I left? I toss and turn all night, throwing the blanket off, then yanking it back over me.

A protein shake is all I can manage for breakfast before I'm back on the ATV. I gun it, gripping the handlebars like they might slip away if I let up even a little. When I reach the cave, I cut the engine, barely waiting for the ATV to roll to a stop before I jump off and sprint inside.

The second I slip into the chamber, I feel it—a low hum, a static charge in the air that raises the hairs on my arms. The waves distort the cave wall like a mirage. A choked laugh escapes me, half disbelief, half sheer relief. "Hell yeah," I shout. My hands shake as I run them through my hair. One more deep breath, then I square my shoulders. "Okay. Let's do this."

I exit on the other side and head directly to Grace's apartment, keeping an eye out for Hoodie. I make it there without incident and climb the steps to her apartment. Raising my fist to knock, my heart pounds harder than it did the first time I stepped on stage. Before I can even lower my hand, the door flies open, and there she is. Her green eyes are ablaze with a fury that hits me like a slap in the face.

"You've got some nerve." Her voice is low and sharp. Before I can get a word out, she slams the door so hard it rattles the frame.

"Grace, wait!" I call out, but my plea is cut short when the door reopens enough for her to thrust a crumpled wad of cash in my direction. The bills hit me in the chest and flutter to the ground.

"There's your cut from the last gig. Take it and go." Her voice trembles with anger. The door slams again and I hear the chain slide into place.

"That went well," I mutter, as I kneel to scoop up the money and collect my thoughts. This isn't how I imagined it. I take a shaky breath, my hand on the door frame as I gather my courage.

"Grace." My voice is firm. "Please, give me a minute. I can explain everything. I promise."

Silence.

"You need a guitarist for tonight's gig, don't you?"

Still nothing. I lean against the door, my forehead pressed against the wood. "I screwed up. I know that. But if you let me explain—if you hear me out—I'll leave you alone after that. I swear."

There's a long pause, then the sound of the chain being slid free. The door opens, and Grace stands there, arms crossed, her face an unreadable mask.

"You've got two minutes," she says flatly. "And it better be good. You're not getting off the hook that easy."

Her words sting, but I nod, grateful just to have the chance. As she steps back to let me in, the weight in my chest eases—but only a little. I have a feeling this isn't over, but at least it's a start. She wouldn't be so mad if she didn't care. I'll hold on to that.

I step inside, but I don't get far. She plants herself in the entryway to the living room, arms still crossed, shoulders squared like she's ready to throw me out at the slightest provocation. The small foyer feels even smaller under her gaze.

"I'm guessing you're pissed." Not a great lead, but I'm out of my element here.

"Whatever gave you that idea?"

Her eyes are sharper than I remember, like two green lasers that cut me to ribbons.

"Two minutes." Her voice is clipped. "Start talking."

I let out a breath, rehearsing the words in my head, but they sound ridiculous even to me. I glance around the room for something, anything, to buy me a second more, but it's just me, Grace, and the ticking clock.

"Why did you run?" she demands. "Last week, when the cops showed up."

I rub the back of my neck. "I… I can't… talk to the police, okay?"

"Why not?" Her voice is razor sharp, and I can feel her study every hesitation, every flicker of doubt in my eyes.

"It's complicated."

"Complicated?" She pauses to let the word hang in the air. "That's what people say when they're hiding something. What is it? Are you wanted for something?" For a moment, her eyes flash terror. "Did I just let a serial killer into my house?"

"What? No!" I blurt out. "It's not like that."

"Then what is it like, Angus?" She takes a step forward, her tone shifts between anger and something else—wariness, maybe. Her face is unreadable, but her eyes stay locked on mine.

I press my back against the wall, cornered by her gaze. More lies aren't an option—I can't dig the hole any deeper. But how do I explain something like this?

"It's going to sound crazy…"

She snorts. "Try me. At this point, I'm pretty open to crazy."

My pulse hammers in my ears, and I hesitate. "Grace, I'm… not from around here. And I don't mean Denver. I mean…" I trail off with a vague gesture. "I'm from somewhere else. Some… time else."

She stares at me, her expression unreadable. "Are you seriously telling me you're some kind of time traveler?"

"Yes." I force the word out before I can second-guess myself. "That's exactly what I'm saying."

Her brows knit together and her mouth opens as if to say something, but I keep going, desperate to get it all out.

"I'm from 2024." The words land like a load of bricks. "I didn't run from the cops because I've got a record. I ran because I *don't* have a record. Nothing. I don't exist."

There. It's out. I brace myself for laughter, for shouting, for a punch in my face.

Chapter Twenty-Seven

Tight Rope – Leon Russell (1972)

Grace doesn't move. She just stares at me, her expression frozen.

Say something. Anything's better than this silence.

She blinks, her expression blank, but something flickers, like recognition. But then it's gone.

"That's insane." Her voice isn't as sharp as before. It wavers a little. "You actually expect me to believe that?"

I step forward, my chest tight. "Grace, I know how it sounds. But I'm not lying to you. I can't lie to you."

Her expression hardens again, though I can see something bothers her. Her arms fall to her sides, and she exhales slowly, almost like she's trying to steady herself.

"You ran off without an explanation. Then I don't hear from you for a week."

"I wasn't trying to hurt you." I don't even know how to explain the regret that's been gnawing at me since I left—how it's chewed me up inside and spit me out. "I swear to you, I've been trying to come back. But the portal—"

"The *portal*," she cuts me off, shaking her head. "Unbelievable."

I study her face for a sign she believes me, even just a little. But all I see is her frustration.

"You've got guts, I'll give you that," she says finally, her voice softer, though still guarded.

"Grace..." I start, but she holds up a hand.

"You've got until tonight." She turns toward the door. "If you want to play the gig, fine. But if you show up, you better have a proper explanation ready. One that doesn't sound like the plot of a bad sci-fi movie."

I swallow hard. "Fair enough."

I'm screwed.

She opens the door again and waits for me to leave. I step out, feeling like I've been hit by a train. As I turn back to look at her one last time, I swear I catch it again—that flicker in her expression, like she knows something more than she's letting on.

And then the door closes, leaving me alone, my head pounding.

It wasn't a total loss. On the bright side, I can still play the gig tonight. Wait. Where are we playing? I check my pockets for the band's schedule, but it's not there. I raise my fist to knock and get the details but think better of it. I'll give her some time to cool off.

The good news is we don't go on for another ten hours. The bad news is we don't go on for another ten hours. What am I going to do with myself? I don't want to risk going home for fear there could be issues with the portal that would keep me from making it back for the show.

I walk to the diner across from Thunder Road to get some lunch.

The owner, Carl, remembers me. "Hey, there. Where's your friend?"

"Just me today."

"Did you find what you were looking for the last time you were here?"

I have to think about what that was. "Oh, yeah. Hallowed Ground. I found them. Thanks for the help."

"There was a lot of commotion here last week. Cops all over the place. It might have been the same band."

I lower myself onto one of the counter stools. "I heard something about a fight after the show."

He pulls a towel from his shoulder and wipes the counter in front of me. "I saw them take a big weirdo with blond hair away in one of the patrol cars."

"Yeah, I heard he started it."

Carl exhales and shakes his head. He flips the towel back over his shoulder. "So, what can I get you…?" he says, fishing for my name.

"Angus. My name's Angus. I'll have a BLT and a glass of iced tea."

"Coming right up, Angus." He sets my tea on the counter and disappears into the kitchen.

When I've finished eating, he places the check on the counter. I pull a couple of singles from my wallet and freeze. Carl waits as I stare at them in my hand. I suddenly realize how I can prove my story to Grace.

"It's a buck and a quarter," Carl says.

"What? Oh, yeah." I set the money on the counter. "Keep the change."

I can prove I'm not lying by showing her something from the future. I'll pop back to 2024 to get some new money and a newspaper. While I'm there, I'll print off the article about her trip to the hospital. She needs to know so she can protect herself. Will it mess with the timeline? I hope so.

The thought of her taking a beating from Lars if I could have prevented it… I can't live with that.

The portal hums in front of me, its surface shifting like liquid glass, and my pulse stutters. I rake a hand through my hair. There has to be another way to convince her, right? Something safer? But she needs proof. Something undeniable. If I don't do this, she might never believe me.

What if something goes wrong? What if I can't get back? I could lose Grace before I even have the chance to prove to her who I am. I shake my head. *No.* I can't think like that. Every second I waste is another second she spends doubting me. I swallow hard, shifting my weight from one foot to the other. *Screw it.* I can't let fear decide this for me.

After I gather what I need, I'm back in 1978 an hour later. I shift from foot to foot as I stand at Grace's door, the crumpled newspaper in my nervous grip. I take a deep breath and knock.

The door opens a few inches. Grace's green eyes are narrow. "You again?"

"Uh… yeah. Sorry to bother you." My voice cracks, and I clear my throat. "I forgot to ask where we're playing tonight."

"Rhythm & Riffs in Lakewood."

"I don't know where that is." My eyes beg her to offer me a ride.

She exhales. "Come back at four, and you can ride with me."

"Thank you." Before she can close the door, I speak again. "Listen, I can explain everything. Please, just… let me in."

"You going to do better than the last time?"

"Can't do much worse, can I?"

She smiles, but it's only a flicker. "You've got five minutes."

The faint scent of incense mixes with the aroma of coffee as I step into her apartment. Her denim jacket is draped over a chair, and her guitar leans against the couch.

I hold out the newspaper first. The tremor is back, and I switch hands. "Here. This is from 2024. Look at the date."

She unfolds it carefully and her skeptical expression falters. Her lips move silently as she reads the headlines: *Climate Summit Reaches Deadlock, AI Takes the Wheel in Self-Driving Revolution.* She looks up at me, confused but intrigued.

I reach into my pocket, pull out a twenty-dollar bill, and hand it to her. "Check the date on that bad boy."

She flips the bill over. "Huh. This feels different... what is this, counterfeit?"

"No. New technology... from the future."

I pull out my trump card and hand it to her.

"What is it?"

"Push the round button on the bottom."

The screen lights up. "Oh." She giggles.

"It's made by a three-trillion-dollar company that, right now, operates out of a garage in Los Altos, California."

"Are you going to tell me what it is?"

"It's a phone. Plus a lot more."

"This... this is... a phone?" She turns it around in her hand. "There's no wire. How does it work?"

I touch the screen, and the dial pad displays. "Everyone has one back home. You can take and make calls from anywhere."

Her eyes sparkle with wonder like a child's on Christmas. "Can I try it?"

"I'm afraid it won't work here. The technology doesn't exist yet to route the calls. But I can show you something else pretty cool."

She hands me the phone, and I tap the camera app. I hold it up and snap her picture, then show her the screen. "There."

Her mouth opens and closes like she's searching for words. "It's a camera, too?"

"And a hundred other things. Pretty cool, huh?" I hand it back to her. "Here you try it."

I show her what to do, then let her snap a picture of me. "Watch this." I lean in close, hold the phone up in front of us and take another. "That's called a selfie, because you can take your own picture."

Her face lights up with a smile. "We look pretty good together."

We look awesome. That's a keeper.

She shakes her head and sits heavily on the arm of the couch. "Okay, so maybe you're actually telling the truth."

"Maybe?" I throw up my arms. "What more proof do you need?" I have a brilliant—or maybe terrible—idea. "After the show, come back to 2024 with me."

She blinks a few times. "What? No. That won't be necessary. I believe you."

Relief washes over me so hard I nearly collapse. "Finally. You have no idea how long I've wanted to—"

A knock at the door cuts me off. Grace freezes.

"Expecting someone?"

She doesn't answer. She crosses the room, her movements wary, and opens the door a crack. Then, with a sigh, she swings it open.

My blood turns to ice.

Hoodie steps inside, his presence filling the room. Are they working together? How stupid can I be? I let my rookie heart lead me right into his trap. I'm pretty sure I'm about to pass out.

"What's *he* doing here?"

Chapter Twenty-Eight

Right Place Wrong Time – Dr. John (1973)

Grace looks at me, her face drenched in confusion. "You two know each other?"

"You can say that." My eyes cut back and forth, looking for a way out if I need it. "This man stopped me on the street when I first arrived in Denver and told me I didn't belong here. He told me to go back to where I came from. It freaked me out."

He pulls off his hood. He's not as scary without it, but I want to know why he's here.

"He's been following me around. Told me he was a time traveler who came through a portal like I did."

"Angus… this is my father, Sam."

Sam smirks. "Miss me, kid?"

"This man is your father?!" I sputter, backing up as Hoodie—now Sam—steps further into the room. The floor feels like it's shifting beneath me.

"If he's your father, then you knew. All this time, you had me sweating bullets over trying to tell you the truth and prove my crazy story."

"No." She holds up her hands. "I didn't know your story until you told me."

I glare at her. "You said I was insane."

"I said *it* was insane, which it is."

I glance at Sam, then turn my attention back to Grace.

"Angus, please, sit," she says.

I try to wrap my head around this new development as I pace around the room.

Grace turns to her father with her hands on her hips. "What are you doing here?"

"He's right. I followed him, and when I saw him come in here, I got worried. I want to make sure you're all right."

"I'm fine. Now's not a good time."

"Be careful. He knows that jujitsu shit."

I stop and square my shoulders. "It's judo… and you started it."

"He's not going to hurt me. Please go. Angus and I have some things to talk about before our gig tonight."

I resume pacing.

"You two are messing with the timeline," he says.

"Dad." Her voice is stern. "We've talked about this. Now go."

"Okay. But I warned you."

"Fine. Consider me warned. Again."

"I'll check in on you later."

"No, Dad. That won't be necessary. We need to leave in a couple of hours, anyway." She glances at me, then back to Sam. "Why don't you come back around five. You can take a shower and fix yourself something to eat."

"Thanks, I could use a shower."

"I'm aware."

His gaze lingers on her for a moment before he turns to me. Although I feel the uncomfortable intensity of his glare, I stay locked on his eyes until he turns back to Grace.

"Okay, goodbye."

She closes the door behind him.

I shake my head. "I didn't see that coming."

"There's no need to be afraid of him."

"Really? He attacked me this morning."

She slumps like a wilted flower. "I'm sorry. He's not well."

"Aren't you afraid he might hurt you?"

She shakes her head.

A sudden realization hits me like a sucker punch. "How long has your father been here in Denver?"

"Maybe we should sit."

I ignore her.

She hesitates. "You don't have to do the math. I came with him."

"I'll take that seat now."

I collapse onto the couch and lean my head back. A sharp pain snakes its way between my eyes and coils up at the base of my brain.

"In my defense, I was three years old."

I close my eyes, remain silent, and wait for the pain to subside.

"It's a long story."

"I have time," I say without opening my eyes.

"My parents were both in the foster care system in Montana. They aged out, moved in together, and eventually got married. I wish I could say it was all sunshine and rainbows. Mom got pregnant and things got worse. She wanted an abortion, but Dad talked her out of it. After I was born, she resented him for it, and me by association. She couldn't handle motherhood and started taking pills."

She pauses, and I want to say something, but I don't know what.

"My dad made the best of it. He provided for us by working construction. In 2014, while tearing down an old building, he stumbled into a portal, probably like the one you came through. He ended up here in Denver in 1960. A month later, he packed me up and brought me here. I was three years old, and my mom wasn't fit to take care of herself, let alone a child. He said he could give me a better life… and I guess he did."

She's a kindred spirit, a fellow traveler, but she lied to me… or at least withheld the truth. I open my eyes. "I'm sorry. That must have been difficult for both of you."

"He went back once a few years ago, after I moved out. He said things were different, and not in a good way."

"What kind of things?"

"He wouldn't say." She looks at the floor. "I'm never going back there, so I guess it doesn't matter."

Once again, I'm at a loss for words.

"Actions in the past have consequences in the future. He's obsessed with warning anyone who might have traveled. It's taken a toll. People tend to write him off as some kind of wack job."

"No offense, but I thought the same thing." I frown. "Have there been other travelers?"

"I don't know. He doesn't talk about it. You're the first one I've ever met." Her sad eyes hold mine. "He's not a bad man. He's my father. He sacrificed to give me a better life."

"Where does he live now?"

"He rents a small apartment about a mile from here. He's not well. I feed him once in a while."

"Why did you give me such a hard time when I told you? You made my time travel sound insane—your word—when you'd done the same thing?"

"It surprised me at first." She tucks a lock of hair behind her ear. "Once I got over the initial shock, I had to protect myself. What if you were a time cop or something, who traveled here from the future to punish other travelers?"

"Is that really a thing?"

Her gaze muddies, and she looks down at her hands. "I don't know. My father seems to think so."

I wouldn't believe everything he says. Just sayin'…

Her uncertain gaze meets mine. "You're not, are you?"

"A time cop?" Amused, I let myself grin. "I can assure you, I am not a time cop."

Another knock at the door interrupts our conversation. This one is more than a knock. It sounds like Thor pounding the door with his hammer.

I jump to my feet. "Don't answer it."

Lars yells for her to let him in.

"Call 911."

"What?" A mix of fear and confusion clouds her expression. "Whose number is that?"

Shit! That won't work for a few more years. "Call the police. NOW."

Chapter Twenty-Nine

Baby It's You – Smith (1969)

Grace dials the police and tells them to hurry. She's crying. Lars is still shouting. There's a tortured screech of metal followed by a sharp pop as something gives way outside. Grace covers her mouth, so she doesn't scream.

I hold my finger up to my lips. She throws her arms around me and buries her face in my chest. I hold her tight until a siren wails, stopping abruptly in front of the building.

"Cops are here," I whisper. "I can't stay. They'll want to see some ID."

I have to pry her arms away so I can step back. "You'll be fine. Wait until you hear the police speak before you let anyone in."

"Okay. You can go out the back door and hide in the record shop." She mouths the words *thank you.*

"I'll be downstairs. Don't forget to show them the hole in the wall."

I wait for the police to leave with Lars in handcuffs. I'm not sure if they can charge him with anything yet, but perhaps they can hold him until after the show. I don't want a repeat of last week's kerfuffle. Grace needs to get a TRO.

I climb her stairs when the coast is clear. The coach light hangs from its wires near the front door. Maybe they can hold him overnight for destruction of property. The doorknob turns in my hand, and I find Grace alone on the couch.

"Are you okay?" I ask.

"A little shaken up. I'll be fine."

"I think you should consider a temporary restraining order so he can't do this again. It will also prevent him from showing up at your shows."

She nods.

"We've got a couple of hours before we need to leave. We should go down to the courthouse and file for one now. Otherwise, you'll have to wait until Monday. If the judge is there, he might grant it on the spot. Did you get a police report?"

She nods.

"Then, let's go."

"Let's... as in, you'll go with me?"

"Of course, I'll just need to keep a low profile."

The wheels of justice, which often grind slowly, spin like they've been sprayed with WD-40. When Grace tells the judge she has a show tonight, he informs her that Lars is being held until his arraignment on Monday. While he doesn't pose a threat for now, the process is nevertheless expedited, and an officer dispatched to deliver the news to Lars in jail.

With our minds temporarily at ease, we put on a kickass show. We get back to Grace's place well past midnight, the kind of hour where the world feels quiet but heavy, like it's waiting for something to happen. She doesn't have to twist my arm to convince me to stay over. We step inside and flip on the light to find Sam sprawled across the couch like he owns the place.

The sight stops me dead in my tracks. The temperature in the room shoots up ten degrees. "Uh... does he do this often?" I whisper.

Grace shrugs, unfazed. "Once in a while. I usually don't mind, as long as he showers first."

I glance at the couch and hesitate. "I kinda thought I would sleep there."

"You can sleep in the bedroom with me."

I take a second to process her words. I'm as nervous as a prize turkey the week before Thanksgiving, and she senses it.

"Relax, Angus. No expectations. Sometimes, it's just nice to have a warm body to lie next to."

I nod, trying to seem cool about it, but my insides are doing somersaults. A warm body? That's me, I guess. She's been with Lars. How the hell am I supposed to follow *that* act? He's the guy with all the swagger, the confidence—so worldly. And I'm... not. Maybe it's better she finds out now rather than later, when I'm fumbling around naked under the sheets.

"Are you okay?" Her voice is softer now, her brow creased with concern.

"I've never, you know..." I rub the back of my neck, my face burning. "Slept with anyone before."

Grace smiles, reassuring and kind. "I'm getting that vibe. It's okay. Nothing like that has to happen tonight." She squeezes my hand gently. "Let's just get in bed and talk until we fall asleep."

I let out a breath I didn't realize I was holding. "Okay. I can do that."

While Grace is in the bathroom, I pace the bedroom like a lunatic in an effort to calm my racing thoughts. I inhale deeply, exhale slowly. Rinse and repeat. My anatomy isn't exactly cooperating, and the article in my back pocket—the one about her hospital stay—feels like it's burnt a hole through the fabric. It would be a good distraction, but this is definitely not the time.

The bathroom door creaks, and I quickly drop trou, dive into bed, and yank the covers up to my chest.

I don't know what to expect when she comes out of the bathroom. This may sound strange to some, but I hope she's not wearing anything too sexy. On the other hand, I wouldn't want to see her in something Gran would wear to bed.

She steps into the room wearing something simple—soft, fitted pajama pants and a tank top. My heart stops trying to escape my chest.

"I'll leave the light on for a bit." She climbs into bed. "We can talk."

We lie next to each other, close enough that I can feel the heat from her body. It's both comforting and terrifying. My pulse won't settle. *Isn't this what you've dreamed about, Angus? Relax. Enjoy it. You've got this.*

"So, Angus Walker, tell me about the future." Her voice is light but curious.

I hesitate. "That's not a good idea."

"Why?"

"Your father can probably explain it better than I can."

She pouts for a moment. "Okay. Then why are you here?"

I prop myself up on my pillow. "Here?"

She mirrors me, propping herself up. "In 1978."

Relief washes over me. For a second, I thought she was asking why I was in her bed.

"Oh." I glance at her, then down, gathering the nerve to say it out loud. I finally look back into her expectant eyes and find the courage.

"You're why."

Her brows knit together and a flicker of confusion crosses her face as she studies me, waiting for more.

"Not at first. That was an accident." I see her expression and backpedal. "But after I met you that night at Thunder Road, I… I had to get to know you, so I came back."

Her posture softens, and a smile plays on her lips. "Yeah, you were a breath of fresh air compared to most guys I meet. It didn't feel like you were just trying to get into my pants."

"I wasn't." My face heats up. "I assure you, that was the furthest thing from my mind."

"Really? The furthest?"

"Well… maybe not the furthest, I…"

She's clearly enjoying this. "Am I making you uncomfortable?"

"Maybe a little bit," I admit before I look away.

"Hey." She touches my cheek, guiding my gaze back to hers. "I felt the same thing."

My heart skips a beat, and I find my voice again. "So, you never answered my question that first night."

"Which one?"

"Soulmates. Do you believe that's a thing?"

She hesitates, her eyes distant, thoughtful. "I think it's possible. I mean, it's kind of crazy, but I believe there's someone out there who totally gets you. Who understands your music, your vibe… everything."

I nod, the weight of her words draws us closer. "That's how I feel. Like two people who are meant to be together from the start."

The unspoken words linger between us, but neither of us is ready to say them out loud.

"Maybe the universe is waiting for you to take a chance." Her smile is contagious.

I take her advice and close the distance between us. The moment our lips touch, the world tilts on its axis. Her lips are softer than I imagined, and my hands, awkward but eager, find their place on the back of her neck. Our lips part for a moment before I pull her into me for another round. It's overwhelming, electric, and I don't want it to end.

When we finally pull back, she smiles. "We should probably get some sleep."

"Yeah. Sleep," I echo, even though my mind is miles away from rest.

A silence stretches out between us.

"What about Lars?" I ask.

"He's out, and you're in."

"Are we talking about the band, or your relationship?"

Her playful smile comes with a wink. "Maybe both."

As the light clicks off and the room fades to darkness, her voice cuts through the quiet. "You're easy to be with, Angus. Lars was… a handful. Thank you for being here with me."

"Anytime," I whisper. After a pause, I add, "We still need to be careful. He's going to be hotter than a dumpster fire when he gets out of jail."

Chapter Thirty

Look Into the Future – Journey (1976)

The smell of coffee pulls me out of sleep before the light streaming through the blinds. I blink at the unfamiliar ceiling and roll over to see Grace seated cross-legged on the bed, sipping from a mug.

"Morning." Her voice is still husky from sleep.

"Morning," I mumble, rubbing my eyes. My brain reminds me where I am—her bedroom. Her bed. And that nothing scandalous happened here last night.

She grins like she can read my mind. "Coffee's in the kitchen. Better grab some before my dad drinks it all."

Sam. Right. I groan as I pull myself out of bed and steel myself for another encounter with Grace's father. "You got any aspirin?"

"Medicine cabinet. Bathroom."

When I make it to the kitchen, Sam's already at the table with a mug of coffee, flipping through the morning paper. His hoodie is gone, revealing a weathered face and a tousled mess of salt-and-pepper hair. His sharp eyes glance up at me when I enter.

"Morning." I grab a mug from the counter and pour myself some coffee.

He grunts, which I decide to interpret as progress.

"Rough night?"

"No rougher than usual," he replies from behind the paper.

Grace breezes in a moment later. "How does scrambled eggs and bacon sound?"

"Perfect."

"Are you boys getting along?"

I wait for Sam's answer, but there's only silence.

"That good, huh?"

I clear my throat. "I'm willing to try."

She pauses. "Dad?"

He lowers the paper. "If it wasn't for the fact he doesn't belong here, he might be okay."

"Look who's talking."

Sam sets the paper down, fixing me with a look. "I'll give you that." He turns to Grace. "He's an improvement over that big scary dude you've been sleeping with. But that's not saying much."

"Dad, leave him alone. He's not Lars, and I'd like to enjoy my breakfast without a lecture."

Sam shrugs. "Just sayin'. You've got a habit of picking musicians with more ego than sense. Maybe this one's different."

"I'll take that as a compliment." I meet his gaze and try not to flinch.

"Good news, Dad. You don't have to worry about Lars anymore. He's history. In fact, he's in jail right now."

"Had a run-in with your porch light?"

"That's part of it."

"That TRO is only good for two weeks," I say. "You'll have to attend a second hearing to get a permanent one."

Grace sets a pan on the stove and turns to me. "Will you come with me?"

"Sure. If I'm here," I reply, unaware I've opened a can of worms.

Grace's eyes narrow, and she tilts her head. "What do you mean? You're going back?"

"Of course I'm going back." She had to have assumed that, right? "I only left for a day, all my stuff's there."

"So, one minute we're soulmates, and the next you're leaving? Good thing nothing happened last night. Otherwise, I'd think you were just like all the rest."

I hold up my hands. "Wait a minute. I never said I wasn't coming back."

"You never said you were."

Sam watches us volley like he's sitting center court at a tennis match. I want to tell her I love her and never want us to be apart, but it's too soon, and we have a potentially hostile audience.

"Let's all take a breath."

I sit across from Sam and nurse my coffee, while Grace busies herself at the stove.

Sam snorts. "Maybe we should all go back. Where'd you say you were from?"

"Northeast Utah, 2024."

"Maybe we've been here long enough, caused enough trouble."

"No, Dad. I can't leave. I have the band to think about."

He looks at me. "Do they have live music in Utah?"

"Yes, sir, they do." I figure it can't hurt to be polite. I might need his blessing someday.

"Stop it, Dad. That's not the point." Grace blows out a frustrated breath. "I have a career. I like it here."

"Well, I don't." Sam leans back in his chair with a groan. "Look at me. This hasn't exactly worked out well for your old man."

Grace's eyes narrow and her jaw tightens. "And whose fault is that? If you weren't so *obsessed* with that portal—" She stops herself, the words hanging heavy in the air.

Sam takes a long sip of his coffee. "Somebody has to keep an eye on it."

"You told me you used a different one," I cut in as he sets his mug down. "Do you watch that one too?"

"Don't have to." He shrugs. "It's gone."

I shift in my seat. "What do you mean, gone?"

"I mean gone." He waves his hand like he's brushing away a fly. "Poof. Kaput. One day it was here, the next it wasn't. That was six months ago. Haven't seen it since."

A cold knot tightens in my stomach. Could that happen to my portal? If it disappears, I could be stranded here—or worse, stuck back home, unable to return to Grace.

"You're sure it's gone?"

Sam smirks. "I may look like someone who's a few bricks short of a load, but up here?" He taps his temple with a finger. "Sharp as a tack."

I glance at Grace. Her worried eyes meet mine. She understands the risk.

"Sam," I say, trying to keep my voice steady, "do you know a man named John Walker?"

He tilts his head. "Should I?"

"He came through the same portal I did around 1964."

"Walker." He repeats the name like he's tasting it. "You related?"

I nod. "He was my grandfather." My hand shakes as I pick up my cup, and I set it down quickly.

Sam notices, and our eyes meet for a moment before I look away.

"Was?" Grace asks, reaching for the coffee pot. She warms her father's mug, then lifts it, silently offering me some. I shake my head.

"He left in 2010," I explain, my voice tight. "We never heard from him again."

Sam takes another sip, his gaze distant. "Doesn't ring a bell. Never met him."

"But you've been watching the portal, right?"

Sam sets his mug down, a wry smile tugging at the corner of his mouth. "I didn't become"—he throws Grace a sideways look—"obsessed…"

She rolls her eyes.

"… until about 1970. Could've missed him if he came through before that."

My heart sinks. "Okay. I hoped I might find him while I'm here."

Sam softens, a rare flicker of sympathy in his eyes. "I could ask around."

"Thanks." I stare at my coffee, spinning the cup slowly in my hands. "What happened in 1970?"

He pauses to fold the newspaper in front of him, like he needs the time to gather his thoughts. "Didn't know about your portal until I stumbled on it in 1970. I was in that basement"—he gives Grace another sideways glance—"partying with some friends when I stepped into the other room to relieve myself. Next thing I know, I'm standing in a cave."

"My cave? The one on my ranch?"

Sam shrugs. "Didn't have a clue I was in Utah until you told me." He fiddles with the edge of the folded newspaper. "Took three hours to pile rocks at the mouth of the cave to hide it. Left just enough room to crawl back inside and return here. After that, I kept an eye on that basement."

I take a deep breath to center myself. "I know you think I'm the enemy, but I'm not." I sit up straight and let the conviction in my voice take over. "I'm not here to cause trouble. I'm here to prevent it."

That gets their attention. Grace turns off the stove and joins us at the table, her expression wary but curious. "What do you mean?"

I pull the printout from my pocket and slide it across the table to Grace. She stares at it, her hand trembling as she picks it up.

Her eyes widen in shock and her free hand flies to her mouth as she reads. "This is dated a week from now. Where did you get this?"

"I Googled your band the last time I went home."

"Googled?"

I squeeze my eyes shut. "Right. Sorry. It's a way to search for news articles online."

She shakes her head, confused. "I don't even know what that means."

"I do," Sam whispers.

"Maybe I'll show you someday." I offer a small, hopeful smile. Grace doesn't return it. "The point is, that was your future when I printed this. You didn't have a restraining order yet. I'm hoping what we did yesterday will change it."

Grace stares at me as something clicks behind her eyes. "That's why you suggested the TRO. Why you pushed so hard to get it done right away."

"Exactly." Relief washes over me.

Sam nods, his tone thoughtful. "That's a significant event. No doubt you changed something."

I exhale, my voice quieter now. "I won't know for sure until I go back home and Google it again."

The three of us sit in silence, the weight of the conversation pressing down on the room. Somewhere outside, a bird chirps, oblivious to our timeline manipulations.

Chapter Thirty-One

I Wanna Be Sedated – The Ramones (1978)

I kiss Grace goodbye, and she holds on a little longer than I expect. I'm not complaining.

"When will you be back?"

"I'll shoot for Thursday, but it might be Friday morning."

"We have a gig Friday night."

"I'll be there."

"Be careful," Sam says.

I think he's coming around.

Knowing the other portal recently ceased to exist, I can't be sure this portal will stay open much longer, let alone still be there. Could there be an expiration date on this one as well?

My palms are slick as I make my way down the basement stairs, each step measured, each breath shallow. What if it's gone? I need to get back to 2024 to see if we've shifted history, but if this portal has disappeared like the other one… I shake off the thought and push forward. Hesitation won't change anything. Either it's here, or it's not. And if it's not? Well, I'll deal with that if and when I need to.

The portal is still here, and I blow out a long breath. I swear it flickers a time or two, so I hurry through before it vanishes. Now that I have a place to stay, spending a week in

1978 looks a lot more appealing. But not this time. I need to Google Grace to see if the restraining order saved her from the hospital. I can't rest until I know she's safe. Ironically, returning home to check means I won't be there to protect her until next week.

The ATV is not where I left it. Big red flag. I walk to the house, nervous about what might have changed. The door is unlocked. It creaks as I push it open, and a strange smell hits me—not the faint trace of weed and stale pizza I expect, but baked goods—fresh bread, maybe. The floorboards groan beneath my weight as I step inside.

I draw in a sharp breath. My stuff—my life—is gone. In its place is an alien landscape: a floral rug sprawled across the floor where my threadbare carpet used to be, an upholstered couch instead of my old recliner. I barely recognize my own home.

Footsteps on the stairs make me turn. A woman I don't recognize freezes halfway down. Her wide eyes meet mine as she clutches the banister. And then she screams.

I raise my hands, palms out. "I'm not going to hurt you."

"You need to leave. Now."

"Okay." I hold my position, hands still in the air like I'm some kind of criminal. "My name is Angus Walker. I used to live here."

Her grip on the banister relaxes, but not much. "What are you doing here?"

"What are *you* doing here?" I counter, my voice sharper than I intended.

"This is my house."

A chill runs through me. "Since when?"

"About six months ago." Her voice softens, like she's explaining to a lost child. "We—my husband Jason and I—we bought it from the bank."

The bank? Six months? My brain stumbles, unable to connect dots that don't line up. "Foreclosure?"

She nods. "The couple who used to own it passed. They had a son who owned it for a while after that. I don't remember his name."

I do. I swallow hard, the words thick in my throat. "His name is Angus. I'm the son."

"Oh." She hesitates as her brow furrows. "I still don't know what you want."

"I'm not sure I do, either." My legs feel unsteady, so I pull out one of the kitchen chairs and sink into it. The chair is too clean, too solid. It doesn't belong in this house.

She descends the rest of the stairs, her eyes still wary. "Are you okay?"

No. I'm not okay. My chest feels like it's caving in. Everything that mattered—gone, sold to strangers. "I'll live."

I press my fingers into my temples to knead away the dull throb that drills its way behind my eyes. It's the third headache this week, and I'm running out of excuses to convince myself it's nothing. They started after I went through the portal for the first time. I don't want to believe they're connected.

"Can I get you a glass of water or something?" she offers, her tone cautious but kind.

I shake my head and force myself to stand. "I don't want to trouble you." My legs feel heavy as I shuffle toward the door. "I'll be on my way."

The cold metal of the doorknob is under my hand when I stop. "I did some camping up in the mountains before I came down here." My voice is strained. "I left some equipment in one of the caves on the property. If you'd be so kind as to let me back to retrieve it someday, I'd appreciate that."

Her expression softens and her suspicion ebbs. "Of course. Anytime. We don't go up there much."

Her kind eyes meet mine, and something twists in my chest. I nod stiffly and step out into the sunlight. The door closes behind me with a soft click that feels like the end of life as I knew it.

I drop onto the warm wood of the porch steps and pull out my phone. My hands shake as I unlock the screen. I feel her eyes watch me through the glass and sense her hesitation, her lingering doubt.

My fingers tremble as I dial Waldo's number. The phone rings twice before he picks up.

"Hold on," I say into the receiver as the door creaks open. She steps out, her arms crossed against the breeze.

"I'm calling for a ride," I explain, holding her gaze for a moment. She seems to consider something, then nods and steps back inside.

I bring the phone back to my ear. "Sorry about that. It's Angus."

"Hey, Angus." Waldo's voice on the other end is a lifeline, tethering me to something solid. My stomach unwinds a little as I exhale. He remembers me, but nothing feels right, and I need answers—fast.

"When was the last time you saw me?" My voice wavers slightly, betraying the storm of confusion that swirls inside.

"It's been a few days. I was getting worried."

"I need a ride. Can you come get me at the ranch?"

There's a pause, long enough that I pull the phone away to check if the call's still connected. "Waldo?"

"What are you doing at the ranch?" His voice is cautious now, as if he's trying to piece together a mystery.

I close my eyes. "Can you come and get me? Please?"

Another pause, shorter this time. "Sure, I'll be there in ten."

"Thanks, buddy."

I lower the phone and stare out at the driveway, where weeds poke through the cracks in the pavement. Waldo remembers me, but everything else feels precarious, as if the ground beneath my feet could shift again at any moment. It sounds like he's aware of the ranch sale. I hope he knows where I live now and whatever else I might need to know about Angus Walker.

The breeze picks up, rustling the wind chimes that hang from the porch. I glance back at the door, where the faint shadow of the woman flickers behind the curtain. I can't shake the feeling I don't belong anywhere anymore.

Chapter Thirty-Two

Smoke on the Water – Deep Purple (1972)

I ease into Waldo's passenger seat, the familiar creak of the old upholstery grounding me for a moment. "Thanks."

He gives me a once-over, his brows knitting together. "You're a sight for sore eyes."

"Why do you say that?"

"You disappeared for almost a week without saying anything." He glances at me sideways, the concern in his voice barely masked. "Where did you go?"

The question hits me harder than I expect. Does he not know about the portal? We've always shared everything—at least in the timeline I remember. My head aches thinking about it.

"It's a long story."

He snorts. "They always are with you. Can you at least tell me where I'm supposed to drop you off?"

"Just take me home."

Waldo nods and turns the car toward town. I settle back into the seat, trying to piece together what I'll say when we get wherever we're going.

He pulls into Rusty's Auto Parts and swings around to the back.

"What are we doing here?"

He parks and throws me a puzzled look. "You said you wanted to go home."

My stomach drops. I follow his gaze to the steep wooden stairway leading to a second-floor apartment above the store. The building looks as tired as I feel, the whole structure sagging under its own weight.

"I live up there?"

"Last I checked." His tone carries a hint of amusement. "You work downstairs. You love the convenience, remember?"

And the hits just keep on coming. I don't respond. What could I possibly say?

Waldo leans closer and studies me like he's trying to decipher a puzzle. "Are you high?"

"Can you come in with me for a few minutes?"

He shrugs and climbs out of the car. I follow him up the stairs, the wood groaning under our weight. At the top, I hesitate then reach into my pocket. Panic flares—I don't have a key.

"There's a key under the mat." Waldo's amusement is replaced with concern.

"Oh. Right."

My hand trembles as I slide it into the lock. I brace myself for whatever version of my life exists on the other side.

The first thing I notice is the smell—familiar but different. The furniture is the same tired assortment. My guitar stands in the corner next to my amp, a reassuring beacon in the chaos of mismatched timelines.

I step inside and take a slow breath. It's not the ranch, but it's something.

Waldo brushes past me, grabbing two beers from the fridge like he owns the place. "You gonna tell me what's going on now?"

"Sure." I twist the top off with a satisfying hiss as I drop into the nearest chair. "But you're not going to believe me." The beer bottle dangles from my fingers. I'm not sure which one of us will need it more.

Waldo settles onto the couch and kicks his feet up on the coffee table. "Try me." He cracks open his beer and waits, eyeing me expectantly. "All right, spill it. Where the hell have you been?"

I stare at the bottle in my hands, twisting it while I sort through the tangled mess in my head. How do I even start? I set it on the coffee table and rub the back of my neck.

"There's… someone…"

Waldo blinks at me. "Someone?" A grin tugs at his lips as he leans forward. "Like a girl someone? Since when do you have a girlfriend?"

I hesitate. "I don't know anymore. My sense of time is…" My voice trails off. "Her name is Grace."

Waldo narrows his eyes, clearly skeptical. "And this Grace just appeared out of nowhere? What's her deal?"

"She's in a band." A small smile creeps in despite myself. "She's amazing, Waldo. Plays bass and sings like she was born to do it."

"Is she from around here? Where did you meet her?"

"She's not exactly from around here. I met her in—" I stop myself. "It's complicated."

"When isn't it complicated with you?" He gives me a pointed look. "Keep going."

I take another swig of beer and try to explain. "It all started when Jackson showed up out of the blue. He claimed he could make me rich if I helped him find some lost Aztec gold he says is buried on the ranch."

Waldo straightens. "Jackass Carr? I thought you hated him."

"I do… or I did."

"Wait. When did this happen, and how come I don't know about it?"

"Let me finish, and hopefully it'll become clear."

I take another drink before I continue. "He didn't find anything, but I did. A portal."

"A portal," Waldo repeats, amid nervous laughter. "Like, to another dimension?"

"Close. Another time."

His laughter dies in his throat when he sees my face. "You're serious."

I nod. "It took me to 1978. That's where I met Grace. She's…" I pause, searching for the words. "She's everything, Waldo. And she's why I left."

Waldo sits back and shakes his head, somewhere between exasperation and disbelief. "So, let me get this straight. You traveled through time, met the girl of your dreams, and now you're here. I'm flattered, but why would you come back?"

"Because I have to do something here that I can't do in 1978. Grace is in trouble. Her ex-boyfriend, Lars, who used to play guitar in her band, is going to put her in the hospital."

"Is? How do you know that?"

"I got curious and Googled her. I found an article that says Lars beats her up. I went back again to stop him."

"You've been going back and forth? How does that work?"

"Not as well as I'd like. The portal is only open for a couple of days each time the moon enters a new phase. You figured that out and told me I have a three-day window about once every week."

Waldo takes a measured sip of his beer as a profound confusion clouds his face. "I don't remember any of this." His gaze never leaves mine. "Where are we now?"

"I'm back in the present—just not the one I left."

He exhales sharply. "You changed something in the past. So, for you, this is a new timeline, while I've always been here, unaware of anything you did in any alternate time-line."

"That seems to be what's happening. Anyway, I convinced Grace to get a restraining order. I'm here to see if it worked. Fingers crossed, because I'm stuck here for a week."

"I feel like I'm in a sci-fi movie."

"Thankfully, you're still my friend. I couldn't have done this alone."

Waldo stares at me, his beer halfway to his mouth. "Okay. What's our next move?"

I open Google on my phone and type her name into the search bar. The letters feel electric under my fingers.

Scrolling, I can't find anything about an altercation be-tween Grace and Lars. I exhale. "Looks like it worked."

"Guess you made a difference after all."

I scroll further down. "Wait. What's this?"

Chapter Thirty-Three

Carry On Wayward Son – Kansas (1976)

Waldo watches me as I skim the article. "What? What is it?"

"There's a songwriting contest," I say, tapping the screen.

He squints at me. "Okay… and what does that have to do with you? Far as I know, you haven't written any songs."

"Not in this timeline."

His feet drop off the coffee table as he leans forward. "Wait—are you saying I knew about this in another version of reality?"

I nod as the weight of everything that's changed settles in. "Yeah. You knew."

His eyes go wide, and he motions for me to keep talking. "What's it called? Have I heard it? Did I like it?"

"I played it for you." My face betrays me with a proud little smirk. "You liked it. It's called 'Waiting for a Girl Like You.'"

Waldo nods. "Fitting."

I scan further. "Says here Lou Gramm is one of the judges. Winner gets their song on the next Foreigner album."

He tilts his head. "You've got all their albums. Is there a song like that on any of them?"

I flash him a grin. "Not yet."

His eyebrows shoot up. "You're going back? You're actually entering this thing?"

"Absolutely." My voice softens. "Why wouldn't I?"

He shrugs. "I don't know… maybe because you could get stuck in the past and never see me again?"

I laugh. "I'll take that risk. I found my soulmate, Waldo. I can't just walk away from that."

"So… you're planning to stay?"

I glance out the window, then back at him. "Would that really be so bad?"

Waldo shakes his head in disbelief. "What else did you find?"

I scroll through a few smaller articles. "Nothing bad. Just a couple of references to the band's new guitarist." I flash a modest grin and turn the phone toward him. It shows a photo of the band with me holding Grace's black guitar.

"No way." His mouth falls open. "Do they say he's any good?"

"They don't say he isn't."

Waldo and I spend the next hour swapping memories of lives that feel like they belong to strangers. He tells me about an Angus I barely recognize, and I return the favor with stories of a Waldo that might as well be someone else. The entire exchange leaves me disoriented, like we're reminiscing over pieces of a puzzle we'll never finish.

I take stock of my new home after he leaves. It's smaller than the ranch—a generic apartment with a faint smell of leftover takeout. All my stuff seems to be here, though. I run a hand along the back of my couch, my fingers catching on a rip I don't remember. What happened to the ranch? I was getting by. Wasn't I? My gut twists as I realize I need to find a bank statement or something to figure out where I stand financially, though it's hard to care too much. What's the point when the next trip could rewrite everything again?

My head still hurts. I pop a couple aspirin and wash them down with a swig of stale coffee. Falling apart isn't an option—not with Grace out there, waiting for me.

In the kitchen, I open a cupboard and find it crammed with the same junk food I threw away weeks ago. I slam the door shut. I'm not holding out much hope that I still have a gym membership.

Another loose end—my job. If I've been AWOL like Waldo says, Rusty will surely fire me as soon as I step foot in his store. Not that I care much. It's a crappy job. As far as the apartment, I'm sure he'll find some reason to throw me out at the end of the month.

Rusty doesn't disappoint. He fires me before I can finish saying hello, muttering about reliability and respect and some other word I don't bother to process. I take it on the chin and head back to the apartment as his grumbling fades behind me.

I tell myself not to get too attached to anything. Everything's different each time I come back, and "home" is just another word I don't trust anymore.

That's when I see it.

In the corner of the lot sits a 1970 GTO. It's rough—primer gray with a few patches of Bondo—but it's solid. No rust, sitting on fresh white-letter tires. My heart skips a beat. Could it be mine?

I scan the lot for Mom's old car, but it's not here. I jog upstairs and find a set of vintage GM keys on a hook by the door. My pulse quickens as I grab them and sprint back down.

The key fits. The lock turns with a satisfying click.

I open the door and grin like a kid on Christmas morning. Unlike its stripped-down counterpart in the barn, this one has seats—actual seats.

I run my fingers over the worn steering wheel, then slide the key into the ignition. A quick twist, and for a split second, everything holds its breath. Then it happens—a deep, feral roar erupts from under the hood, and I feel the vibration through the steering wheel and seat. My grin stretches wider as the sound fills the air.

When I throw it into first gear, the car lurches forward, prowling across the lot like a lion sizing up its prey. The engine purrs, and I can't wait to let it loose.

I reach the street, pop the clutch, and stomp on the gas. The tires squeal, and the GTO surges forward like it's been waiting for this moment. Wind tears past the open window, and the engine's rumble turns into a wild roar as I push it harder. The kid-at-Christmas feeling is back in full force, and I feel alive.

By the time I reach the gym, I'm practically buzzing. I'm ready to kick some ass—metaphorically speaking, of course.

Chapter Thirty-Four

Your Song – Elton John (1970)

Friday morning, I'm eager to get back to Grace. I pause in front of the bathroom mirror, pleased with what I see. Another week at the gym has made my face look leaner and the soft edges that used to round my jaw sharper, more defined. Stepping on the scale reveals I've lost twelve pounds.

I pull up my shirt and run a hand over my stomach, where the faint outline of muscle is beginning to show, and a wave of pride surges through me. It's not just the weight—it's the proof that I can take control of at least one aspect of my life when everything else feels like chaos. For the first time in a long time, I feel… capable… and, dare I say, confident.

I drive the GTO out to the ranch and park it at the side of the road. I'm uncomfortable leaving it there, but I'll only be gone for a day or two. And it won't matter, anyway, if I never return to this timeline.

By ten o'clock, I'm climbing the stairs to Grace's apartment with my song notes tucked in my back pocket. Only a week ago, I stood here with my heart pounding and the weight of rejection on my shoulders as Grace slammed the door in my face. Today, the memory feels distant, like a bad dream.

The door opens before I knock, and Grace's face lights up with a contagious, megawatt smile that makes everything else fade. "Angus!" She throws her arms around my neck.

For a moment, I freeze, caught off guard by the warmth of her embrace. Then I let myself melt into it. "I missed you, too."

She clings to me as I step inside, her arms strong but comfortable, like I belong here. My eyes scan the room, relieved to find no sign of Sam or any other unwelcome surprise.

Once we settle in, I broach the topic carefully. "So, uh, have you heard anything about a songwriting contest?"

Her shoulders slump a little. "Yeah, I've heard of it. But nothing I've written is good enough to enter."

I let the silence stretch long enough for her to remember the song I'd told her about.

"You wrote a song, right?" She tilts her head, with that curious spark in her green eyes. "When are you gonna let me hear it?"

"It's not finished." I pull the crumpled pages from my pocket. "But I'll play it for you if you like. Maybe you can help me figure out the arrangement."

Her eyes light up. "Really? I'd love to." She grabs her guitar from the corner and hands it to me. "Go ahead. Play it."

I sit down, adjust the strap, and let my fingers warm up with a few familiar chords. "Okay." I take a deep breath. "But it's still rough."

The first notes fill the room, tentative at first, then growing stronger. I keep my eyes on the fretboard as I sing, but I can feel Grace's gaze on me. When I glance up, she's swaying, her eyes closed like she's letting the music seep into her. She doesn't move right away when I finish.

I clear my throat, suddenly unsure. "Well?"

Her eyes open, and her expression floors me. It's not just approval—it's something deeper. "Angus... I don't know what to say."

"Say you like it."

A smile spreads across her face. "I *love* it."

Relief washes over me, and I manage a tentative smile. "Good. I was hoping you'd say that." I feel the weight of the moment. "I, uh, wrote it for you."

Her mouth falls open, and she stares at me like she's trying to solve a puzzle. "For me? But... we've only known each other for three weeks."

I shrug as my heart pounds in my chest.

"When did you write it?"

"A couple of days after we met at Thunder Road."

She looks stunned. "You're kidding." She stands and paces. "And this is the only song you've ever written?"

I smile and nod. "Guess I needed the right inspiration."

She stops pacing and grabs her bass. "Let's try it out."

"It needs a keyboard."

"We'll do a guitar-only version. First chord is A-minor, right?"

I nod. "Chorus begins on D-minor."

We dive into the song, and the music comes together in a way that feels effortless, like it was meant to be. Her suggestions tighten the arrangement, and by the time we've played through it twice, the song feels alive.

"It's got potential, Walker. And your voice isn't half bad, either."

"Let's try it out at tonight's gig. We can do the stripped-down version."

She shakes her head. "Contest rules state the song can't have been performed in public prior to the judging."

I fiddle with the dials on the guitar. "Okay. I can live with that. Any more rules I should know about?"

"It's two weeks from today." Grace's voice buzzes with excitement. "During the Foreigner concert at McNichols Sports Arena. The top three songs get performed live, and the crowd votes for the winner. If we win, they'll record our song on their next album. Oh, and there's a five-hundred-dollar cash prize!"

I blink at her, stunned. "Wait… we have to perform our song? In front of all those people?"

"Of course! It's going to be amazing."

Amazing for her, maybe. My stomach's already doing backflips. "I've never played in front of a crowd that big before."

"Neither have I," she admits. Her grin doesn't falter. "But that's the dream, right? If we're going to be rock stars, we'd better get used to it."

I nod slowly as the reality of it sinks in. Standing on a stage like that? With thousands of people watching?

Grace tilts her head as she studies me. "What's wrong?"

"Nothing. Just… processing."

"Well, process faster, because there's one more thing." Her tone takes on a sharper edge, though her excitement still bubbles underneath. "We have to submit our entry by midnight tomorrow."

"Tomorrow? As in… twenty-four hours from now?"

"Yep." She gathers my notes and the scattered scraps of paper we've written on.

I reach out to grab one of the papers, my pulse racing. "This isn't finished, Grace. It's barely legible. We can't submit this. We don't even have proper sheet music." I can hear the finished version of our song in my head, but it doesn't exist yet—not in this time.

"So, let's fix that. They sell blank sheet music downstairs. Let's go."

Ten minutes later, we're back at her place, hunched over the table with fresh sheet music and sharpened pencils. The pressure's on, but Grace's determination is unshakable. Her energy is contagious, and despite my nerves, I find myself caught up in the momentum.

As the song takes shape on paper, Grace pauses, tapping her pencil against the table. "How should we list the song-writing credit?"

"Both of us." I say it without hesitation. "It's our song."

She glances at me, her expression softening. "Our song." She smiles and nods.

When we finally finish, Grace leans back with a satisfied grin. "Well, Mr. Walker, we've got ourselves a song."

I stretch, crack my knuckles, and manage a confident smile. "We do... and it's a good one."

Her eyes shine as she laughs. "Damn right it is."

"Here's another good one." I play another song as she sits and watches, her face full of approval.

"I love it," she says when I finish. "Did you write that one, too?"

"I wish. That was 'Summer of '69' by Bryan Adams."

"I've never heard it before."

"I'd be surprised if you had. It was on his fourth album, *Reckless*, released in 1984."

"You're lucky. You've got forty more years of music history than me."

***

Thunder Road's sticky floors and dim lighting do not dull the electric energy of the crowd. Grace and I are in sync, every chord and lyric lands perfectly. For a moment, I let myself forget about timelines, contests, and Lars.

But then he walks in.

He leans against the bar, his eyes locked on me like a predator sizing up his prey. He raises two fingers to his eyes, then points them at me. It's the second time he's shown me that gesture, and it sends a chill down my spine. He has it in for me because he thinks I stole his girl. The truth is, if he treated her better, I wouldn't be here and he wouldn't be having this problem.

During the break, I pull the pirate bartender—whose name is Randy—aside. "He's got a restraining order. He shouldn't even be here."

Randy sighs, his expression unreadable. "Cops will kill the vibe. Let me handle it." He replaces Sasquatch at the door to keep an eye on Lars, and we finish our set without incident.

After the show, while our drummer, Jake, and I load our equipment into the van, a familiar voice calls and my stomach bottoms out.

"Hey, shithead."

That's not a name I respond to anymore, but the voice belongs to Lars, and it's dripping with malice.

Jake looks at me, alarmed. "Uh, I'll go get the bouncer," he whispers then darts back inside.

Lars stumbles closer, his eyes bloodshot and wild. "You think you're tough? Think you can just take what's mine?"

My heart pounds as I step back. "Go home, Lars. You're drunk."

I can probably avoid him for a couple of minutes, but even in his drunken state, he'll eventually get his hands on me, and I'm sure I won't like what happens after that.

Sasquatch bursts through the back door and stands between us. "Come on, Lars. Let's not do this. Go sleep it off."

He stumbles then mutters something about ripping my head off and stuffing it down my neck hole. The other bouncer and a few of the patrons join us outside. Lars glances their way and hesitates.

"You're in violation of a restraining order," Sasquatch says. "We don't have to call the cops if you leave now."

After a long, tense pause, he glances at the gathering crowd, then points a finger at me. "This isn't over."

You can almost hear the collective sigh of relief when he turns and walks away.

Sasquatch disperses the crowd, then looks at me. "Sorry about that." He shakes his head. "Lars can be a real dick. It's a shame. He's a damn good musician, and he's got a new band now. He should lick his wounds and move on."

Grace joins me. "A new band?"

He nods. "Yeah, Steel Mirage. They're playing here next week."

The ride back to Grace's apartment is quiet. She maintains her silence when we climb into bed, but she moves closer. I close my eyes, but I can't ignore the gnawing fear in my chest.

This isn't over. Lars's words echo in my head, a dark promise I can't ignore. For Grace's sake, I need to stop him—before it's too late.

Chapter Thirty-Five

More Than a Feeling – Boston (1976)

Morning sunlight filters through the curtains and casts a warm glow over the kitchen. I tell Grace I need to go home to take care of something. She's disappointed and tries to persuade me to stay. She pours two cups of coffee, the rich aroma filling the air, and hands one to me.

"I'll make it worth your while." Her voice is low and teasing, laced with a playful edge that makes my pulse quicken.

I almost drop the cup. She's not subtle, and I'm pretty sure I know what she's hinting at. My heart skips a beat as anticipation collides with a familiar wave of insecurity. She's a rock star. She's used to men who can deliver swagger and seduction on command. What if I don't measure up? What if I ruin this perfect, once-in-a-lifetime connection?

I clear my throat. "As awesome as that sounds—"

"Really?" Her eyebrow arches, her tone a mix of surprise and irritation.

I offer a nervous shrug and try to muster some charm. "Rain check?"

Her shoulders slump, and the flicker of disappointment in her eyes stings. "I thought you—"

"I do. I really do," I cut in, my voice earnest. "But I'm worried about Lars. You saw him last night. He's not taking this well, and it doesn't seem like he'll let it go until I'm…" My voice trails off, and I glance away, unable to finish the sentence.

She sets her coffee down with a sigh and crosses her arms. "How will running back to 2024 help with Lars?"

I try to make light of it. "I have a crystal ball back home." Her confused look tells me the joke didn't land. "I need to Google us. If something bad is about to happen, I can find out before it's too late. That's how I knew to get the restraining order, and that's why you're not in the hospital right now."

Her expression softens and the tension between us eases. She nods, taking a sip of her coffee as she considers my words.

"I'll be back on Friday for the next gig," I promise.

"We're off next week."

"Even better." I grin and lean forward. "I'll take you out to dinner."

Her face lights up, and the sparkle in her eyes is enough to banish any lingering doubts. "Now you're talking."

I raise an eyebrow as a sly smile creeps across my face. "That rain check will still be valid by then, right?"

Before I can react, she throws her arms around my neck. Her momentum nearly knocks me off balance. The hug is warm, fierce, and unguarded, and it ends with a kiss that makes my thoughts scatter like leaves in the wind.

"Absolutely," she murmurs against my lips.

I hold her close for a moment longer, breathing in her scent and wishing she had an Internet connection so I didn't have to leave. Here, there's no signal, no Google, no way to foresee the future. I could take her with me and never look back, leaving this mess behind for good, but that's asking a lot of her.

"What would you be willing to sacrifice for love?" I ask, my voice softer than I intend. It's not just any question—it's the one that's gnawed at me since I met her, since I stumbled into this whole impossible situation.

She hesitates, her head tilted as if weighing her words. "I don't know."

"Really?" I press, searching her face for an answer.

"Why? What would you give up?"

"Everything."

It hangs between us like an unspoken dare. She pauses to consider my answer like it's a challenge she didn't expect.

"Move in with me." Her words hit me like a chord I wasn't ready for—unexpected, resonant, perfect.

It's not like I haven't thought about it a hundred times since we met, but hearing her say it makes it real. Can I give up my life in 2024 to stay in the past with Grace? The answer leaps into my mind: yes, absolutely, a thousand times yes.

But the paradoxical questions creep in. What happens when the years roll by? I'll be forty-six years old when 2002 comes around, and Angus Walker is born on a ranch in Utah. Will there be two of us? What if we meet? What if I go to his school and kick the crap out of the jerks who call him names and give him wedgies? The thought makes me grin—until I realize how tangled the timeline could become.

"Angus?" Grace's voice pulls me back.

"I'd need to be sure that's what you want."

"I wouldn't have suggested it if I wasn't sure." Her eyes don't waver as they lock on mine. "I want this. I want you."

I reach for her hand and run my thumb over her knuckles. "What if we take it slow? When I come back, I'll bring some of my things and stay for a while. See how it feels."

Her lips curve into a smile, relief softening her features. "That sounds like a plan."

We linger over breakfast, talking about everything and nothing, but eventually, reality sets in. Grace heads to the local radio station, KAZY, to register our contest entry while I make my way back to the portal.

The journey feels heavier this time, like each step pulls me away from something I don't want to leave behind.

I'm relieved when I step out of the cave in 2024 and see the ATV exactly as I left it a week ago. It wasn't there the last time, and I found my home occupied by strangers. The ranch looks quiet as I approach. Familiar. Still mine. I peek inside the barn for further confirmation. The tarp still hides the same rusty GTO, a stubborn reminder that I don't have a stellar track record of fixing things.

The door creaks as I step inside. I call out Ozzy's name, hoping for the impossible. But the house is silent. No bark. No warm, wagging tail to greet me.

The place looks just as I left it—the couch, the guitar propped in the corner, the photo of my parents on the mantle. I drop onto the couch, kick off my shoes, and stretch out. My head falls back, and I stare at the ceiling, running through every conversation with Grace, every warning from Sam.

His voice echoes in my mind. *By simply being here, you can disrupt the timeline.* Waldo's explanation of chaos theory follows close behind. The butterfly effect, he called it. Small changes, big consequences.

It seemed so abstract at the time. A butterfly flaps its wings in Brazil, and a week later, a tornado tears through Texas. But now, I'm living it. Every step I take in 1978 ripples through time. A minor decision might cause a completely different history to unfold.

And yet, I didn't ask for this. I didn't ask to find that portal, to step into the past, to meet Grace. Was it all just an accident? Or something more? Something meant to happen?

Speaking of Grace...

I sit up and pull my phone from my pocket. My fingers hover over the keyboard for a moment, nerves tightening my chest. What will I find this time?

Chapter Thirty-Six

Hold the Line – Toto (1978)

The search results fill the screen. Most are dead ends—random Graces who aren't my Grace. But one headline grabs me. It's an archived article from a local Colorado paper, dated 1978. My breath hitches as I click.

Rising Rock Stars Take Top Honors at KAZY Songwriting Contest.

There's a photo.

Grace is center stage, bass slung over her shoulder, her smile lighting up the frame. She's holding a trophy—and next to her, arm draped casually around her, is… me.

I'm standing there, grinning like I belong. Like I've always belonged. The caption reads: *Grace Monroe and Angus Walker celebrate their victory at the KAZY songwriting contest. Their original track will appear on Foreigner's upcoming album.*

I drop my phone and dive toward my record shelf. Flipping past rows of alphabetized sleeves, I stop at the Fs. *Foreigner 4.* Released in 1981, it would have been their next album. Hands shaking, I pull it out and scan the back. Track four. There it is. Our song.

Written by Angus Walker and Grace Monroe.

A surge of pride swells in my chest for both of us. We did it. I feel like I'm helping Grace fulfill her dream, and I couldn't be happier.

I slip the vinyl from its sleeve, gently place it on the turntable, and drop the needle. The speakers crackle to life with a synthesizer melody—different from our original piano version, but unmistakably our song. It works. I sink into the couch, letting the music wash over me, a goofy grin plastered on my face.

When it ends, I reach for my phone, still buzzing with excitement.

Then I see it. My celebration is short-lived. Beneath the article, there's a suggestion for a related piece:

Tragedy Strikes at Local Music Contest: One Dead, Suspect in Custody.

My stomach drops. I hesitate. My thumb hovers over the link before I tap it. The page loads slowly, and I swallow hard as the article comes into focus.

Angus Walker, 22, was fatally shot last night outside McNichols Arena in Denver. Witnesses say the gunman, Lars Steele, a rival musician, confronted Walker after the contest results were announced. The confrontation escalated, leading to a violent altercation. Police apprehended Steele at the scene. Walker, a promising talent and recent addition to the Colorado music scene, was pronounced dead upon arrival at Denver General Hospital. Authorities are investigating the motive behind the attack.

The words blur as my mind struggles to process what I see.

I never considered I might die in the past. I hadn't been born yet. Is that even possible? I'll be caught in an endless time loop.

This isn't real. It can't be real. I'm sitting here, alive, in 2024. But the photo, the article—it's all there in black and white. The band breaks up shortly after the incident. I derail Grace's career. How can I live with that?

My hands tremble as the pressure in my head builds, and I drop the phone onto the couch. My breath comes in short, shallow bursts as I lean forward to bury my face in my hands.

Sam's warning roars back. *You don't belong here.*

My thoughts race as I piece together fragments of memory, conversations, and possibilities. Lars—that self-absorbed, narcissistic prick. Grace said he was talented but temperamental, prone to jealousy. He thinks I stole his girl, and he wants me gone. Did our victory push him over the edge?

My fingers curl into fists. It doesn't matter how or why. What matters is that this happens. It will happen unless I stop it.

I grab my phone again and scroll frantically through the article for clues. The three finalists are Hallowed Ground, Steel Mirage, and a singer-songwriter named Dann Walsh. *Steel Mirage.* The name sounds familiar. Then it hits me. Sasquatch said Lars joined a new band named Steel Mirage. I only have two weeks to change things.

But how? If I pull out of the contest, does that ripple out into something worse? Do I risk Grace losing her chance at the recognition she deserves? Or do I confront Lars and try to de-escalate things before they spiral out of control?

My mind spins with possibilities, each one more dangerous than the last. I've already disrupted the timeline just by being there. I look back at the phone, where my obituary stares back at me. I can't sit still anymore.

I dial Waldo's number on the way out the door. It rings, then goes to voicemail. His familiar, laid-back voice greets me, a small reassurance that not everything in my life has changed. He's probably at work—wherever that might be now. I can't be sure of anything anymore. "It's Angus. Call me when you get a chance." I try to sound normal, like my world hasn't just been upended.

I toss my phone on the passenger seat and head for the gym. I still have my locker key. The locker hasn't been cleaned out, so I guess I'm still a member in good standing.

I need this workout. I push myself hard—weights, cardio, anything to burn off the nervous energy that courses through me. Grace might not care about my soft edges, but I do. I don't want her to feel like she's sleeping with the Pillsbury doughboy. I want to be the kind of guy she deserves.

By the time I'm done, I'm drenched in sweat and my arms feel like lead, but at least I'm too tired to overthink my own mortality for a while.

Waldo calls on my way home. I pick up, relieved to hear his voice live this time. "Hey, man. You free for dinner?" I ask.

"Sure. What's on the menu?"

"Salmon, quinoa, and a guilt-free salad. I'm on a health kick."

Waldo chuckles. "Who are you, and what have you done with Angus?" He pauses. "Alright, I'll be there by six."

I stop by the market to pick up the salmon. The barbecue ribs at the deli counter tempt me for a second, but I ignore their smoky allure. The things we do for love.

Waldo pulls into my driveway at five-thirty. I meet him on the porch, and we exchange a brief handshake-hug combo before we head inside. By now, he knows most of the craziness—sparing me the need to start every story with, "So, there's this portal…" We stand by the grill as I lay the salmon filets on the grate.

While we watch the fish sizzle, I tell him about the last time I was here—the new ranch owners, my apartment, and the GTO.

"The GTO part is cool. The rest, not so much."

"I'm glad you're caught up." My hand trembles as I flip the fish. "Because it gets worse."

"Worse?"

I glance at him, steeling myself. "I Googled my obituary this morning."

Waldo freezes. "You what?!"

"Yeah. Apparently, I get shot in 1978. Lars pulls the trigger after Grace and I win a songwriting contest."

"Okay, first: congrats on winning. Second: ARE YOU OUT OF YOUR MIND? This is your cue to stay put and stop messing with the timeline, Angus!"

"I can't."

"Then it's been nice knowing you." He throws up his hands. "You didn't invite me here for dinner—you invited me to your last supper! Forgive me if I don't toast your impending demise."

"Before you waste a perfectly good piece of fish, hear me out."

He folds his arms. "I'm listening."

"Information is power," I explain. "I know when and where it happens. That means I can stop it."

"And how, exactly, do you plan to stop a jealous psycho from putting a bullet in you? What's your plan, Angus?"

I shrug. "I don't know yet."

Waldo groans as he paces a tight circle on the patio. "Don't you see what's happening here? You two are Romeo and Juliet."

"What… like an epic love story? I'll take that."

"Yeah, except they both die in the end."

My smile fades. "Okay, so maybe I didn't read the whole thing."

"You and Grace are the textbook definition of star-crossed lovers." Waldo's voice is heavy with frustration.

"Star-crossed?" I scoff. "Is that a thing?"

"It's a real thing," he insists. "Two people drawn together by fate but doomed by forces beyond their control. Romeo and Juliet are separated by a family feud. You and Grace are separated by time itself, Angus. Time. You can't beat that."

"I don't buy it." I flip the salmon with a little too much force, and my hand trembles. "We're meant to be together."

"Still having tremors, I see."

I glare. "It's just nerves."

"You can believe what you want, but you're risking everything. Not just your life, Angus. Hers, too."

I swallow hard as his words land heavier than I expected. "So, you think there's no hope for us?"

Waldo shakes his head. "I'm afraid not."

"Harry and Sally made it work."

"Yeah. Eventually, they get together. But that's a movie, a rom-com. It *has* to end that way. This is real life."

Our eyes clash in the hostile air. The gravity of his concern is undeniable. "As your best friend, I'm begging you not to go back."

A deafening silence follows.

I try to lighten the mood. "I might be 68 years old the next time you see me."

Waldo points an index finger at me. "That's not funny."

I pull the filets off the grill and onto a plate. "Dinner's ready. Let's eat."

Waldo shakes his head and mutters under his breath as we head inside. The conversation might be over for now, but the storm it stirred in my head rages on.

Chapter Thirty-Seven

I'm Coming Back for You – Elf (1972)

After dinner, the air between us feels heavy with words unspoken. We agree to disagree, silently promising not to let this rift drive a wedge between us. Waldo's been my only real friend for as long as I can remember, the one constant in my chaotic life. I can't shake the guilt that comes with keeping him in the dark about my plan to stay there permanently. Every trip to the past risks unraveling the fragile thread of our friendship. How long before the Waldo I know is gone—or worse, before he doesn't know me at all?

We step out into the cool night air of the porch, the only light bleeding through the screen door from the kitchen. The sound of crickets fills the silence between us, and I feel like a traitor. I know which way my heart pulls me, and it's not here. I thought this would be easier.

"I'd better go." Waldo shoves his hands into his pockets. "Thanks for dinner."

"Sure. Anytime." The words taste bitter and hollow. When will I tell him I'm leaving for good?

Before I can second-guess myself, I step forward and pull him into a hug. It catches him off guard, and I feel him stiffen for a moment before he awkwardly pats my back.

"Thanks, man." My voice is fragile. "You're a good friend."

"Uh… okay," he says, clearly confused but trying to roll with it. "So… so are you."

When I let go, he studies my face. I can't meet his eyes. If I do, he'll see right through me.

"You feeling okay?" he asks with a cautious voice.

"Yeah. I'm…" I trail off, forcing a weak smile. "Have a good night."

Waldo hesitates like he wants to say something more, but instead, he nods and heads for the stairs. I watch him walk to his car. The sound of his engine fades into the distance, leaving me alone with my thoughts.

The kitchen greets me with the aftermath of dinner—dirty plates and utensils scattered across the counter. I stare at the mess, aware that I should clean it up, but my limbs feel like lead. It can wait.

As I climb the stairs, Grace's voice echoes in my head, "What would you give up?"

"Everything," I whisper into the empty house. The word lingers in the air like a vow, unshakable and absolute.

I reach my room and sink onto the edge of the bed and stare at the floor. I'm leaving Waldo behind. I'm leaving *everything* behind.

But Grace is worth it. Isn't she?

The question echoes in my head until I cross the border into sleep.

My mind is already spinning as the sun crests the horizon. Nothing gets solved lying in bed, so I get up, scarf down a quick breakfast, and head out to the barn. The ATV needs gas, and I've put off refilling the cans.

I grab the first can and shake it. Empty. The second isn't much better—just a slosh of fuel at the bottom. *Great.* Looks like I'll have to head into town.

As I turn toward the ATV, my eyes drift to the tarp-covered GTO in the corner of the barn. For a moment, I let myself imagine driving it to the gas station, heads turning as I cruise by. But that's a fantasy. I pull back the tarp to reveal the rust and neglect beneath.

The car stares back at me, unchanged since the day I bought it. Maybe it's for the best. Even if I'd restored it, I can't drive it through the portal. It's another piece of this life I'll have to leave behind. I let out a hopeful sigh. Someday, I'll buy a pristine one in Denver. Something that doesn't look like it survived a junkyard apocalypse.

For now, I focus on what I can control. I hit the gym harder than usual, pushing through the ache in my muscles. Sweat pours off me in rivers. When I finally step into the shower, my arms and legs feel like they belong to someone else. The plan for the rest of the day is simple: stop for gas on the way home, then collapse into bed until dinner.

The rest of the week follows a similar rhythm—gym, eat, sleep, repeat. By Thursday night, I'm down six more pounds. Grace says she likes me the way I am, but I can't help wanting to be better for her. I pack a suitcase with clothes and toiletries, then zip my guitar and sheet music into a gig bag and leave it all by the door.

Friday morning, I check Google one last time. Nothing has changed. Part of me wants to bail, to stay here and avoid the storm brewing in 1978. But I can't. Tonight isn't just any night—it's the night Grace and I have been building toward. If I can find a way to stop Lars, to rewrite my fate, there will be many more nights like this one.

I chug a protein shake, load the ATV, and head for the portal. A half hour later, I'm standing on Grace's porch, suitcase in hand and guitar slung over my shoulder. I knock several times with no answer, then peer inside the window. Her stuff is still there.

She'll be back soon, I tell myself, then drop my bags on the porch and perch on the top step. I play a game of identifying the vintage cars that go past, but my thoughts grow heavier with each minute. Did she change her mind about getting involved with a guy from the future?

After twenty minutes, I decide to kill some time in the record store downstairs. The scent of vinyl and wood grounds me. Grace is behind the counter, ringing up a sale. She looks at me and her face lights up like a stage under a spotlight.

She works here? I haven't known her all that long, but long enough to know if she has a job and where she works. I guess I never asked. What else don't I know? Perhaps she wonders the same about me. I can't get into one of those conversations about secrets. Not yet.

I wait until her customer walks away, then plant my hands on my hips, barely able to hold back a grin. "Are you trying to ditch me?"

"I obviously didn't try hard enough," she says with a smirk.

She runs around the counter, grabs my hand, and tugs me toward the back.

Before I can say a word, she pulls me into the same nook where Sam and I had our first real conversation. She leaps into my arms, wraps her legs around my waist, and presses her lips to mine.

I stumble back, knocking over a stool, but manage to keep my balance.

"I'm disappointed." I catch my breath. "I thought you'd be excited to see me."

She narrows her eyes. Confusion swirls before she punches my chest. "You jerk."

Our laughter mingles as our lips meet again.

"I'm so glad you're back," she says when we finally pull apart, her green eyes sparkling. "I'll be done here in a couple of hours. I'll give you my key so you can wait upstairs."

When she gets home, her smile widens at the sight of my suitcase and guitar. She clears out a drawer and shifts hangers in her closet to make space. The gesture feels monumental—this is getting real.

I remind her about my dinner offer a week ago and ask her where she'd like to eat. She picks a fancy restaurant and calls to make reservations for seven o'clock. As she hangs up, she looks at me with a grin that lights up the room.

"Tonight will be perfect," she says.

I return her smile, doing my best to ignore the week ahead and focus on what's right in front of me. "Yeah. Perfect."

The restaurant is dimly lit. The candles flickering on every table cast shadows that seem to dance in time with the soft jazz that drifts through the air. Grace looks stunning in her emerald-green dress, her hair tumbling in loose waves over her shoulders. I can't stop glancing at her, and every time our eyes meet, she gives me that little smile that makes my chest tighten.

She runs her finger along the edge of her wineglass. "This place is beautiful."

"A friend of mine recommended it." I smile. "She has good taste."

Grace studies the menu in mock concentration, but a faint smile flashes across her lips. I grin, but inside, my stomach churns. How do I sit here and make small talk, knowing that, in a week's time, I might be dead and her future ruined? Every laugh feels borrowed, every smile a lie. But tonight isn't about that. It's about Grace—about us. *Enjoy yourself, Angus.*

The waiter arrives, takes our orders, and disappears.

"So," she says, folding her hands on the table and tilting her head at me, "you plan to stay the whole week?"

"That's the plan."

"Good." Her voice is soft but firm. "Because I'm not ready to let you go yet."

The way she says it sends a shiver down my spine.

The jazz trio starts a new tune, something slow and romantic. Grace looks over at the band with a wistful expression. "You know, I've been dreaming about a night like this for a long time."

I lean closer. "Really?"

"Yeah. Great music, great food, great company. Lars would never have taken me to a place like this."

The sound of his name strikes a raw nerve.

"It's almost like it's too perfect, you know?" She looks back at me, and for a moment, her playful demeanor gives way to something deeper. "Like it's all happening too fast, but you don't want it to stop."

I swallow hard. Her words hit closer to the truth than she realizes. "I know exactly what you mean."

The waiter returns with our meals. The conversation flows easily as we eat, filled with playful banter like I'd seen in movies, but never imagined I would someday experience. For a little while, I forget about Lars, the contest, and the ticking clock. Grace has that effect on me.

After dessert, we linger over coffee, neither of us in any hurry to leave. I'm more relaxed, but the undercurrent of tension—of what's waiting for us back at her place—remains. She leans forward, resting her chin on her hand, and watches me with a gaze that feels like it's peeling back every layer I have. Her lips part as if she's about to say something, but she changes her mind. She stands and grabs her clutch. "Ready to head out?"

"Sure."

I pay the bill, and we step into the cool night air. Grace loops her arm through mine, leaning her head against my shoulder, and for a moment, I believe it's all going to work out. But the clock is ticking, and I have one week to rewrite our future.

Chapter Thirty-Eight

Stairway to Heaven – Led Zeppelin (1971)

On the way home, I clear my throat and glance at Grace. "Hey, can we make a quick stop at Thunder Road?"

Her head whips toward me. "Thunder Road? You're kidding, right? Lars is playing there tonight."

"I know." My voice is calm. "It'll only take five minutes. I'll be in and out before you know it."

She lets out a frustrated sigh as her grip tightens on the steering wheel. "Why? What are you trying to prove?"

"It's not about proving anything," I reply, even though we both know that's a lie. "Trust me, okay?"

She exhales sharply and pulls the car up to the curb in front of the packed venue. "Fine. Five minutes. And don't make me regret this."

"Promise." I lean over and kiss her cheek, but she doesn't turn to look at me, her gaze fixed firmly out the windshield.

The place is a wall of noise and bodies as I step inside. The band is mid-set, the pounding beat vibrates through my chest as I weave through the crowd to get close to the stage. There he is—Lars, larger than life, his guitar slung low as he commands the spotlight.

It doesn't take long for him to spot me. His fingers falter for a fraction of a second. His eyes narrow as they scan the room, likely searching for Grace. When his gaze lands back on me, I make my move: two fingers to my eyes, then a sharp point directly at him.

His lip curls in a sneer, his teeth bared like a cornered wolf. Message received.

My pulse races as I push my way back through the crowd and step outside into the cool night air. Grace's car idles at the curb. I climb in, closing the door with a soft click.

She turns to me, her expression unreadable. "Are you going to tell me what that was about?" Her voice is calm, but there's an edge beneath it that makes me hesitate.

"And spoil the rest of the evening?" I force a grin. "Not a chance."

She stares at me like she's waiting for something.

"Grace." My smile falters. "We can go now."

As we drive, the tension in the car feels as thick as the air inside the bar. I glance at her, searching for a way to ease it. "The band really sucked," I say, testing the waters.

Her lips twitch, and a smile tugs at the corners of her mouth. It's subtle, but it's enough to give me hope.

Back at her place, she locks the door behind us, then leans against it, her arms crossed and her gaze locked on mine.

"You didn't have to try so hard to impress me tonight." Her tone teases but her eyes are serious.

"I wasn't trying to impress you." I step closer until we're inches apart. "I was just trying to keep up."

Her breath catches, and for a moment, the space between us is charged with unspoken words and raw emotion.

"You're doing great," she whispers, her voice barely audible as her hands slide up to tangle in my hair.

For a heartbeat, I hesitate as nerves and excitement battle inside me. But then her lips brush against mine, soft and certain, and something clicks into place.

With a burst of courage and determination, I lift her into my arms, her laugh warm against my neck as I carry her toward the bedroom.

"Why, Angus Walker," she murmurs, her voice playful, "you're full of surprises tonight, aren't you?"

I smile, pressing my forehead against hers, and finally let go of everything else and focus on this moment. On her.

Tonight, there's only us.

★★★

The morning light streams through the sheer curtains, bathing the room in a soft, golden glow. The unfamiliar warmth of a naked body pressed against mine pulls me from the haze of sleep. Grace's hair spills over the pillow in a messy tangle, her cheek resting against my chest. I don't want to know what time it is. I just want to lie here and not break the spell.

Last night was... perfect. Better than anything I could have imagined.

Her lashes flutter, and she blinks up at me. A slow, lazy smile spreads across her face. "Morning," she murmurs, her voice husky and soft.

"Morning." My lips twitch into a grin. "Sleep okay?"

"Best sleep I've had in ages." She props herself up on one elbow. "And you?"

"Pretty sure I'll never top that."

She laughs, low and throaty, and the sound wraps around me like a warm blanket. "Don't set the bar too high, Walker. We've got a lot of mornings ahead of us."

God, I hope so.

We linger a little longer in bed, tangled together in a comfortable silence, before Grace stretches and pulls away. "Come on, lover boy. If we don't get up now, we'll never get up."

I follow her into the kitchen, where she pulls out eggs and bread. She moves with an effortless grace, humming under her breath as she works. I grab the coffeepot and start a fresh brew, feeling more at home here than I ever expected.

"Toast or no toast?" she asks, glancing over her shoulder.

"Toast. Burnt, if you can manage it."

"Burnt toast, coming right up," she says with a wink.

We sit together at the small kitchen table. The smell of coffee and eggs fills the air. She's wearing an oversized T-shirt, her hair still mussed from sleep, and I can't stop staring at her.

"What?" she asks, when she catches me.

"Nothing." I shrug, trying to play it cool. "Just wondering how I got so lucky."

She rolls her eyes but smiles. "Flattery will get you every-where."

Over breakfast, we fall into easy conversation. She tells me about her plans for the day—an afternoon shift at the shop and maybe some time with the band in the evening.

"And you?" She raises an eyebrow as she sips her coffee.

"Oh, you know. I'll find something to keep me busy. I've got to get the lay of the land if I plan to live here."

In truth, I already know what I'll do, and the thought weighs heavily on me. I need to see Sam.

It's a risk, sneaking off like this, but I need to talk to him. If anyone knows how to deal with Lars—or how to change the course of events—it's him. I can't talk to anyone else about this. Not even Grace. Not yet.

As we finish breakfast, she glances at the clock and sighs. "I should get ready for work."

"Don't let me keep you." I stand to clear the plates.

She places a hand on my arm, stopping me. "You're not keeping me. Just… don't disappear on me, okay?"

"Wouldn't dream of it."

She lingers for a moment as her eyes search mine, before she gives me a quick kiss and disappears into the bedroom.

As soon as I hear the shower, I exhale and lean against the counter. My hand trembles, and I grab the edge of the sink. This feels wrong—keeping secrets from her—but what choice do I have?

I'll head straight to Sam's place when she leaves for work. I need answers. I need a plan. And most of all, I need to make sure I'm still alive next week.

Chapter Thirty-Nine

You Really Got Me – Van Halen (1978)

Grace steps out of the bathroom, steam following her as she tightens the towel wrapped around her. Water beads glisten on her shoulders, and her hair clings in damp waves to her neck.

"Is there any hot water left?" I ask, though my mind isn't focused on the question.

"You might have to wait a few minutes." She casually brushes a stray strand of hair from her face.

"Not a problem. I'll stay here and enjoy the view while I wait."

I lean against the bedroom wall, grinning like a tick on a fat dog.

"Like hell you will."

"Come on. You're a rock star. This morning-after stuff has to be old hat for you by now."

She snorts as she walks past me toward the dresser. "I'm hardly a rock star, Angus. Let's not get carried away."

"Okay, but you've been with other guys." The words slip out before I can stop them, and I instantly regret how clumsy it sounds.

She glances over her shoulder. "Not as many as you might think."

The reply is casual, but it lingers in the air between us, and I turn it over in my mind. Before I can say anything else, she gestures toward the bathroom with a wave of her hand.

"There's probably enough hot water by now." Her tone is light but commanding. "Go."

"Fine, fine." I grab a towel and pause in the doorway to glance back with a mischievous smirk. "But I've got a great idea for how we can save water next time."

Her laugh follows me into the bathroom. "Dream on, Walker."

The hot water pounds against my back, a stark reminder not to lose focus. As much as I want to revel in the memory of last night, there's a darker shadow that looms over my thoughts—saving my life and Grace's future. The first step is clear. I need to talk to Sam. The problem? I have no idea where he lives.

I could ask Grace, but I'll need a solid reason. A lie won't cut it. By the time I dry off, I've settled on the perfect excuse, and it's not a lie. If I'm going to live here permanently, I'll need papers—birth certificate, driver's license, the whole deal. Grace once mentioned Sam had arranged all of that for the two of them. Hopefully, he can do it again.

When I step out of the bathroom with a towel around my waist, I find Grace on the edge of the bed, her arms crossed and a mischievous grin on her face.

"Don't you have somewhere you need to be?" I ask, heading for the dresser to grab some clothes.

She checks her watch dramatically. "Plenty of time to watch you get dressed."

I walked right into this. "Suit yourself." A faint blush creeps up my neck as I pull out a T-shirt and shorts. "Since you're so keen on staying, maybe you can do me a favor."

Her eyebrows lift in amusement. "I didn't expect you to give up so easily." She leans back on her hands, her head tilted. "All right, one favor. Within reason."

"I need your dad's address."

Her playful expression falters. "What?"

"It's a reasonable request." I pull my shirt over my head. "Why?"

"If I'm going to stay here, I'll need papers. You said he did it for you. Maybe he can help me too."

Grace exhales and her posture softens. "I guess that makes sense." A small smile tugs at her lips. "I love that you're serious about this—about staying."

My chest tightens, and for a second, I almost tell her I love her. Instead, I manage, "I'm serious about *you*."

Her breath catches, and she pauses for a moment, but recovers with a teasing smile. "I got that impression when you showed up with your guitar yesterday. Speaking of which, when are you going to show it to me?"

I grin, grateful for the shift. "How about now?"

Grace lights up as I pull the Flying V from its case. Her eyes widen as she runs her fingers along the neck. "This is gorgeous."

She grabs her bass from the corner, and before I know it, we're sitting on the floor, running through a couple of songs.

The way she locks into a groove makes me feel like we've been playing together for years.

"You need to bring that to the contest," she says when we finish.

"That's the plan." I flash her a grin, but my thoughts are already darkening. I might have to use it for more than music if Lars doesn't back off. And just like that, my mission takes center stage again, heavy as ever.

Before Grace leaves for work, she writes Sam's address on a piece of paper, folds it, and hands it to me with a tentative smile. "Play nice."

She offers to let me take her car. I decline, not willing to risk a situation where I might need to produce identification. I'll walk or take the bus. She kisses me and wishes me luck.

Sam's been unable to hold down a job for years because of his obsession with keeping the timeline safe from meddling time travelers. A noble endeavor, but not something you talk about around the water cooler. He'd spent some time in an institution before Grace convinced them he could take care of himself under her supervision. Social Services found him a subsidized apartment, where he survives on his monthly disability check. I'm not sure what to expect when I get there.

The building sits on the corner of a quiet street, a tired-looking brick building with faded numbers above the door. I check them against the paper in my hand. It's the kind of place where neighbors keep to themselves, and the landlord probably hasn't updated the paint since the Eisenhower administration. A faded "Apartments for Rent" sign hangs in the front window.

I push open the door and step into a dimly lit lobby that smells faintly of coffee and old carpet. I check the directory on the wall. Monroe, S. is in Apartment 2B. I glance at the other names, hoping one of them might belong to Gramps. No such luck.

A narrow staircase creaks under my weight as I climb to the second floor. Apartment 2B is at the end of the hallway, and I knock twice. Someone or something shuffles inside, and the door opens enough to reveal Sam's wary expression.

He stares for a moment with those piercing gray eyes, and I want to turn and run. An unfamiliar determination holds my feet in place. I've never wanted anything more in my life than to be with Grace, and I'll need Sam's help with that.

"You lost?" he asks, his voice gruff but not unfriendly.

"No, sir. It's Angus. Grace's..." I falter. What am I? Boyfriend? Time traveler with benefits?

His eyes narrow as he recognizes me. "You've got nerve, kid."

Chapter Forty

Dirty Deeds Done Dirt Cheap – AC/DC (1976)

I'd asked Grace not to call Sam ahead of my visit. If he knew I was coming, there was a chance he'd vanish before I got here.

His eyes narrow. "What are you doing here?"

"Can I come in?"

He hesitates, leaning against the door frame. For a second, I think he's going to slam it shut. Then he sighs and steps aside. "Guess you're not the type to take a hint."

The place is small but neat. A bed is pushed against one wall, with a simple nightstand beside it. A wooden table is covered with papers, a couple of coffee mugs, and an old portable radio. His blue hoodie hangs on a coat rack near the door, and a beat-up guitar leans in the corner, its finish all but worn off.

I glance at the guitar. "You play?"

"Used to."

Sam gestures to the only chair. "Sit." He crosses his arms and leans against the wall. "What do you want?"

I sit, gripping my knees to keep my hands steady. "I, uh... I need your help."

He remains silent, his lips pressed together, waiting for me to continue.

"I plan to stay here. In 1978. With Grace."

His face tightens, and his eyes narrow again. "I thought I made it clear you don't belong here."

"With all due respect, sir, neither do you."

Sam's eyes flash. "Careful, kid. You don't know a damn thing about me."

"I know enough." I hold his gaze. "You stayed here for her. I'd like to do the same."

He studies me, his jaw working as if deciding whether to throw me out. Finally, he exhales sharply. "Keep talking."

"I need papers—a birth certificate, driver's license, the works. You can do that. You did it for yourself and Grace."

"That's a big ask."

"I'll cover whatever it costs. I just need your help to make it happen."

He exhales through his nose, his gaze sharp. "If you care anything about your life in the future, then I suggest—"

"That's just it," I cut him off. "I only care about my life with your daughter. Grace is happy. And I don't want to mess that up. I'm serious about staying. About her."

That gets his attention. His arms uncross, and his expression softens a fraction. "You'd really risk everything to stick around for her?"

"In a heartbeat."

Sam studies me for a moment, then nods. "All right. I'll help you with the papers."

I hand him my license. "Can you use the picture from this?"

He inspects it. "I don't see why not." He sets it down and fixes his gaze on me. "Something tells me that's not the only reason you're here."

I take a deep breath and steel myself. "You're right. There *is* something else."

His posture stiffens, his eyes narrowing again. "What?"

"It's about Lars."

"What about him?"

"Last time I went home, I Googled the songwriting contest Grace and I entered. We win, by the way. That's the good news. The bad news is that, a week from now, I get shot and killed at the competition by Lars."

"You must have really pissed him off."

"He claims I stole his girl, which I guess I did. Then, when he attacked me outside the club a couple weeks ago, I humiliated him in front of a crowd of people."

"You fought with that monster and lived to tell about it?" He shakes his head. "That's impressive, I'll give you that. Sounds like he's not going to let it go."

"I need your help."

Sam's expression hardens. "The way I see it, she wouldn't be in this trouble if you hadn't come around."

"No, but she'd still be with Lars. I don't see how that could end well."

"You planning to take him on again?"

"Not exactly." I rest my elbows on my knees and lock eyes with him. "I plan to sneak into his dressing room and steal his gun while he's on stage. But I need you to be there so you can get rid of it. Somewhere it'll never be found."

"That's risky. If he catches you..." His voice trails off.

"He won't," I say quickly. "I'll be careful. But I can't do this without you."

Sam shakes his head, muttering under his breath.

"I'm not doing this for me. If I die, it breaks up the band. Grace loses everything. Her band, her future. I can't let that happen."

"You're playing with fire, kid. And fire's a damn hard thing to control."

"I'm willing to take the risk for her."

That seems to hit a nerve. Sam leans back, and his gaze softens. "You really care about her, don't you?"

"I do." My voice is steady. "More than anything."

He studies me for another moment, his gaze sharp and searching. Then, finally, he sighs. "Okay, I'll help you. But this better work. For Grace's sake."

"It will. Thank you."

"You're lucky she likes you."

"Roger that." I feel a surge of relief as I stand. "One more thing. I don't want Grace to know about this."

He exhales slowly, then nods. "Okay. I agree it's for the best. This time stuff... it's tricky. One wrong move, and it could all go to hell."

"I can't just do nothing."

Sam's eyes meet mine, and for the first time, there's a glimmer of respect in his gaze. "Neither can I." He closes the door behind me.

I feel a lot better about my chances on the walk back to Grace's. Having Sam in my corner feels like a game-changer, and it's clear he's beginning to accept me. If I want to be with Grace, having her dad's support—or at least his cooperation—can only help. The fact that he's willing to set me up with the papers I need to stay? That's a big step in the right direction.

On the way, I stop by the record store to let Grace know I'm back. She's at the counter, sorting through a pile of new arrivals, and her face lights up when she sees me.

"How did it go?" she asks, coming around to meet me.

I try to sound more confident than I feel. "We're all set."

"How was Dad? Did he treat you okay?"

"He was great."

Her eyebrows shoot up in surprise. "Really? I was afraid—"

I cut her off with a reassuring smile. "It's all good."

Grace exhales. Her shoulders relax as a grin spreads across her face. "Oh, Angus, I'm so excited about our future."

"Me too, Babe. Me too."

But even as I say the words, Sam's warning echoes in my mind. I might stop Lars from pulling the trigger this week, but what about next week? Or the week after that? As long as he's out there, I'll be looking over my shoulder—and Grace might end up caught in the crossfire.

I pull her into a hug and hold her a little tighter than usual. If I want a real future with her, I'll need to make sure Lars can't ruin it.

Chapter Forty-One

Rock and Roll Fantasy – Bad Company (1979)

Grace walks in an hour later as I'm lounging on her couch. Her face is bright but guarded.

"I have good news and bad news," she announces as she kicks off her shoes.

"Lay it on me."

"They announced the finalists for the songwriting contest. We made it."

"I assume that's the good news." I think I already know the bad.

Her nose wrinkles as she tilts her head. "Of course, silly. The bad news is, Lars's new band is in the finals, too."

I shrug, trying to play it cool. "I wouldn't worry too much."

Grace sits next to me, her expression skeptical. "Lars can't write his way out of a paper bag, but I don't know about the rest of his band. They're solid musicians."

I slide an arm around her and pull her into a hug. "We got this."

She leans back enough to peer into my face. "Do you know something I don't, future man?"

"Remember? No talk about the future."

She narrows her eyes and searches mine for a clue before she wrinkles her nose. "Wait, what's that smell?"

Before I can answer, she perks up, realization dawning. "You made dinner?"

"I'm a man of many talents." I grin and lead her into the kitchen, where I've set the table for two.

"This is such a pleasant surprise." She beams. "Thank you."

"We're having pasta, garlic bread, and a salad. It'll be ready in ten."

Grace presses a quick kiss to my cheek and disappears to freshen up.

After dinner, she sets her napkin on the table and leans back in her chair with a contented sigh. "Dinner was fantastic, Angus. Let me return the favor. How about a movie tonight?"

"What's playing?"

"There's a double feature at the drive-in—*Jaws 2* and *Close Encounters of the Third Kind*."

"A drive-in? I've never been."

"Oh, you're gonna love it. You sit in your car with a speaker hooked on the window. It's private." She raises an eyebrow above a teasing smirk. "If you know what I mean."

I chuckle. "Do they have popcorn?"

She crosses her arms. "Seriously? You're alone in a car with a beautiful woman, and all you can think about is popcorn?"

"You didn't mention there'd be beautiful women there."

With a laugh, she punches my arm. "You're such a jerk."

Our laughter mingles as she leans in, and our lips meet.

After a moment, she pulls back. "The first *Jaws* is my favorite movie of all time. Have you seen it?"

I grin. "You're gonna need a bigger boat," I say, mimicking Chief Brody.

Her eyes go wide. "Oh, my God. You sound just like him!"

At the drive-in, Grace parks in the middle row. The speaker crackles as she hooks it onto the window. The sun sets in vibrant streaks of orange and pink, casting a magical glow over the lot.

I look around at the activity. "This is amazing."

Grace pops open a bag of licorice she brought along and offers me a piece. "Told you it's cool. Wait until the movie starts."

The giant screen flickers to life with a preview for *Animal House*. As we settle in, Grace leans her head on my shoulder, her voice soft. "Thanks for tonight, Angus. I needed this."

I slip an arm around her, feeling the warmth of her body against mine. "I think we both did."

Grace clutches my arm when the shark's fin appears. "Okay, I forgot how intense this is," she whispers.

I smile in the dim glow of the screen. "Don't worry. You've got me to protect you."

"From a shark? In Colorado?"

I squeeze her tight. "Always."

For a little while, the chaos of the contest and the looming threat of Lars melt away, leaving just us, a screen full of adventure, and the magic of the moment.

That night, Grace wakes up mumbling something about a shark attack. I hold her close, murmuring reassurances until we both drift back to sleep. By morning, the nightmare seems forgotten.

We're at the kitchen table, enjoying the kind of Sunday morning I could get used to—coffee, bacon and eggs, and the Sunday paper spread between us.

"Richard Nixon made his first public appearance since resigning," Grace says, folding the front page.

I flip to the sports section. "Ron Guidry just had his thirteenth straight win for the Yankees. That's a team record."

She smiles over her mug. "Think Foreigner's next album will make the headlines?"

"With our song on it? No doubt."

By Wednesday, the carefree vibe is gone. I visit Sam while Grace is at work, and we go over the plan one more time. With no metal detectors at concerts in 1978, there's nothing to stop Lars from bringing in a gun. Best case scenario, we perform before Steel Mirage. It'll be easier for me to slip away unnoticed if we're not stuck backstage waiting to go on. Plan B requires Sam to steal the gun, but I'd feel better if I did it myself. Either way, I'll need Sam to dispose of it.

That night, I tell Grace Sam wants to come to the contest. She raises an eyebrow but agrees he can ride with us.

Friday night arrives in a blur of pre-show chaos. Sam sticks close as we navigate the crowded backstage area. I'm more nervous about stopping Lars than playing our song on stage in front of fifteen thousand people. I exhale a little when I hear we're up second, followed by Steel Mirage. Timing is everything, and so far, it's working in our favor.

Still, I avoid Lars, even as I tell myself he's probably not crazy enough to walk around with a loaded gun and take his shot before we go on. This is a contest, after all, and I'm sure he wants his chance to beat us on stage. Or perhaps his plan is to eliminate the competition before it ever gets that far. My nerves are like frayed wires about to snap.

Grace squeezes my hand when our name is called. "You ready?"

"As I'll ever be."

We step onto the stage, and the roar of the crowd hits like a tidal wave. I focus on the music and let the melody carry me through. By the final chord, the applause is deafening. Grace hugs me, eyes bright with excitement.

"You killed it," she says, and I can't help but laugh. If she only knew.

As we head offstage, I kiss her cheek. "I need to hit the bathroom."

"I'll go too. I don't want to miss Steel Mirage."

We reach the restrooms, and she gets in line outside the women's while I duck inside the men's.

"Sam?" I scan the stalls. Nothing. My pulse spikes. Where the hell is he?

I poke my head outside. Grace is still in line, but Sam is nowhere to be found—until I spot him in line at the concession stand. I wait until Grace is inside, then sprint over to Sam and grab his arm. "No time for that. Move!"

He mutters a protest but follows me toward Steel Mirage's dressing room. "You owe me a beer," he grumbles.

"If I'm still alive, I'll buy you two."

I station him outside the door as a lookout and step inside. The room is empty, silent except for the pounding of my heart. A frantic search of the lockers and shelves turns up nothing. My gaze falls on three guitar cases in the corner.

The first is empty. So is the second. I open the third and flip the small compartment at the top. My stomach drops. Nestled inside is a Smith & Wesson .38 revolver, fully loaded.

Damn it, Lars, you were really going to kill me.

There's a knock at the door. "Hurry up," Sam whispers. "The song's almost over."

I crack the door and shove the gun into his hands. "Dumpster. Out back. Now. Make sure no one sees you."

Grace gives me a skeptical look when I rejoin her backstage. "What took so long?"

"Crowded bathroom." I force a shrug.

Her eyes narrow. "You okay?"

"Better now."

Grace slips her hand into mine, and I hold on tight. It's amazing what cheating death can do for your mood.

Chapter Forty-Two

We Are the Champions – Queen (1977)

The crowd roars as they announce our song as the winner. Grace screams with joy and throws her arms around the other two band members. Then she turns and leaps onto me, her legs wrapped around my waist as she kisses me hard. The world blurs for a second—just her and me in a whirlwind of elation. I'm so damn excited for her. For us.

Hallowed Ground is called back to the stage for a bow. The applause is electrified and surreal. I catch Grace's eye as we bow together. She's radiant, and for once, I feel like I might actually belong in this moment.

The stage manager ushers us toward Foreigner's dressing room, where we're greeted with warm handshakes and congratulations. Lou Gramm, the voice behind some of the greatest rock anthems of all time, smiles and says, "Great song. Seriously. With a few tweaks to the arrangement, this is going to be killer on our next album."

My heart skips. Lou Gramm loves our song. Our song. It's like stepping into a dream. They're one of my all-time favorite bands, and now they tell me I've made the cut. My head spins, and I try not to freak out. *Who's a shithead now?*

The stage manager reappears to let us know Foreigner has to take the stage. He promises their people will be in touch with our people, which makes me chuckle. We don't have people. Guess we'll need to fix that. Fast.

As we head back, Steel Mirage crosses our path. They offer their congratulations, but I stay alert, positioning myself between Lars and Grace. Technically, he's violating the restraining order, and I won't let him get within arm's reach of her.

Lars stares me down, his face unreadable—until he flashes that familiar gesture. This time, though, he adds a new twist. He drags his index finger across his neck, his meaning unmistakable. My stomach tightens, but I don't flinch. Let him go look for his gun. It's long gone.

We meet up with Sam and settle into our seats for Foreigner's set. The lights dim, the crowd erupts, and the first notes hit like a freight train. It's an incredible show, everything I'd imagined and more. But even as I'm swept up in the music, I can't stop replaying the night's events in my mind.

Against all odds, we're here, in this impossible moment. After cheating death, I'm watching a band I thought I'd never be able to see live. It feels like victory. It feels like magic.

And for tonight, at least, it feels like we're unstoppable.

★★★

Morning comes with a stark clarity that makes everything sharper. The glow of last night's victory has faded, leaving me face-to-face with the reality I've been trying to avoid. Lars won't let up. If anything, it feels like he's ramping up. I need answers—answers I can only get from the future.

Over coffee, I break the news to Grace. "I have to go back today. To get more of my stuff." It's not a lie, but it's not the full truth either. "And it probably won't be the last trip. It's not like I can drive a U-Haul through the portal."

She sets her mug down, frowning. "Angus, I don't like this. Can't it wait? What if—" She stops herself. "Be careful, okay? I can't wait until you're here for good and we can destroy that damn portal. Then maybe my dad's life can get back to normal."

Destroy the portal? My heart skips. I didn't know that was the plan. Sure, I've told myself I'll stay here—for Grace, for this life we're building—but the portal is more than a doorway. It's my lifeline to where I'm from, to the person I used to be. Losing it feels like cutting the last thread that ties me to my identity.

"Angus?" Her voice cuts through my spiraling thoughts.

"What? Oh, yeah. Of course. I'm always careful."

She leans in and kisses me lightly, but the unease lingers like a shadow between us.

By the time I step through the portal and onto my ranch, the familiar sights are almost a comfort. The GTO still sits beneath its tarp in the barn, rusting quietly into oblivion. The house is untouched, every room just as I left it.

Traveling back and forth is taking its toll—physically and mentally. It's hard to pretend that the headaches and tremors are not a result of my travels. But it's my only way to foresee the future, which has become more of a necessity than a luxury.

I collapse onto the porch swing and pull out my phone to call Waldo. He's my anchor, my link to sanity in this shifting timeline.

The phone rings, and then—"Hello?" A woman's voice.

My brow furrows. "Uh… is Waldo there?"

"I'm sorry, you have the wrong number."

"Wait! Do you know if this number used to belong to a Walter Hastings?"

There's a long pause. Too long. "I'm sorry, I don't know. I've had this number for the last four years."

Four years?

"Sorry to bother you," I manage, before ending the call.

My thoughts race as I stare at the empty horizon. Waldo is gone—or at least, his connection to me is. Another ripple in the timeline, another soul lost in the fallout of my meddling. I sink deeper into the swing, weighed down by a crushing sense of displacement.

I've really screwed things up. Every trip through the portal seems to widen the gulf between the worlds, leaving me stranded in between. I don't feel like I belong in 2024 anymore, but I'm not sure I truly belong in 1978 either.

But then I think of Grace. Her smile, her laugh, the way she looks at me like I'm her whole world. She's my anchor now, the reason I move forward, even when everything feels like it's falling apart.

Grace is worth it.

Right?

Of course she is. Stop wallowing, Angus. I close my eyes and shake my head, like a kid erasing a mistake on an Etch A Sketch. Okay. Focus. It doesn't matter what 2024 looks like anymore. My future is with Grace Monroe in 1978. I'm a rock star.

With renewed determination, I grab my phone and type "Grace Monroe" into Google. It takes a moment to load, but when it does, my breath catches as I read the first headline:

Green Diamond Records Signs Local Band to Record Deal

Rock star, indeed. I smile as my chest swells with pride. "We did it," I whisper. "Attagirl, Grace." She deserves this—every bit of it.

For a moment, I think about breaking my no-future-talk rule. Wouldn't it be worth it to see her face light up when I tell her the good news? But then my thumb scrolls further, and my heart stops cold.

Local Musician Gunned Down Outside Green Diamond Records

No. No, no, no. I don't want to believe it. My hand shakes as I click the link, and the words blur in front of my eyes:

August 2 - Angus Walker, 22, was fatally shot yesterday outside Green Diamond Records in Denver. Police say the shot came from a nearby rooftop. A suspect is in custody, but no arrests have been made. Walker, a promising talent and recent addition to the Colorado music scene, was pronounced dead upon arrival at Denver General Hospital. Authorities are investigating the motive behind the attack.

My stomach churns as I stare at the screen. I squeeze my eyes shut and pray it won't be there when I open them. But when I do, it's still there.

I force myself to keep scrolling, and it only gets worse.

Double Trouble for Local Band as Green Diamond Records Cancels Contract

The police identified Lars as the shooter, and Green Diamond Records immediately severed ties with the band. The fallout was swift and brutal. The band dissolved within days, and Grace... Grace vanished from the music scene altogether.

I stand abruptly, the porch swing creaking in protest. The phone feels like a lead weight in my hand. I chuck it into the yard, but the rage inside me doesn't dissipate. My chest heaves as I pace back and forth, unable to make sense of what I read.

This isn't happening. It can't happen.

But it will—unless I stop it.

It won't be so easy this time.

Chapter Forty-Three

I'm Losing You – Rare Earth (1970)

I pace back and forth on the porch with no one to talk to, no one to pull me back from the edge. Waldo has always been the voice of reason, the guy who could untangle my scrambled thoughts and help me make sense of the chaos. But that's another bridge I've burned, another casualty of my time-traveling misadventures.

The portal will close soon, and if I miss it, I'll be stuck here for another week—alone with my thoughts, my failures, and no way to fix any of it.

I sink back into the swing and stare out at the horizon. The cicadas buzz in the distance, their drone amplifying the noise in my head. I have some serious decisions to make, and their weight crushes my chest.

First, how much of this do I share with Grace? No future talk—I know the rules—but if I don't tell her what I've learned, how can I protect her? Or myself?

Second, do I even belong in 1978? Maybe Sam was right all along. I'm living a life that was never meant to be mine. As much as I want to believe Grace is my soulmate, and as much as we've accomplished together, my presence could be the thing that ruins everything for her. Her dreams, her career, her safety—it's all at risk because of me.

The swing creaks under my weight as I lean forward and bury my face in my hands. Every choice feels like the wrong one. But I can't stay paralyzed by indecision. The clock is ticking, and Grace is waiting for me.

I throw a few of my things into a battered old suitcase. My gaze lingers on a photo of Waldo and me that I used to keep by my bed. The last time we were together, he begged me not to go back to Denver. I almost grab it, but what's the point? That version of my life feels like it belongs to someone else now.

On the way to the cave, I stop to pick up my phone. The screen is cracked, but the phone is working. The portal hums and crackles with energy as I step through. And then, just like that, I'm back. The faint scent of Grace's favorite jasmine incense greets me when I open her door. I'm relieved she isn't home.

The thought hits me like a slap. Relief? Since when am I relieved not to see her? I set the suitcase down. How could I feel this way about Grace? About us?

I run a hand through my hair and try to make sense of the knot in my chest. This isn't how it's supposed to be. When I first met Grace, I couldn't get enough of her. Her smile, her laugh, the way her eyes lit up when she talked about music. She filled up every empty space in me. And now? Now I'm standing in her empty apartment, grateful for the silence, for the space between us.

What kind of person does that make me? I love Grace—I know I do—but the secrets are piling up between us like bricks in a wall I never meant to build. I don't want to be the guy who hides from the person he loves, who lets fear and guilt gnaw away at the best thing that's ever happened to him.

But the truth is, I don't know how to stop.

An hour later, after I've had time to take a hot shower and decompress, the front door opens.

"Angus? Are you home?"

I slap on a smile and meet her in the kitchen. "I got back an hour ago."

She sets two paper grocery bags on the table. "Did you miss me?"

"Always."

The smell of fresh groceries—bread, fruit, coffee—fills the kitchen. I lean against the counter and watch her unpack. Her energy lights up the room like it always does.

We have twenty-four days until Lars pulls the trigger. I don't need to tell her anything today. It sounds cowardly, and maybe it is, like if I ignore it, it's not real.

I can't put it off for too long. If I can't figure out a way to stop Lars, and I have to leave, she'll need time to get a new guitarist up to speed before the first recording session. It's the least I can do. But for now, it's business as usual.

"Did you get anything good?" My cheery voice masks the storm swirling in my head.

She grins and holds up a box of Cap'n Crunch.

"Perfect. Thanks." I need some comfort food.

I help her put away groceries like everything is fine. It's easier than it should be. Grace is so full of life, so excited about the little things, that it almost makes me believe nothing bad could ever happen. Almost.

The days pass in a strange rhythm, a careful dance between the life I've always wanted and the one I can feel slipping through my fingers. Every time she flashes me that radiant smile, I tell myself it's not the right time to bring up the truth. Not today. Maybe tomorrow.

On the third day, she hangs up the phone on the wall and turns to me, her face glowing with excitement.

I never understood the term "hang up" the phone… until now.

Her phone is big, blocky, and the color of old oatmeal, with a rotary dial that reminds me of a safe from an old heist movie. A long, coiled cord dangles from the receiver like a snake that's been stretched and tortured, knotted and kinked in ways that defy physics.

"You'll never guess what just happened," she says.

I lean back in my chair. "Try me."

"That was the A & R man from Green Diamond Records!" She practically bounces on her toes. "They've offered us a contract! We're going to make a record!"

Her joy is contagious, but it hits me like a fist to the stomach. Of course. This is how it happens. Everything is falling into place, leading us straight to that rooftop. My stomach churns as I try to process it all.

"That's incredible, Grace." I plaster on a smile. "I'm so proud of you."

She frowns, her head tilted. "Don't you mean *us*? You're part of this, too, Angus."

"This is all you, Grace. I'm just lucky to be along for the ride."

Her frown deepens, but she lets it go, spreading papers across the table—notes, lyrics, ideas for the album she's already building in her mind.

I watch her for a moment as the weight of my secrets presses down on me. I can't keep this up much longer. Every moment I stay, every lie I tell, feels like another step toward the edge of a cliff I can't avoid.

Who can I turn to for help? Waldo's gone, and I can't drop this on Grace. That leaves Sam. I'm running out of time.

"Hey." I force a smile. "I need to take a walk. Clear my head."

"Okay." She glances up from her notes. "Don't be too long. I want to brainstorm some ideas for the album."

"Sure thing."

The weight in my chest eases when I step outside. The afternoon sun is warm on my skin, and I take a deep breath.

I hope you've got some answers, Sam, because I'm running out of time.

Chapter Forty-Four

Bad Time – Grand Funk Railroad (1974)

My heart pounds harder than my fist against Sam's door.

"Sam! It's Angus. Open up!"

Silence.

I knock again, louder this time. My voice cracks. "I need to talk to you. Please."

Nothing.

I press my forehead against the door and let out a frustrated groan. Eventually, I walk outside and slump onto the stoop, elbows on my knees, head in my hands. The minutes crawl by, each one louder than the last in my mind. Grace's face flashes before me—her wide smile, the light in her eyes. That light will dim every second I stay away, and still, I can't bring myself to go back. Not yet.

The stillness is unbearable. Sam said he still watches the portal; maybe he's there.

The building is cold and empty. No sign of Sam or the portal. I leave disappointed, hoping I can spot him on the street.

The newsstand guy casts a wary gaze as I inquire about the man in the blue hoodie.

"A blue what?"

"Uh… you know, a sweatshirt with a hood attached."

"Crazy Sam?" The man squints at me. "Haven't seen him today."

"Thanks." My voice is flat, the word hollow.

It's past dinner time, and I'm hungry. I'm sure she's eaten by now, so I'm on my own for dinner. I stop at the diner, where Carl fixes me a plate of his world-famous meatloaf. His words, not mine.

I push the food around on my plate. Grace must be worried. I've been gone for hours with no explanation. She's at home waiting. Or maybe not waiting—fed up with me after I walked out when she needed me.

The longer I'm out, the deeper the hole I dig for myself. I pay the bill and leave. The streetlights flicker on, casting long shadows across the pavement. Grace's face flashes in my mind—excited, hopeful—and the realization that I've left her hanging twists the knife deeper. She wanted to celebrate, to start planning for the album. I've ruined that.

My footsteps echo in the quiet night. The apartment is dark except for the faint glow of the living room lamp. Grace is on the couch, staring at a blank TV screen. She doesn't look up as I close the door behind me.

The stack of papers is gone, replaced by a half-empty bottle of wine on the coffee table.

"Grace—"

"Don't." Her voice is flat, tired, and it cuts through me worse than if she'd yelled.

I stand there, the silence stretching between us like a canyon. The weight I carried out the door earlier feels even heavier now that I've made things worse.

"Where the hell have you been for four hours?" she asks, her tone sharp, though her gaze remains fixed ahead.

"I went to see your father."

That gets her attention. She sits up straighter, her eyes narrow. "You two have been getting pretty chummy lately. What's going on?"

I avoid her gaze. "He wasn't home."

Her lips press into a thin line, and she shakes her head. "I'm disappointed, Angus. I was so happy when I got the news today. I wanted to share that with you, to celebrate us. But you left me hanging, like you didn't know or didn't care about my feelings."

Hearing it laid out so plainly makes me feel like a jerk. "I'm sorry. I've just… I've got a lot on my mind."

Her arms cross over her chest, a clear wall going up between us. "Why would you want to talk to my father about it instead of me?"

Good question. One I don't have an answer for. "It's complicated."

"Angus, what's really going on? You're not yourself lately."

I keep a careful distance as I sink onto the couch beside her. "What if we moved to 2024?"

I have to at least float the possibility of her coming back with me. It might be the only way we can stay together.

She blinks at me, stunned. "What? I thought we decided to stay here and live the rock and roll dream together."

"Yes, but… would you ever consider it?"

"Where's this coming from?"

"Just… keeping our options open."

Her face hardens. "Well, I don't see that as an option. We've just signed a record deal, Angus. That's huge. It's what I've wanted since I was a little girl. I thought it's what you wanted, too."

"What I want is *you*." The words spill out before I can stop them.

She stands abruptly as anger flashes in her eyes. "Come on, Angus. You're scaring me. What's this really about?"

I rise and move toward the kitchen to put some distance between us. "Never mind," I say over my shoulder. "Forget I asked."

She follows me. "No, I won't forget it. What aren't you telling me?"

I grab a glass of water, chug it, and slam it down on the counter. The sound reverberates through the kitchen. "I said forget it."

Her face falls as hurt overtakes the anger. "Fine. I'll give you some alone time to think about it on the couch tonight."

She spins on her heel and marches toward the bedroom. The door slams behind her with a resounding finality.

I lean against the counter and stare at the empty glass. Every instinct tells me to chase after her, to fix this before it spirals further. But what can I say? That I've seen the future, and it doesn't include me? That staying here might destroy her dreams?

The silence after Grace's door slams is deafening. I lean against the kitchen counter, and the weight of everything—the lies, the impending disaster, the fractured trust—presses down on me.

Smooth, Walker. Real smooth.

But she's right. She should be scared. I've done nothing but mess things up since I got here. Grace deserves better than half-truths and my constant hedging. I sigh and grab the glass again. I fill it halfway before drinking slowly, as if the water could somehow cool the fire that rages in my chest. Every part of me wants to storm into the bedroom, apologize, and promise her everything will be okay. But how can I do that when I don't even believe it myself?

The faint creak of the bed tells me Grace has settled in for the night, and it makes my heart ache. I want to be with her, to hold her, to pretend for a few hours the future isn't a ticking time bomb.

But pretending is what got me here.

I glance at the couch, then at the door Grace slammed moments ago. Every instinct tells me to let her cool off, to give her space. Instead, I knock softly on her door.

"Grace?"

Silence.

"I'm sorry." My voice is just above a whisper. "You're right. I've been acting weird, and it's not fair to you. I… I don't know how to do this. Any of it."

Still nothing.

I lean my forehead against the door and close my eyes. "I love you, Grace. That's all I know for sure."

The bed creaks again, followed by soft footsteps. The door opens a crack. Her eyes are red, her expression guarded.

"You don't get to drop cryptic comments and then say you love me and expect that to fix everything." Her voice is shaky.

I swallow hard. "I need you to trust me for a little longer while I try to figure this out."

She stares at me for what feels like an eternity before sighing and opening the door wider. "You'd better. Because if you shut me out, Angus, you're going to lose me."

"I know. And I'm terrified of that."

She steps aside and lets me in.

Chapter Forty-Five

Tangled Up in Blue – Bob Dylan (1975)

A knock at the door pulls me from sleep, though I can't tell if it's real or part of my dream. Morning sunlight streams through the sheer curtains and makes the room feel too bright for the emotional hangover I carry. As the fog in my head clears, I remember—Grace left for work early this morning, still angry. Another knock comes, this one louder, and I groan as I drag myself out of bed. I grab yesterday's shorts and t-shirt off the floor, pulling them on as I shuffle to the door.

"Coming."

I open it to find Sam wearing a rare smile. It doesn't last. He gives me a once-over, and the smile slides off his face.

"You look like you just woke up."

"Grace isn't here," I say, my voice groggy. "She had to work."

"That's fine. I'm here to see you."

That's not ominous at all. I step back to let him in.

"Want some coffee?" I ask as we head to the kitchen.

"Sure, if it's not too much trouble."

As I start a fresh pot, he pulls a couple of papers from his pocket and sets them on the table.

"Got your new ID."

I pick up the license and birth certificate and study them. "These look legit."

"Angus Walker, age twenty-two, native of Denver, Colorado." He smirks. "Lives right here in this apartment."

I hold up the new license. "How about that." I'll hang onto both until this Lars thing gets resolved. I slip them into my wallet.

"What do I owe you?"

"I told you it wouldn't be cheap. It's going to set you back two hundred."

I grab the money from my bag and peel off an extra fifty for his trouble. "Thanks."

He nods as he wraps his hands around the cup of coffee I set in front of him. For a moment, he sits there, staring into the steam like he's gathering his thoughts. Then, his voice drops, quieter, more serious.

"I never told Grace," he begins, "but over the years, I've seen a few travelers come through the Montana portal. Most keep a low profile. A few… not so much."

"I haven't caused any trouble."

"That depends on your definition of trouble. Let's see—you've moved in with my daughter, got a band member fired, won a songwriting contest, stole a gun and disposed of it—"

"You disposed of it," I cut in.

"Which I wouldn't have had to do if you'd stayed in Utah."

I lift my coffee. My hand trembles enough that I quickly set the cup back down. Sam catches the movement and his eyes narrow.

"How long have you had the tremor?"

"A couple weeks."

"Triple T," he says matter-of-factly, then sips his coffee.

"What?"

"Time Traveler's Tremor."

"There's a name for it?"

"It's not an official medical term. I made it up. But I've seen it before. Headaches, too?"

I nod.

"A guy from Montana had it. Stubborn bastard. I warned him to stop, but he kept bouncing back and forth. It got bad enough that he eventually stayed home for good. Don't know if he's dead or alive."

Sam pours himself another cup, lifting the pot toward me. I shake my head, throat too tight to trust my voice.

"You've traveled." I press him. "Any symptoms?"

"I've only gone through a few times—first time by accident, the second time to get Grace, and another to see the shit show my actions here created in the future. I walked through that portal six times. I don't think that's enough to cause any side effects." He leans forward. "How many times have you gone through?"

Obviously, too many. I take a sip of lukewarm coffee while I do the math. "I'm not sure. Sixteen. Give or take."

He lets out a low whistle. "You'd better slow down, son."

He's right, of course. If I'm going to stay in 1978, which doesn't seem as likely as it did a week ago, I have to live here—really live here—one day at a time, like everyone else.

I need to change the subject. "There's something else we need to talk about."

"Let me guess—Lars."

I nod.

Sam's expression hardens. "That lunatic isn't going to stop until you're…" His voice trails off, but we both know how the sentence ends.

"That's the problem. We may have won a battle, but this war isn't over. And it's not one I think I can win."

"What are you saying?"

"I'm considering going back to 2024. For good."

Sam's eyebrows shoot up. "You can't."

Who are you and what have you done with Sam? I frown. "Isn't that what you wanted from the start?"

"At first," he admits. "But I've never seen Grace so happy."

"You don't understand."

"Enlighten me."

I need movement to settle my nerves, so I get up and rinse my cup. This is the part I've dreaded. Can I trust him to keep my secret?

"Lars is going to kill me, and this time, I don't think there's anything I can do to stop it."

That catches him off guard and he shifts forward in his seat. "I'm guessing you read this online."

I nod and slide the article I printed before leaving 2024 across the table. He reads it and his face darkens.

"Holy shit," he mutters.

"Yeah. That's what I said."

"He did a tour in the army, you know. Sniper."

This just went from bad to worse. "Of course he did."

For a moment, the room is silent except for the tick of the kitchen clock.

I grab my cup from the sink, fill it halfway with coffee, and lean against the counter. "The band got offered a record contract."

Sam taps the paper in front of him. "Green Diamond Records?"

"Yeah. Grace found out yesterday. You should've seen her face. Do me a favor—act surprised when she tells you."

He exhales through his nose and his expression tightens. "That puts you at the scene of the crime."

"August 2, 1978." I shake my head. "Even if we stop him this time, he'll keep coming. The only way I can stay ahead of him is by bouncing back and forth to Google his next move. Clearly, that's not an option. It's too much pressure, too much of a risk for myself and for Grace. I don't want to spend the rest of my life kicking the can down the road, lying to Grace about it, and hoping I'm alive to kick it again the next time."

"What about another restraining order?"

"I have no proof, no grounds to justify it. How would I explain knowing about a future event? People don't put much stock in time travel. You, of all people, should know that."

He has no response. What could he say?

"I don't know how to stop him this time," I add. "And I sure as hell don't want to be the one who ruins Grace's career in the process."

Sam slides the article back across the table, his fingers tapping lightly against the edge. "Grace doesn't know any of this?"

"No." My voice is firm. "And I want to keep it that way. Yesterday, I floated the idea of moving to 2024, but she shot it down. She loves it here. Her career's finally taking off. I can't stand in her way."

He studies me for a moment before leaning back in his chair and folding his arms. "So, if you stay, you're a dead man, and her career's over."

"Hardly the happy ending I hoped for." The words stick in my throat. "But if I leave, she'll find another guitar player. Someone who can keep the dream alive for her. I need to give her time to find that person, and time..." I stare into my coffee. "Time is the one thing I don't have."

Sam exhales heavily, his gaze narrowing. "What's waiting for you back home?"

"A whole lot of nothing," I admit, my voice flat. "Actually, I don't even know anymore. Every time I go back, things are worse than before. But this isn't about me. I have to think about what's best for Grace."

His sharp eyes cut through the silence. "You're serious about this, aren't you?"

I meet his gaze, letting the silence speak for me.

He runs a hand through his hair and lets out a sharp breath. "For the record, I'm sorry for the way I treated you when you first got here. You're a stand-up guy. The kind of man I always hoped Grace would settle down with."

You and me both. "Bad timing, I guess."

Sam shakes his head. "I don't want to see you go, but I respect the hell out of you for putting her dreams above your own happiness."

I force a nod, but it doesn't soften the blow. His approval doesn't make this hurt any less. It's the right thing to do. Grace and I were doomed from the start—like Romeo and Juliet. I hate that story.

"What are you going to tell Grace?"

"I don't know." I set my coffee on the counter. "But I need to walk away from the best thing I've ever had."

"What if you tell her the truth?"

I let out a bitter laugh, shaking my head. "I can't force her to make that kind of decision."

"So, you're going to make it for her?"

"There's no win-win here, Sam. I'm doing this because I love her. Because I want the best for her."

"And you don't think that's you?"

"Unfortunately, no," I whisper.

Chapter Forty-Six

Love Hurts – Nazareth (1975)

The front door opens, and Grace steps inside, a thin layer of sweat on her brow from the heat outside. She stops short when she sees Sam at the table. Her eyes dart between the two of us.

"Well, this is unexpected." She sets her bag down by the door.

Sam stands and gives her a small nod. "I'm on my way out."

Grace arches an eyebrow, clearly suspicious. "What's going on?"

"Nothing you need to worry about." Sam pats her shoulder as he moves toward the door. "You had a good day at work, I hope?"

"Yeah, it was fine." She's cautious, her gaze shifting to me.

Sam pulls the door open but pauses. "Take care of yourself, Angus." His tone is laced with something heavier than usual. He doesn't wait for a response before he steps out and lets the door click shut behind him.

Grace crosses her arms. "What was that about?"

I rinse out my cup in the sink. "He stopped by to drop off my new ID. No big deal."

"That's great." She watches me for a moment and walks to the fridge. She pulls out a soda, cracks it open, and leans against the counter, her eyes fixed on a distant spot on the floor.

"You're home early." My voice is light, testing the waters.

"A little. Is that a problem?"

And there it is. A remnant of last night's fight, still lingering in the air between us. I swallow hard and glance toward her, but she's not looking at me.

"I, uh…" I hesitate as I search for the right words. "I've been thinking about what you said yesterday. About staying here."

She looks up. "Yeah?"

My heart pounds in my chest, every beat echoing in my ears. I can feel the weight of the words I need to say, and they're stuck in my throat, refusing to come out.

"You're right," I say finally, the words awkward and stiff. "This is where you belong. You've worked hard for this, and you shouldn't have to give it up for anything."

Her eyes soften, but the tension in her shoulders doesn't fade. "I wasn't trying to be harsh, Angus. I… I'm happy here. I thought we could be happy here together."

"I know."

The silence stretches between us, heavy and unbearable.

She sighs and sets her soda down. "Look, I'm sorry about last night. I shouldn't have snapped at you. It's just… everything's moving so fast. The band, the contest, the record contract. It's all I've ever wanted, and now it's happening, and I feel like I'm barely keeping up."

"You don't have to apologize." My voice is just above a whisper. "You've got nothing to be sorry for."

She steps closer, her hand brushing against mine on the counter. "I don't want to fight with you. We're supposed to be in this together, right?"

I glance down at her hand, her fingers so close to mine. I want to grab her hand, pull her into me, and tell her everything. Tell her why I have to leave, why it's the only way to keep her safe and happy. But I can't.

Instead, I nod and force a tight smile. "Yeah. We're in this together."

She studies me for a moment, her eyes searching mine. "You're acting weird. Did something happen with Sam? Is there something you're not telling me?"

I shake my head. "No. Nothing happened."

She doesn't look convinced, but she doesn't push. "Okay." She pulls her hand away. "I'm gonna grab a quick shower."

"Sure."

She disappears down the hall, and I let out a shaky breath. The sound of the shower echoes through the quiet apartment, and I stare at the floor, my chest heavy with the weight of what I'm about to do.

The shower stops, and a few minutes later, Grace emerges from the hallway, her hair damp and curling around her shoulders. She's wearing one of her oversized band T-shirts. She glances at me as she towels off her hair.

"You still look like something's eating at you."

"I'm fine," I say too quickly, my voice sharper than I intended.

She narrows her eyes. "You sure? Because now you're snapping at me."

I push off the counter and walk toward the living room, needing the space to think, to breathe. "I said I'm fine, Grace."

She follows me. "No, you're not. You've been on edge ever since I walked in the door. If something's wrong, just say it."

"Why does it always have to be about what's wrong?" I snap, spinning to face her. "Can't we let it be for once?"

Confusion clouds her eyes. "Where is this coming from? Are we seriously fighting again? I thought we talked about this."

I hate myself for every word that comes out of my mouth, but I can't stop now. I need to push her, to make her angry enough to shove me out the door so I don't have to be the one to leave.

"You talked." My voice is cold. "I listened. That's all we ever do—your plans, your career, your life. Did you ever think about what I want?"

Her mouth drops open in shock, but she recovers quickly, her tone sharp. "That's not fair, Angus. I've always considered you. You're the one who keeps pulling away."

"Maybe because I realize I don't fit here, Grace. I don't fit in your world, and I never will."

"Where is this coming from?" she demands, her voice rising. "Yesterday, you were the one talking about a future here. What changed?"

"I finally opened my eyes and realized we're fooling ourselves. This isn't going to work."

Her confusion gives way to hurt. "You don't mean that," she whispers.

I look away, unable to meet her gaze. If I see the pain in her eyes, I'll break. I'll never find the strength to leave.

"I do." My voice is low and unsteady. "I've been lying to myself, thinking I could make this work, but I can't. You deserve someone who can actually keep up with you, Grace. Someone who belongs here."

She takes a deep breath. "What are you willing to sacrifice for love, Angus?"

Shit! "Don't go there, Grace."

"Don't go there, *Grace*?! I'm not the one who's bailing."

Her breath catches, and when she speaks again, her voice trembles with anger. "You're such a coward, Angus. You're not even giving us a chance."

"Maybe I am a coward," I say, turning toward the door. "But it's better this way."

She steps closer, her voice breaking. "You don't get to make that choice for me. I love you, Angus. Doesn't that mean anything?"

Every fiber of my being screams at me to turn around, take her in my arms, and tell her I love her too. But instead, I harden my voice. "It doesn't change the fact that I don't belong here."

Her silence is deafening.

Finally, she steps back, her voice cold and hollow. "Fine. If that's how you feel, then go."

I nod, but the lump in my throat makes it impossible to speak. I open the closet door and grab my guitar and the suitcase I packed after Grace left for work this morning.

Grace plants her hands on her hips. "Seriously?! Your bags are already packed?"

Her glare follows me outside before I let the door close behind me. I flinch as something shatters against the inside of the closed door.

The warm air hits me like a slap, and I stumble down the steps, my vision blurry. Every step feels like a betrayal, but I force myself to keep walking.

I'm not sure who I hate more right now—myself, for breaking her heart, or the universe, for making this the only way to save her.

Chapter Forty-Seven

Don't Look Back – Boston (1978)

My timing is off once again. I stop and drop my suit-case in the middle of the sidewalk. It's Wednesday afternoon. The portal won't be open until Friday, if I'm lucky. I walk aimlessly through the streets, my guitar slung over one shoulder, while the summer heat clings to me like a second skin. I don't have a destination, not really. I just know I can't go back to Grace—not after the way I left.

The familiar orange roofline of a Howard Johnson's up ahead brings with it a sigh of relief. I shuffle into the lobby, where the air conditioner hums. The desk clerk looks up with a polite but detached smile. I slide some cash across the counter, and within minutes, I'm alone in a standard–issue room with pale blue walls and a bed that's too neatly made.

I drop my suitcase on the floor and sit on the edge of the mattress. The silence presses down on me, broken only by the muffled hum of traffic outside. My stomach growls, but I can't bring myself to eat. Every bite would taste like regret.

My mind spirals again. I pull up the photo app on my phone and stare at her picture. Tears fall as I tap the trashcan icon. My finger hovers over the confirmation button for a moment before I tap *Cancel* and toss the phone on the bed.

The next day crawls by in a haze. I wander the town like a ghost, drifting from one unfamiliar street to another. Coffee shops, diners, benches in the park—nothing holds my attention for long. I avoid anywhere I might run into Grace. Every time I pass a phone booth, I fight the urge to call her.

Friday morning finally rolls around, and my appetite is making a comeback. I check out of the hotel and buy a light breakfast at the coffee shop. My plan is to slip into the building, head to the basement, and wait for the portal to open. One step into the future, and all of this will be behind me—at least, that's what I tell myself.

Sirens cut through the hum of conversation and clinking plates. I pay my bill, gather my bags and step outside. As I approach my destination, my stomach drops, and my breakfast nearly makes another appearance.

Fire trucks and police cars block the street. First responders swarm the building, stretching yellow caution tape around the crumbling facade. A crowd has gathered, their eyes wide as they murmur and point at the damage.

My heart pounds as I push my way closer.

Part of the building has collapsed. Bricks and debris have spilled onto the sidewalk. Faint tendrils of smoke rise from the wreckage, and I feel like the air's been knocked out of me.

"Angus!"

I turn to see Sam weave through the crowd toward me. He grabs my shoulder.

"What happened?" I manage, my voice hoarse.

"The building partially collapsed early this morning," he says. "No one's allowed near it."

"The basement," I whisper. "Do you think it's still intact?"

"I don't know. There's no way to check right now."

I glance back at the wreckage as a cold weight settles in my chest. If the portal's gone, then what?

Sam pulls me aside, his voice low. "Grace told me you left."

I close my eyes and brace for what comes next.

"She's pissed," he continues. "She told me you didn't even try to fight for her. She thinks you gave up."

The words hit hard. I open my mouth to respond but stop. What's the point?

Sam's expression softens. "I know what you're doing. But I have to ask—are you sure about this?"

"It's the only way," I snap, louder than I intended. Heads in the crowd turn briefly, but I don't care. "She's better off without me."

Sam studies me for a moment as his jaw tightens. "You're leaving her with a lot of questions and no answers."

I look away, unable to meet his eyes.

The crowd stirs as a firefighter steps forward and warns everyone to back up. "This building's unstable. We need everyone to clear the area."

People start to disperse, but I stay rooted to the spot. My escape plan is crumbling, literally and figuratively.

Sam grips my arm. "I hope you know what you're doing."

He walks away, leaving me to stare at the wreckage.

The day stretches on endlessly. I find a quiet spot at the end of the alley where I can watch the wrecked building without drawing attention. I have no plan, just a gnawing sense of desperation.

Firefighters come and go. They cordon off more of the site and mark it with warnings I can't afford to heed. The heat bears down on me, and my stomach growls, but I ignore both.

By dusk, the activity around the building dwindles. The crowd thins to a handful of curious stragglers as the yellow caution tape flutters in the evening breeze. The light casts long shadows that make the building look even more foreboding.

I wait, every nerve taut. A few more minutes pass, and the last firefighter pulls away in his truck. The street falls silent.

This is my chance.

I move quickly, keeping to the shadows. When I reach the perimeter, I duck beneath the caution tape and make my way to the side of the building where the damage looks the least severe.

The faint hum of crickets plays like static in my ears as I step cautiously over broken glass and fallen bricks that shift under my feet. The blocked entrance leaves me no choice but to climb over a jagged pile of rubble where the wall has partially caved in.

I pull out my phone and turn on the flashlight. The bright beam cuts through the encroaching darkness, but I keep it low, to avoid unwanted attention.

Halfway up the unstable pile, I stumble. My heart lurches as I catch myself on a twisted beam, but the sudden jolt sends my phone flying from my hand.

"No!"

I watch in horror as it tumbles and disappears into a narrow crevice between the rubble. The faint glow of its flashlight flickers like a taunt before it vanishes completely.

Panic sets in. My hands scrape against jagged edges as I search frantically for the spot where the phone fell. My mind races. I can't leave it here. A piece of future technology lying around in 1978 could change everything.

I drop to my knees and paw through the debris. The crevice where it fell is barely wide enough to fit my arm. My fingers brush something cold and metallic, but it slips further out of reach.

"Damn it," I mutter, my voice shaky.

Minutes stretch into what feels like an eternity. Sweat drips into my eyes as I pry away smaller chunks of debris and strain to reach the phone. The sharp edge of a brick cuts into my palm, but I barely notice.

Finally, my fingers close around the smooth surface of the phone. Relief floods through me as I pull it free. The crack in the screen has spread, but the flashlight still works.

I let out a shaky breath and sit back for a moment. *Focus, Angus!* I stand and turn back to the task at hand, weaving my way deeper into the building. Every step feels like a gamble, but I press on.

I pause at the basement entrance and test each step as I descend into the darkness.

The air grows colder as I reach the bottom, and my pulse quickens as I feel the hum. The portal is intact.

My footsteps echo in the quiet space. I hesitate for a moment as my thoughts flicker back to Grace. Her smile, her laugh, the way she'd look at me like I was the only person in the world.

"I'm sorry," I whisper.

With a deep breath, I step into the portal. The world blurs around me and swallows me whole.

Chapter Forty-Eight

Just What I Needed – The Cars (1978)

The portal spits me out like a bad memory it wants nothing to do with. I stumble and land on my hands and knees. The weight of the journey clings to me as I struggle to my feet—relief to be back in 2024, dread for what might have changed, and a hollow ache that echoes with Grace's absence. The warm night air wraps around me as I step out of the cave, but it does little to comfort me. I'm three hundred miles and forty-six years away from the only woman I've ever loved.

The ATV sits near the mouth of the cave, but something's off. My pulse quickens as I notice it's not the same one I left behind. It's a newer model—sleek, polished, and unfamiliar. My fingers hesitate as I set my guitar and suitcase in the back and start it up. The engine hums smoothly, a sound that feels wrong.

The house is quiet when I arrive, but the back porch light is on. My stomach sinks. I never replaced that bulb. Everything about this feels foreign, like I've returned to someone else's life. My hands tremble as I slide open the barn door enough to slip inside.

The smell of hay and animals hits me immediately, earthy and sharp. The barn is alive. A commotion erupts to my right—hoof stomping, snorting, and the unmistakable neighing of horses. Horses? My barn hasn't housed animals in years.

I slide the door closed behind me and fumble for the light switch. The sudden brightness reveals two horses in separate stalls, their dark eyes wide and fixed on me. I freeze, hands raised.

"Whoa. Steady, now." My voice is low and even, though inside I'm unraveling.

I approach the first horse from the side, my movements deliberate. "Easy, boy. I'm not here to hurt you." He watches me closely, his ears twitching. He nickers softly when I stroke his neck, and the tension in his frame eases.

The second horse shifts in his stall, craning his head toward me. I move over and repeat the same calming gestures, and he snorts, his warm breath brushing my hand. I stroke his neck and whisper reassuring words until both horses settle.

With the barn quiet again, my eyes sweep the space. My gaze lands on the corner where my GTO should be, but all that remains is the folded blue tarp that had covered it for years. I swallow hard. Someone's been here. Someone else lives here now.

I sit down on a bale of hay, my guitar and suitcase beside me. I'll have to figure out who owns this place in the morning. For now, emotional and physical exhaustion drag at me. The hay isn't much of a bed, and a folded tarp isn't much of a pillow, but I lie down anyway and close my eyes. Sleep takes me faster than I expect.

A loud scrape jolts me awake. The barn door slides open, and sunlight floods the space. I sit up, groggy and disoriented, rubbing my eyes. My jaw drops as I squint toward the light.

"Gramps?"

There he stands in his worn John Deere cap and faded denim overalls, hands planted on his hips. His weathered face is unmistakable.

"Angus? What in the world are you doin' in here?"

I scramble to my feet, my legs shaky as I cross the barn in a few stumbling steps and throw my arms around his chest. "What are *you* doing here?"

He takes a step back to steady us, his eyes wide with alarm. "What am I doing here? Last I checked, I live here!"

I pull back, staring at him like he's a ghost. "You're alive." The words tumble out before I can stop them.

He grips my shoulders, squinting into my eyes. "Why wouldn't I be? Angus, what's gotten into you, son?"

Where do I even begin? "Nothing," I lie, shaking my head. "I… I'm just glad to see you."

His hand drifts to the back of his neck, his expression caught between curiosity and concern. "Well, all right, then. You're actin' mighty strange. Your gran's been worried sick about you."

"Gran?" My heart skips a beat.

"Yeah, Gran. You sure you're feelin' all right?"

"Yup."

He watches me gather my things. "What the—?"

Before he can finish, I dart past him, grinning despite myself. "I'll tell you later. I gotta go see Gran."

★★★

I barrel into the house. My guitar case thumps against the doorframe as I stumble into the kitchen. The warm scent of biscuits and sausage gravy wraps around me, dragging memories behind it. Everything looks familiar but off, like someone rearranged my life while I wasn't looking. The worn carpet has been replaced, Gran's patchwork quilt is folded over the back of my chair, and the rooster-shaped cookie jar is back on the counter.

"Gran?"

She appears in the doorway, her hair still pinned in that no-nonsense bun. It's like seeing a photograph come to life. The moment she sees me, her expression hardens.

"Well, look what the cat dragged in." She crosses her arms. "You got some nerve, boy."

I blink, taken aback. "Gran?"

"Don't you *Gran* me," she snaps, planting her hands on her hips. "You been gone for days without a word. You think this house runs itself?"

"I—what? I mean, I—"

"Don't you stutter at me like a busted record. Spit it out. Where in Sam Hill have you been?"

This isn't the Gran I saw at my parents' funeral, bitter and broken. This is the woman who raised me—sharp-tongued and unyielding as a summer drought.

I have to ask. "Are Mom and Pop..." My voice trails off.

She scrunches up her face like she just smelled something awful. "Mom and Pop? Are you feeling all right, son?"

"I'm fine, I think." I set my guitar and suitcase down. "I—I didn't mean to worry you. I just needed... some time."

"Time?" She narrows her eyes. "You've had more 'time' than a preacher on Sunday, and what do you have to show for it? Lookin' like you ain't had a decent meal in days. Lord help me, Angus, you're as thin as a fence rail."

I can't help the small, relieved smile that tugs at my lips. She's chewing me out like I'm a kid who missed curfew, and I've never been happier to hear it.

"I'm sorry, Gran," I whisper. "Really."

Her eyes narrow further, and for a moment, I think she's going to let loose again. But then her shoulders sag, and she shakes her head with a sigh. "What am I gonna do with you, huh?"

Before I can answer, she pulls me into a hug, her arms strong and sure. I freeze for a second, caught off guard, then wrap my arms around her. The familiar smell of lavender soap and old wood fills my nose.

She pulls back and studies me. "You scared me half to death, Angus. You can't go runnin' off like that."

"I'm sorry."

"You're still a boy. And without a mama and papa to raise you right, that responsibility falls on Gramps and me. We're old, Angus. We don't have that much fight left in us."

I nod, respectfully. "Yes, ma'am."

She lets out a huff and shakes her head. "Well, go call your gramps and wash your hands. We're havin' biscuits and gravy for breakfast."

I do as I'm told, then sink into one of the chairs at the table. The familiar creak grounds me as I watch her. For a moment, I sit there and take it all in—the clatter of plates, the hum of the fridge, the way she mutters to herself as she works. It's like I've stepped back into a life I thought I'd lost.

She sets our plates on the table. We say grace, and dig in.

"So," she says, breaking the silence. "You gonna tell me what's really goin' on, or do I have to drag it out of you?"

I pause, my fork halfway to my mouth, and my hand shaking. I set it down and look at her. She's leaning forward, her sharp eyes boring into mine, but she remains silent.

"Like I said, it's complicated." I rub the back of my neck.

She snorts. "Life's complicated. That's no excuse for keepin' secrets."

I sigh and lean back in my chair. "I… I needed to get away for a while. Clear my head."

"And I reckon whatever's botherin' you has a name."

I hesitate, the word caught in my throat. "Grace."

"You didn't get her in trouble, did you?"

"What? No. Nothing like that." I shake my head and backpedal when I see the look on her face. "It's everything. The past few days have been… intense."

She doesn't respond right away, just watches me with that same steady gaze. Finally, she reaches across the table and places her hand over mine.

"Whatever it is, Angus, you don't have to carry it alone. You've got people who care about you. Don't forget that."

Gramps nods, his mouth full of food.

I swallow the lump in my throat. "Thanks, Gran."

She pats my hand before pulling hers back. "Now, eat up before it gets cold."

I glance at Gramps, who hasn't said a word the whole time, and his eyes meet mine. They tell me he knows more than he's letting on.

Chapter Forty-Nine

Wish You Were Here – Pink Floyd (1975)

Each step groans under the weight as I haul my guitar and suitcase up the stairs. The air carries the same familiar scent of lavender. Gran must still be tucking her little sachets into every nook and cranny like she used to before she disappeared. But that was in a different timeline. Apparently, she stuck around in this one because Gramps came back. Keeping it all straight feels like a losing battle.

I'm relieved to see all my stuff is still in my room. My empty guitar stand and amplifier wait in the corner, like they've been holding their breath for me to come back. Rows of vinyl records line the shelf under the window, every spine a piece of who I was—or thought I was. The posters on the walls are a little faded now, the edges curling. Zeppelin. Pink Floyd. Black Sabbath.

I set my guitar in the stand and drop my suitcase onto the bed. My hands linger on the frayed edge of the old flannel blanket for a moment before I sit down. I'd moved into Mom and Pop's room after they died for the extra space. Now it feels too big, too cold, and too empty without Grace.

I had everything I thought I needed back then—music, my own space, a chance to make it on my own. But Grace changed all of that. She showed me what it felt like to share my life, to have a dream intertwined with someone else's.

What the hell am I supposed to do now? I sit on the edge of my bed, elbows on my knees, and stare at the floor like it might have answers. Grace is out there—forty-six years away—building a life without me. I'm sure she hates me for walking out the way I did. That thought alone is enough to rip me apart.

Did I make the right choice? Could I have stayed? I fall back onto the bed and stare at the ceiling, searching for something—anything—that feels right about what I did.

I'd read my obituary. Twice. Lars wouldn't have stopped until I was dead, and then where would that have left Grace? Her career? Her dreams? All of it would've crumbled because of me. A rock and a hard place.

I sit up with a start and grab my phone. A quick search for *Hallowed Ground* pulls up a few articles, mostly old news about the songwriting contest. The latest article is dated a week after I left—the band broke up before they recorded their first album. My stomach sinks. No mention of what happened to any of the band members after that.

I type Grace's name into the search bar and get the same results.

Blowing out a long breath, I dial Waldo. It rings twice before he answers.

"I guess this means you're back."

I feel him out cautiously, unsure if he knows about the portal. I don't want to sound too crazy if he doesn't. "Back from where?"

"Angus, it's me. I know about your time-traveling escapades."

I let out a small laugh. "Sorry. Can't always keep track of who knows what."

Before I can say more, Gran's voice cuts through the air like a whip. "Angus!"

"Hang on." I pull the phone away, sighing hard.

"I'm on the phone with Waldo."

"I don't care if you're talking to the governor. Gramps needs help with the chores!"

She's still sore because I left for a few days without telling her.

"Be right there!"

"Sorry, I gotta go. I… I just wanted to let you know I'm back in one piece. We'll catch up later."

"Sure," Waldo says. "Thanks for the call."

I take another look around the room, but it's Grace's face that flickers in my mind. I swallow hard, pushing her image away, and head for the stairs to face this strange new chapter of my old life.

Gramps is in the barn when I catch up to him.

"What do you need me to do?" I try to sound like I'm ready for anything.

He waves me off and leans against a post. "Everything's done. I wanted some privacy so we can talk."

I fold my arms and wait, skeptical but patient.

He studies me for a moment. "You found the portal, didn't you?"

"Is it that obvious?"

"And Grace?"

My shoulders slump. The words spill out before I can stop them. "I fell in love with her in 1978."

"I'm sorry, Angus." His voice is soft. "I can't imagine what you're going through."

"Not many people can." My throat tightens, and I pause to clear it. "In the timeline I came from, you went through the portal and never came back. I looked for you in 1978."

He hesitates. "I went back a few times. Stayed long enough to place a few bets. I bet on Cassius Clay in '64, Nixon in '68, and the Jets in Super Bowl III. I could have really cleaned up if Colorado had a lottery back then."

His expression tells me there's more.

"I'm not proud of myself, but I made enough to keep the ranch running."

"No judgment," I say with a reassuring tone. "I thought about it a few times myself."

"I started getting headaches and tremors," he says. "Convinced myself it was the universe's way of telling me to stay put."

He anticipates my next question. "They eventually stopped."

"How did you know about my—?"

"I noticed at breakfast. Didn't want to say anything in front of Gran." He places a hand on my shoulder. "You'll get through this, Angus. Just give it time."

"I think I messed up, Gramps." I spit the words out like they taste bad in my mouth. I spill my guts, telling him about Lars, the record deal, and how I bailed on Grace instead of telling her the truth.

He lifts his cap and scratches his head. "That's a real pickle."

I stare at the floor. "I thought maybe you'd have some grandfatherly advice."

He sets his cap back on his head and straightens up. "Here's what I can tell you from experience. Regret from honesty is easier to bear than regret from deception."

I nod, grateful for his understanding. A silence descends as I absently kick the straw around on the floor.

He places a hand on my shoulder. "Come on. I want to show you something. Maybe it'll lift your spirits."

He leads me to a two-car garage that wasn't there the last time I left.

"How long has this been here?" My heart is already pounding.

"Couple of years."

Gramps pulls the door up on its rails and flips on the lights. My knees nearly give out, and I momentarily forget about my troubles. There, brilliant under the fluorescent lights, is a fully restored, Bermuda Blue 1970 Pontiac GTO.

"No way!" I can't believe my eyes. It's exactly how I always imagined it. "Who did this?"

"You did. With a little help from your gramps."

Who are you, Angus? And what have you done with the shithead? "Can I take it for a spin?"

Gramps beams with pride as he tosses me the keys. "It's your car, Angus. Go on."

Sliding into the driver's seat, I grip the wheel and feel a small flicker of hope. Maybe, just maybe, I can start over.

★★★

They say time heals all wounds, but I call bullshit on that. Gramps says it's a little early to be drawing those kinds of conclusions, but what does he know about losing someone like Grace?

On the third day back, I catch up with Waldo. He has some time off from his summer job, so we meet for lunch. Seeing him again is like coming up for air after being underwater too long. We swap stories, compare notes, and try to make sense of our scrambled memories. Not all of them match. He's at Cal Tech now instead of Stanford, majoring in something I can't even pronounce.

He remembers traveling with me and meeting Grace—that much stayed the same in this timeline. I press him for some much-needed validation.

"Do you think I did the right thing?" As soon as I say it, I want to take it back.

"It doesn't matter what I think. You're the one who has to live with your decision."

Tell me something I *don't* know. The conversation ends abruptly. It's obvious where it's headed. I've asked myself the same question a hundred times, and the answer is always the same.

I tell myself I did the right thing, the only thing I could've done. If I go back, I'm a dead man. Grace's life is ruined. Nobody wins. If only there was some way we could be together. Apparently, our stars are crossed.

But that's not the point, is it? I should have told her the truth. We should have made the decision together. I leave the restaurant feeling worse than when I arrived.

Life on the ranch has settled into a rhythm—or maybe it's a rut. I pick up a few shifts at Rusty's again, mostly for the employee discount. Between chores, work, and music, I stay busy enough to keep from spiraling.

I clean out the loft in the barn and move my electric guitar and amp up there so I can crank the volume past three. Gran and Gramps seem to be hard of hearing when it comes to everything but my music. Gramps felt bad and bought me an acoustic guitar to play in the house. I guess he used money that Treasure Hunt 2.0 never found.

But no amount of work or music makes the pain go away. I don't miss Grace any less, and I still can't picture spending the rest of my life without her. I keep putting one foot in front of the other because, well, what else can I do? And our song? I haven't played it. I can't, and probably never will.

On the bright side, Gran's finally eased up on me. I'm not sure how much she knows about where I went or how I met Grace—we don't talk about it—but she's let go of the drill sergeant routine.

Chapter Fifty

Baby, Come Back – Player (1977)

The bell above the door at Rusty's Auto Parts rattles for the hundredth time as another customer leaves, and I grit my teeth as the sound drills into my skull. The store is quiet again, but my mind is anything but. Images of Grace interrupt my work.

I pull up the selfie I took with her and set my phone next to the register. It's been a week since I left her, a week since I walked away without telling her the truth. You couldn't tell from the two smiling faces that stare back at me. I can't keep doing this.

"Angus, you okay?" Rusty's gruff voice jolts me back to reality. He's leaning on the counter, clipboard in hand, his ever-present cigar clamped between his teeth.

The knot in my chest tightens. "Rusty." My voice cracks. "I need to leave."

"Leave?" He blinks and his cigar bobs. "The hell you talkin' about?"

"I'm sorry. I can't explain. But I have to go. Right now."

He studies me, and his expression softens in a way I don't expect. "You're chasin' somethin', aren't you?"

I nod, swallowing hard. "Yeah. And if I don't do this now, I'll lose it forever."

Rusty sighs and shakes his head. "Fine. Go."

"Thank you." I pull off my apron and toss it onto the counter. "I won't forget this."

"You better not," he grumbles and waves me off. "Now, get outta here before I change my mind."

By the time I get home, my heart is racing. I push through the back door, my boots pounding against the floor.

"You're home early." Gran's voice is sharp with suspicion. "What's the rush?"

"I won't be home for supper," I blurt out, taking the stairs two at a time.

"Angus Walker, you stop right there!" she hollers.

"I can't, Gran. I'll explain later."

In my room, I yank my guitar case out of the closet. I toss a few clothes and all the old money I have into a duffel bag. My hands shake so badly I can barely zip it shut. My mind flashes to Grace—her face when I left her, the hurt in her eyes. She deserves the truth. We'll figure it out together.

I clatter back down the stairs, nearly tripping over the last step. Gran is standing at the bottom, arms crossed. She looks like she's about to tear me a new one.

"Boy, you're gonna tell me what's going on, or I swear—"

I stop cold, breathing hard, my heart caught between panic and purpose. "Please, Gran, I… I need to do this."

"Do what?"

"You wouldn't understand."

Her back stiffens. "I'm old, Angus, not stupid."

"You once told me something when I was a kid, right after you taught me that Dylan song on Stella."

Her brow furrows, unsure where I'm going with this.

"You said, 'What's the point of living if you're not fighting for something?'"

She blinks. The words hit her. I see it.

"Well…" I swallow. "I finally found something worth fighting for."

After an awkward moment, she steps aside, her lips pressed into a tight line. "Be careful, Angus. Whatever this is… just be careful."

"I will." I lean in and kiss her cheek before I bolt out the door.

The ATV roars as I gun it, and the wind slaps my face. I have to tell Grace the truth. I have to make this right.

The heat rising off the ground ahead distorts everything, making the horizon shimmer like a mirage. Something is moving out there, blurred and indistinct. I slow the ATV and squint through the waves. My pulse picks up. Is that… a person? Out here?

I press on until the shape becomes clearer. A figure walking toward me. My hands tighten on the handlebars.

As I get closer, recognition slams into me like a freight train. The way the hair moves in the breeze. The swing of her arms. *It's Grace.*

My vision blurs and my heart hammers so loud it drowns out the roar of the engine. I gun the ATV, the tires spitting up dust as I surge forward, my eyes locked on her. She stops walking and her hand comes up to shield her eyes from the sun. It's her. It's really her.

I slam on the brakes so hard the ATV fishtails, skidding to a stop. My legs move before I even think, stumbling off the seat and running toward her.

"Grace!" Her name comes out as a gasp, carried away on the hot wind.

She stands there, still as a statue, her face unreadable at first. As I get closer, I see the flicker of something familiar—relief, or maybe the beginnings of a smile.

"Angus." Her voice trembles. "I found you."

She sets her bags down, then plants her hands on her hips, barely able to hold back a grin. "Were you trying to ditch me?"

"I obviously didn't try hard enough," I say with a smirk.

She steps forward hesitantly, her voice steady. "I couldn't do it, Angus. I couldn't stay there. Not without you."

I'm afraid if I touch her, she might disappear like a cruel mirage. "How...? You're here. How is this even possible?" My voice cracks under the weight of my disbelief.

"Sam showed me the portal."

I point to my stuff in the back of the ATV. "I was on my way there now. To see you, to tell you the truth."

"He said you'd need me more than the timeline needed me to stay put."

"Is he here?"

She scrunches up her nose. "I hope that's okay." She glances behind her. "He went back to grab the rest of our stuff."

"Back through the portal?"

"It was too much for one trip. He's going to need some help when he gets here."

I nod, my heart racing, then pull her into my arms. I hold her so tight I'm afraid I might crush her, but she lets out a soft laugh against my chest.

"You're here," I whisper, my voice thick with emotion.

She tilts her head to look up at me. Her hand brushes against my cheek. "I didn't belong there alone. I don't care what happens or what it takes—we belong together."

I take her bags and set them in the back with mine while she climbs into the shotgun seat.

"Let's get you home. I'll come back for Sam later."

Gran is in the kitchen cooking supper when we get to the house. She turns.

Before I can say anything, boots thump on the porch behind us, and we turn to see Gramps wipe his hands on a rag as he steps inside. His brows lift in surprise at the scene before him.

"Well, I'll be damned." He mutters as he glances from Grace to me. "Guess this old world ain't done with miracles just yet."

Grace takes a step back and slips her hand into mine. She looks from Gramps to Gran, then back to me, her expression puzzled. "I thought—"

"I know," I whisper. "You can imagine my surprise when I got back and found them both here."

Gran cuts in, her voice sharp but teasing. "Well? Are you gonna introduce us to your lady friend, or do I have to do it myself?"

After I introduce everyone, Gramps gives me a wink, and Gran gives Grace a quick once-over, her eyes narrowing.

"What?" Grace asks cautiously.

Gran smirks. "Angus never brings any girls around here."

"Gran!" I groan, heat rising to my face.

Gramps chuckles, and Grace politely covers her mouth to stifle a laugh.

"Will she be staying for dinner?"

"Yes, but we'll need to set two extra plates."

Gran tilts her head. "Two?"

"Yes, ma'am," Grace says. "Sam will be here shortly. He's getting the rest of our luggage."

I jump in. "Grace and Sam will be staying with us for a little while."

Gran straightens, her eyes wide. "And who might this Sam fella be who you've got hauling your luggage?" she presses, fixing Grace with a firm stare. "You're not one of them snooty rich girls with a butler, are you?"

Grace quickly shakes her head. "Oh no. Sam's my dad. He came with me from—"

"Denver," I cut in, hoping to steer the conversation away from anything timeline-related.

Gran raises a brow. "Well, around here, we show some respect to our elders. Might want to keep that in mind."

"Okay, that's enough," I say, squeezing Grace's hand. "We'll be out on the porch."

Gran waves us off with a smirk. "Suit yourselves. I'll set a couple more plates for dinner."

Grace and I settle on the porch swing, and I can't stop staring at her, afraid she might vanish if I blink.

She catches my gaze and smiles. "What?"

"I still can't believe you're here."

She takes my hand, her touch soft but steady. "Someone once asked me what I'd be willing to sacrifice for love."

I tilt my head and smile. "What did you tell them?"

"I told them I didn't know."

"And now?"

Her grip tightens, her voice soft but firm. "Everything."

We lean in, our lips inches apart, when the door creaks open behind us.

Gran's voice cuts through. "Where are my manners? Would y'all like some sweet tea?"

I roll my eyes and glance at Grace. She nods, trying to stifle a giggle.

"Sure, Gran. Two, please."

As Gran disappears, I turn back to Grace. "I thought your career... What made you change your mind?"

She brushes her thumb over my hand. "It was you, Angus. My dad told me everything. I love that you'd sacrifice so much to save my career, but you didn't have to."

I shake my head, overwhelmed. "I couldn't be the one to take away your dream."

"You couldn't have taken it away." She smiles. "You're my dream. We can write another song. Get another deal. We did it once; we can do it again. Together."

"Okay." My voice catches. "We'll figure it out together."

Sitting there with Grace, hand in hand and fingers intertwined, I lose track of time until I spot Sam in the distance. He's walking toward us, a suitcase in each hand.

"There's Sam now." I stand. "Come on. Let's go get him."

We hop on one of the ATVs and ride out to meet him.

When we pull up, Sam sets the suitcases down and wipes his brow. "Boy, am I glad to see you. I'm getting too old for this."

"Toss 'em in the back. There're only two seats, but we'll make it work."

"There's more stuff in the cave," Sam adds, groaning.

"We'll grab it later."

Back at the house, after we unload the bags, I offer Sam my hand. He takes it, and I pull him in for a hug and a couple of solid slaps on the back.

"Thanks, man." My voice is heavy with gratitude.

"For what?"

"For not listening to me. I should've told Grace myself, let her make her own decision. I was on my way to do that when I found—"

Sam interrupts. "I know. But she was a mess after you left. I couldn't let her suffer like that."

"Well, I owe you one."

Sam follows me inside, suitcases in hand, and I make the introductions.

Gran looks him over with suspicious eyes. "So, you're the butler."

"What?" Sam blinks back surprise.

"Gran's a kidder," I say, then shoot her a glare.

Before dinner, I warn Grace and Sam to refrain from any timeline discussion. Gran's pot roast is as good as I remember, and conversation flows easily. Genuine laughter fills the house like music as we all get to know each other.

After our food settles, Grace agrees to stay with Gran and Gramps while Sam and I retrieve the rest of the stuff from the cave.

Sam follows me out to the barn to get the ATVs.

Once inside, he closes the door behind us. "We need to talk."

Chapter Fifty-One

TNT – AC/DC (1975)

The tone of Sam's voice crawls over my skin like spiders, and I second-guess Grace bringing him here. "What's on your mind?"

Sam's gaze is steady and unreadable. "The portal."

"What about it?"

He takes a deep breath, as if choosing his words carefully. "You know as well as I do that thing is dangerous. I would have destroyed it years ago, if I could have. It's a threat to everything—and everyone—we care about. It needs to go."

"I've thought about it," I admit. "But maybe it's too soon. You should take some time to make sure—"

"Time is the one thing we don't have. Keeping it open is like leaving a loaded gun lying around. Anyone could stumble across it."

I meet his gaze. "I get it, but this isn't just our decision. What about Grace?"

Sam's jaw tightens. "She's already made up her mind. She agrees with me."

"Did she tell you that?"

"She's here now. With you. That's what she wanted. What reason would there be to keep it open?"

I don't answer right away, staring down at the dusty barn floor as I weigh his words. He's right. Everyone is here, where they're supposed to be. But something in me still clings to the idea of keeping it intact, just in case.

Before I can respond, the barn door opens, and Gramps steps inside. His eyes narrow as he looks between us. "Is everything all right in here?"

"Yeah." I clear my throat. "We were talking about the portal."

Gramps lifts his eyebrows. "Oh? What about it?"

Sam answers before I can. "I think it's time to destroy it. For everyone's safety. Angus here needs a little convincing."

Gramps steps farther into the barn, his boots crunching on the straw-covered floor. He studies us both for a moment. "You want my opinion?"

We both nod.

"I reckon Sam's got a point. That portal's nothing but trouble. It's already messed with enough lives—including ours. If everyone's here now, where they're supposed to be, maybe it's time to close that chapter for good."

My stomach twists, but I accept the reality of their arguments. "I… I don't know. Destroying it feels so final."

"That's kind of the point, son," Gramps says. "You've been through enough. We all have. Sometimes moving forward means letting go of the escape hatch."

Sam's tone softens. "We're not saying it's easy, Angus. But keeping it around? It's too big a risk. For Grace. For you. For everyone."

"If we're doing this, it has to be all of us." My voice is firm. "Grace, too. I won't make the call without her."

Gramps nods in agreement. "That's fair. She's earned a say."

Sam looks like he wants to argue but holds his tongue. After a moment, he exhales sharply. "Fine. Let's get her in and get it done."

Gramps offers to fetch Grace. Minutes later, they return.

"Dad? Angus? What's going on?"

"We want to destroy the portal," Sam says matter-of-factly. "But we want to make sure everyone involved agrees."

Grace sighs. "I have no need for it anymore. I left everything behind to be here."

Sam casts me a pointed look. "Told you." He raises an eyebrow. "So, how do we do it?"

I shrug, already feeling the weight of the decision. "I've never destroyed a portal before, but I might have an idea."

I crouch by the workbench and dig around underneath it, praying Jackson's dynamite is still where I left it. My hand finds the box, and I ease it out. Gramps removes his hat as I set the box on the bench. He rubs the back of his neck with a surprised, uneasy look.

Sam's face brightens. "Perfect. Let's go." He heads for one of the ATVs. "I used to work construction back in Montana—we used dynamite for demolitions all the time."

I glance at Grace as she climbs onto the passenger seat of my ATV. "This could be dangerous—"

"After everything we've been through?" Her voice is steady. "I think I can handle it."

I nod, firing up the engine as Sam does the same. Gramps stays behind to cover for us with Gran.

Sam kills the engine first when we arrive at the cave. The pile of stuff inside the cave is bigger than I'd expected.

"Wow." I survey the mess. "Who did your packing, Paris Hilton?"

Grace tilts her head, her face a mix of confusion and mild annoyance. "I packed myself. Who is Paris—"

"Never mind." I smile. "You've got a lot of catching up to do."

I turn to Sam. "Did anyone see you carry all this stuff into the building?"

He grabs one of the bags. "I don't think so."

We load everything into the ATVs and turn our attention to the portal. Sam grabs the dynamite and handles it with confidence.

"The plan is to light the first stick and toss it in. We have to time it so it explodes while it's inside the tunnel. If that doesn't do it, the second stick should," Sam explains, his voice calm, like he's done this a thousand times before.

As he prepares to light the first fuse, I glance at Grace, but before I can speak, she lets out a blood-curdling scream.

I spin around in time to see an arm and leg emerge from the waves of the portal.

"Oh, hell," I mutter as I take an instinctive step back.

A head of long blond hair immediately follows the arm. Lars stumbles through, his eyes wide with confusion that sharpens into a murderous glare when they lock on me.

"I'll kill you, you little shit!" His voice echoes off the cave walls.

Grace screams again as Lars takes a ragged step toward me. My mind races as I consider my options. Suddenly, a bright flash and the sharp crackle of electricity fill the space.

Lars freezes mid-step, his body convulsing violently before he collapses to his knees.

Sam stands rigid, his hands wrapped around what looks like my Taser. Sparks crackle from the leads embedded in Lars's chest.

"Stay down, you son-of-a-bitch!" Sam shouts, his voice trembling but fierce.

Lars crumples into a heap, still twitching. Sam doesn't move, his hands locked on the Taser.

"Sam!" I yell, snapping him out of his trance. "You told me you destroyed that thing."

A crooked smile spreads across his face. "I lied."

"We need to push him back through the portal—now!"

Grace clings to my arm but quickly lets go to join Sam and me as we struggle to push Lars's dead weight toward the waves. He feels heavier with every inch as sweat drips into my eyes.

"Come on!" My voice is strained.

Grace throws her weight into it, and finally, the three of us manage to roll him into the waves. They part and swallow him whole.

Sam bends to grab the first stick of dynamite as the waves part again. He raises the Taser.

"Don't shoot!" I yell as a familiar black shape bursts through.

Ozzy tumbles onto the cave floor and whines when he spots me. He scrambles to his feet and dashes over to lick the happy tears from my face.

"Good boy," I whisper, wrapping my arms around his neck.

The moment of relief costs us precious time. I need to focus. Lars could recover any second.

"Sam!"

He lights the first stick and tosses it into the portal. It vanishes into the waves, but nothing happens.

"Another!"

Sam lights the second stick and lets the fuse burn before he throws it in. For a moment, there's only silence.

Then the ground rumbles. A low vibration builds into a seismic event that causes the walls of the cave to tremble.

"Run!"

We sprint for the ATVs, Ozzy barking at our heels as the cave starts to collapse around us.

Chapter Fifty-Two

All Right Now – Free (1970)

We make it outside in one piece. My heart pounds as adrenaline courses through my veins. Ozzy runs around, barking like his tail is on fire. I collapse onto the seat of the ATV. My hands tremble on the wheel as Grace slides in beside me, her face pale but determined.

My voice is low but steady. "We need to leave. Now."

The ride back to the house is quiet, save for Ozzy's occasional bark and the distant rumble of an aftershock. The vibration is faint but unmistakable. I glance over at Grace as she squeezes my arm, her gaze forward. By the time we pull into the driveway, the world feels calm again, as though nothing out of the ordinary just happened.

We unload everything into the barn and sort through the pile of belongings.

"Gran's no fool. If we try to carry all this in, she'll know something's up."

Sam nods. "I'm okay if we keep some of it out here for a while."

I pick up a bag and laugh. "Lost luggage recently delivered?"

Sam smirks. "It's not the worst story you could come up with."

We're about to head into the house when Gran swings the door open, her face a mask of worry. Gramps is right behind her, and I give him a nod and a wink.

"Is everybody all right?" Gran asks, her voice unsteady. "I thought the house was going to come down around us!"

"Everyone's fine," I assure her quickly. "Nothing to worry about."

"You think it was an earthquake?" Gran asks, her eyes darting toward the barn like she half-expects it to collapse.

Gramps steps in. "Probably one of them military exercises. They blow stuff up out there every now and again."

Gran's eyes are skeptical, but eventually she nods. "Well, I hope they're done. I don't need my nerves frayed any more than they already are."

Her expression brightens when she sees Ozzy. She stoops down as far as her back will allow to stroke the dog's head. "And who do we have here?"

"That's Ozzy," I say. "He's—"

"My dog," Grace cuts in. "I hope it's okay."

She never notices the bags, her full attention on Ozzy. "Sure, dear. He looks hungry. I'll get him something to eat." She holds the door open and follows the dog inside.

Well, that went better than I thought it would.

Later that evening, the next challenge arises: sleeping arrangements.

Gran stands in the doorway of my room, her hands on her hips. "If you two insist on sleeping in the same room," she says, her tone equal parts scolding and resignation, "Grace sleeps under the sheet, and you sleep on top. None of your important parts better be touchin'."

Grace's face turns crimson, and I bite back a groan. "Fine, Gran." There's no point in fighting her on this. I can live to argue this one another day. Sam will stay in my old room for the time being.

Life adjusts in fits and starts. I get used to Gran's hearty breakfasts again, complete with unsolicited advice on everything. Meanwhile, Grace is adapting surprisingly well to forty-six years of cultural and technological progress. She's fascinated by smartphones, though it takes her some time to grasp the idea of apps.

"So, it's like a telephone, a jukebox, a camera, and a typewriter all in one?" she asks, holding up her new phone.

We drive into town in the GTO, which turns more than a few heads. Grace blushes as I tease her. "It's not the car. It's you that's got people staring."

She smirks, but her cheeks flush. "You're such a jerk."

We both need a few things, so we stop at Walgreens on the way home. Inside, we each grab a basket, and Grace marvels at the sheer variety of products. "There's so much! Half of this didn't even exist in 1978. How does anyone decide?"

"You'll get used to it."

She waves me off. "Go on, I can handle myself. I'm not a child."

"Okay, but don't get lost," I joke, then head toward the back of the store.

After I get what I need, I wander through the aisles until I find Grace. She's standing in the health section, her basket hooked over one arm, staring intently at a shelf. She glances over her shoulder when she hears me approach.

"Hey, you good?" I ask, stepping closer.

"Yeah." She flashes a distracted smile. "Is this for real?"

I follow her gaze to the shelf. It takes me a second to process before my heart skips a beat.

"Grace… is that a…?" My voice trails off as I point at the box in her hand.

"Pregnancy test," she confirms, but it sounds like a question. "I'd heard they were working on something like this, but… There are so many options."

I blink a couple of times as my brain catches up. "Wait, you're… you think you might be…?"

She shrugs, and her lips curve upward. "We've been… close, Angus. Like, this-could-happen close." Her laugh doesn't quite hide the vulnerability in her tone.

A rush of emotions wash over me—excitement, nerves, disbelief. "Are you serious? You really think—" I catch myself and lower my voice to keep from attracting attention. "Grace, are we… gonna be parents?"

She holds the box up and gives it a little shake. "That's what I'm trying to figure out, Angus."

I laugh, maybe a little too loudly, which earns a glance from a passing customer. "Right. Of course. Sorry, it's… This is huge!" I rub the back of my neck, grinning like a fool. "Do we need more than one test? Should we buy two or three? You know, to be sure."

Her laughter is soft but genuine, and she hands me the box. "Let's start with one and see how it goes, okay?"

I turn the box over in my hands, reading the fine print like my life depends on it. "This one says it's 99% accurate. That's pretty good, right? Are there any that say—?"

"Angus," She places a hand on my arm. "Breathe."

"Sorry. I… I never thought about… a family. It's… amazing."

Her expression softens, and she leans in closer. "It's a little scary, too," she admits, her voice barely above a whisper.

"Yeah." I nod. "But the good kind of scary. Like… roller coaster scary." I pause to search her eyes. "Are you okay? I mean, how do you feel about all this?"

"I don't know yet." Her smile grows. "But I'm glad you're excited. It makes me feel less… overwhelmed."

"Grace, no matter what, we've got this. Okay? You and me. Together." I place the box in her basket.

As we head toward the checkout, I can't stop glancing at her as the realization settles in that my world might be about to change forever. Again.

Back at the house, Gran is in her usual spot, knitting another afghan, her needles clicking rhythmically. "You missed dinner." She doesn't bother to look up.

"Sorry, Gran."

"I fixed a couple of plates." She sets her needles down and stands. "I'll heat them up for you."

I hesitate and turn to Grace. Our eyes meet.

"Everything all right with you two?" Gran is always reading between the lines.

"Yep. Just fine," I reply, doing my best to sound convincing.

I can't help but grin. If Grace is pregnant, it won't matter which side of the sheet I sleep on anymore.

After dinner, we scurry upstairs to read the instructions on the box, only to learn we'll need to wait until morning to take the test.

Chapter Fifty-Three

Utah Sunrise – Grace Monroe (2024)

I'm off to work early the next morning, leaving Grace asleep in our bed. The day drags at work, my thoughts consumed by Grace and the possibility of our future. When I get home, the house feels quiet, almost too quiet.

"Gran, do you know where Grace is?"

Before she can answer, Gramps steps into the doorway. "She's been in the barn most of the day, strummin' on your guitar."

"Thanks," I call over my shoulder as I head for the door.

I find her in the loft, sitting cross-legged on the wooden floor, my acoustic guitar resting in her lap. She's surrounded by papers—some crumpled into balls, others laid out in a rough semicircle around her. The sunlight streams through the cracks in the barn walls and highlights her face, her expression focused and serene.

"Hey," I call softly, climbing the last few steps. "What you doin'?"

Her eyes sparkle with a mixture of excitement and vulnerability. "I was so flattered by the song you wrote for me, I wanted to return the favor."

I sink to the floor in front of her, folding my legs under me. "You wrote me a song?"

She nods and a hint of shyness creeps into her smile. "I'm still working on the arrangement, but I can let you read the lyrics, if you want."

"Of course I want to see it."

Grace picks up one of the pages from the floor and hands it to me.

"'Utah Sunrise.'" The title rolls off my tongue. "That's a great title."

I hold the page in both hands and read:

[Verse 1]
I left behind the twilight's haze,
A world of echoes and yesterdays.
Chasing dreams that burned so bright,
I found my heart in desert light.
The canyon winds, they whispered clear,
Brought me closer, led me here.
To arms so strong, a love so true,
Under skies of faded blue.
[Chorus]
Utah sunrise, painting the dawn,
A new beginning where I belong.
Mountains rise and shadows fall,
Your forever love outshines them all.
Utah sunrise, light my way,
With you, my heart will always stay.
[Verse 2]
The red rock stands, timeless and free,
Like the strength you've given me.
The past may call, but I won't go,
This is my home, it's where I'll grow.
Your voice is my guide, as together we climb,

Through the ebb and flow of time.
I traded the city for this open sky,
And now, my spirit's free to fly.
[Repeat Chorus]
[Bridge]
Life's a road that twists and bends,
But every journey somehow ends.
In your arms, I've found my peace,
Our timeless love will never cease.
[Repeat Chorus]

By the time I finish, the paper trembles in my hands. My vision blurs, and tears streak down my face faster than I can wipe them away.

"You like it?" Her voice is soft and hesitant.

"Grace…" My voice cracks as I look up at her. "It's… These are the most beautiful lyrics I've ever read."

She smiles, her eyes glistening. "I'll take that as a yes."

Before I can respond, she hands me another paper. "This is how I thought we could end it—right after the final chorus."

I take the page and read the final lines:
So here I stand, your hand in mine,
Underneath this Utah sky.
The past is gone, the future's clear,
With every sunrise, we'll be here…
Together.

Grace leans forward and brushes a tear from my cheek. "Hey, don't cry. It's a happy song, I promise."

I laugh through the tears, shaking my head. "You don't understand. This… this means everything to me. *You* mean everything to me."

She places the guitar on the floor and scoots closer, taking my hands in hers. "I meant every word, Angus. Every single one."

After a long, peaceful moment, I turn to her, a sudden thought striking me. "Hey, I almost forgot… Did you take the test?"

Grace tilts her head, her lips forming a soft smile. Without a word, she reaches into her pocket and pulls out a small, plastic wand that she hands me.

I take it carefully. "Wait… Did you pee on this?" I ask, half-teasing, half-nervous.

She laughs. "Angus, I think we've moved past worrying about that sort of thing by now."

I grin despite myself and lower my gaze to the test. My eyes land on the little window, and my heart skips a beat. "There's… there's a plus sign." I look up at her and my breath catches. "Does that mean…?"

She nods, her eyes shimmering with unshed tears. "You and me *plus*…" Her voice is barely above a whisper as she finishes, "…a baby."

"We're gonna have a BABY!" The words burst out of me like fireworks, and before I can stop myself, I scoop her up in my arms and spin her in a circle as the test falls to the floor.

"Angus!" She clutches at my shoulders, her laughter ringing out in the quiet of the barn.

I set her down and my thumbs brush away the happy tears that spill from her eyes. She smiles at me, her hands resting on mine. "Can you believe it?"

"I don't know if I can believe any of this," I admit, pulling her close and resting my forehead against hers.

We sink down to the floor of the loft and lean back against the wall as the light of the setting sun filters through the cracks in the barn. Ozzy trots up the steps and curls at our feet, as if he knows this moment is something special.

I take her hand in mine, my thumb brushing over her knuckles. "You know," I say, glancing over at her, "it's kind of funny. For so long, I thought I'd lost everything—my parents, my future, you. I didn't think something like this was possible for me."

She squeezes my hand, her voice soft but firm. "Angus, you fought for us. You gave up so much to keep me safe, to give me a chance. You made this possible."

I swallow hard. "You're not scared?"

"Terrified," she admits. "But that's okay. Because we're in this together. And together… we can handle anything."

The words hang in the air between us, as warm and solid as the wood of the barn. For the first time in what feels like forever, I feel at peace.

"We're exactly where we're supposed to be." My voice is quiet but certain.

Grace leans her head against my shoulder, her free hand resting on her stomach. The sun dips below the horizon, casting the barn in twilight, but I don't care. In this moment, the rest of the world could fall away, and I wouldn't even notice.

Chapter Fifty-Four

Epilogue

Today marks one year since Grace Monroe—now Grace Walker—stepped foot in Utah and turned my world upside down in the best way imaginable. Looking back, it's clear we didn't just find each other—we found ourselves. That's the magic of soulmates, I guess. They help you see the person you're meant to be.

Nicole Elizabeth Walker—named after both of our mothers—is four months old now and, thankfully, the spitting image of Grace. She's tiny, with a full head of dark hair and eyes that already sparkle with curiosity. Grace has taken to motherhood like she was born for it. Me? I'd never been up close and personal with an infant before, and I'm still in awe of how small and delicate everything is. Sometimes, I hold her tiny hand and marvel at the fact that she's ours.

We still live on the ranch with Gran and Gramps, but we're making plans to build our own place on the property. Grandpa Sam, who now works for a local construction company and lives in the apartment above Rusty's Auto Parts, is always around to lend a hand—and to spoil his granddaughter.

Gran says having a baby in the house makes her feel young again, and even Gramps seems more energized.

He built Nicole the most beautiful old-fashioned cradle. Watching them both dote on her makes me feel like I've brought something back into their lives that had been missing.

After Grace and I finished arranging and recording *Utah Sunrise*, I showed her how to upload it to YouTube. Within days, it went viral, and suddenly, we were fielding calls from record labels.

Now we play gigs here and there as a duo, calling ourselves Harmony and Grace. Our sound leans more acoustic these days, but we haven't let go of our classic rock roots. Last month, we released our first album, *Utah Sunrise*. It's mostly original songs, with tracks like *Broken Compass, Timeless Grace, The Time of Your Life*, and, of course, *Utah Sunrise*.

As for me? When I'm not spending time with my family—singing Nicole to sleep, writing songs with Grace in the barn's makeshift studio, or horsing around with Ozzy in the yard—you'll find me at the gym or catching up with my oldest and dearest friend, Walter "Waldo" Hastings.

Honestly, I couldn't be happier.

Grace, Nicole, Ozzy, Gran, Gramps, Waldo, and even Sam—they're my everything. My past, my present, and my future.

I've found my home. My family. My forever.

★★★

A Note from the Author

Thank you for investing your valuable time in reading my novel. I hope you enjoyed the story. Please visit my website at **www.davidhomick.com** for more information about me and my books and to sign up for my mailing list using the button at the top of the page. You can write to me through the site if you're so inclined. I'd love to hear from you.

Word of mouth is the most powerful promotion any book can receive. If you enjoyed this book, please tell your friends. A shout-out on your favorite social media sites would be cool, too.

I want you, the reader, to know that your review is very important to me and to others that may be considering buying this book. You can leave an honest review on Amazon. It doesn't have to be long, just a sentence or two. Your comments are greatly appreciated, but a simple star review is also appreciated.

Thank you Karen Siddall, who reviewed my book for Reedsy Discovery and said, "The selections were so perfect that I compiled them, along with additional songs mentioned in the narrative, into a fun, nostalgic Spotify playlist." You can find the "Time Traveler's Playlist" at Spotify.com.

Books by David Homick

Available on Amazon
Time Traveler's Playlist: A Classic Rock Time Travel Adventure
From Time to Time: A Time Travel Romantic Thriller
Karma Dog: Unleashing Redemption
Changing the Station: How One Stray Dog Found Its Purpose
Don't Curse the Rain (Rain Mystery Trilogy Book 1)
Rain Dance (Rain Mystery Trilogy Book 2)
Fire and Rain (Rain Mystery Trilogy Book 3)
Broken Angels
Reason to Live

www.ingramcontent.com/pod-product-compliance
Lightning Source LLC
Chambersburg PA
CBHW032338310726
48973CB00007B/1752